Praise for Keri Arthur

'Keri Arthur's imagination and energy infuse
everything she writes with zest'
Charlaine Harris, bestselling author of *Dead Until Dark*

'Keri Arthur is one of the best supernatural romance
writers in the world'
Harriet Klausner

'This series is phenomenal! It keeps you spellbound and
mesmerized on every page. Absolutely perfect!'
FreshFiction.com

'Ms Arthur is positively one of the best urban fantasy
authors in print today. The characters have been well-
drawn from the start and the mysteries just keep getting
better. A creative, sexy and adventure-filled world that
readers will just love escaping to'
Darque Reviews

'Vampires and werewolves and hybrids ... oh my! With
a butt-kicking heroine and some oh-so-yummy men, Keri
Arthur ... has put her own unique spin on things, and the
results are a sensual and energized fantasy brimming
with plenty of romance'
RomanceReviewsToday.com

'Keri Arthur knows how to thrill! Buckle up and get ready
for a wild, cool ride!'
Shana Abé, *New York Times* bestselling author'

Keri Arthur won the *Romantic Times* Career Achievement Award for Urban Fantasy and has been nominated in the Best Contemporary Paranormal category of the *Romantic Times* Reviewers' Choice Awards. She's a dessert and function cook by trade, and lives with her daughter in Melbourne, Australia.

Visit her website at www.keriarthur.com

Darkness Rising

A DARK ANGELS NOVEL

KERI ARTHUR

piatkus

PIATKUS

First published in the US in 2011 by Dell,
an imprint of The Random House Publishing Group,
a division of Random House Inc., New York
First published in Great Britain as a paperback original in 2011 by Piatkus

A CIP catalogue record for this book
is available from the British Library.

ISBN 978-0-7499-5496-3

Printed and bound by CPI Group (UK) Ltd, Croydon, CR0 4YY

Papers used by Piatkus are from well-managed forests
and other responsible sources.

MIX
Paper from
responsible sources
FSC® C104740
www.fsc.org

Piatkus
An imprint of
Little, Brown Book Group
100 Victoria Embankment
London EC4Y 0DY

An Hachette UK Company
www.hachette.co.uk

www.piatkus.co.uk

For Kasey, my baby girl,
who turned twenty-one this year.
So proud of you!

ACKNOWLEDGMENTS

I'd like to thank:

Everyone at Bantam for all the help and support they've given me over the years, especially my editor, Anne—you've taught me so much, and I really do appreciate it.

I'd also like to add a special thanks to my agent, Miriam, who is my rock when everything goes crazy. I don't know what I'd do without you.

And finally, the Lulus—writing buddies, best friends, five women I couldn't live without.

Chapter One

THE HOUSE STILL SMELLED OF DEATH.

Two months had passed since Mom's murder, but the air still echoed with her agony and I knew if I breathed deep enough, I'd catch the hint of old blood.

But at least there were no visible reminders. The Directorate's cleanup team had done a good job of removing the evidence.

Bile rose up my throat, and I briefly closed my eyes. I'd seen her—had seen what had been done to her—and it haunted me every night in my dreams. But in many ways, those dreams were also responsible for me finally being able to walk through the front door today.

I'd done enough remembering, and shed enough tears. Now I wanted revenge, and that wasn't going to happen if I waited for others to hunt down the killers. No, I needed to be a part of it. I needed to do something to help ease the ferocity of the dreams—dreams that came from the guilty knowledge that I should have been there for her. That if I had, I might have been able to prevent this.

I drew in a deep breath that did little to steady the almost automatic wash of fury, and discovered something else. Her scent still lingered.

And not just her scent. Everything she'd been, and everything she'd done—all her love and energy and compassion—filled this place with a warmth that still radiated from the very walls.

For the first time since I'd scattered her ashes in the hills that she'd loved, I smiled.

She would never entirely be gone from this world. She'd done too much, and helped too many people, for her memory to be erased completely.

And that was one hell of a legacy.

Still, despite the echoes of the warmth and love that had once filled these rooms, I had no intention of keeping the house. Not when all I had to do was step into the kitchen to be reminded of everything that had happened.

I walked along the hallway, my boots echoing on the polished marble floor. Aside from the few items of furniture placed to give prospective buyers an idea of each room's size and purpose, the house was empty. Mike—who'd been Mom's financial adviser and was still mine—had made all the arrangements, talking to the real estate people on my behalf and shifting most of the furniture into storage so I could deal with it later. Only the items in the two safes remained untouched, and that was a task only I could handle—although it was the one thing I'd been avoiding until now.

I drew in a shuddery breath, then slowly climbed the carpeted stairs. Once I reached the landing, I headed for Mom's bedroom down at the far end of the hall. The air had a disused smell. Maybe the people employed to keep the house spotless until it sold hadn't been as generous with the deodorizer up here.

But the soft hint of oranges and sunshine teased my nostrils as I walked into Mom's bedroom, and just for a moment it felt like she was standing beside me.

Which was silly, because she'd long since moved on, but my fingers still twitched with the urge to reach for her.

I walked across the thick carpet and opened the double doors to her wardrobe. Her clothes had already been donated to charity, but somehow seeing this emptiness hit me in a way that the emptiness of the other rooms had not. I'd often played in here as a kid, dressing up in her silkiest gowns and smearing my face—and no doubt said gowns—with her makeup.

She'd never once been angry. She'd always laughed and joined the fun, even letting me do *her* face.

I swiped at the tear that appeared on my cheek and resolutely walked into the bathroom. Most people wouldn't think of looking for a safe in an en suite, which is exactly why Mom had installed her second one here. This was where she'd stored her most precious jewelry.

I opened the double doors under the basin and ducked down. The safe was embedded in the wall and visible only because all of Mom's makeup had been cleared away.

After typing in the code, I pressed my hand against the reader. Red light flickered across my fingertips; then there was a soft click as the safe opened.

I took a deep breath, then sat and pulled the door

all the way open. Inside were all her favorite items, including the chunky jade bracelet she'd bought the last time she was in New Zealand, only a few weeks before her death. There was also a stack of micro-drive photo disks and, finally, an envelope.

There was nothing written on the front of the envelope, but faint wisps of orange teased my nostrils as I flipped it over and slid a nail along the edge to open it. Inside was a folded piece of paper that smelled of Mom. I took another, somewhat shaky breath and opened it.

I'm sorry that I had to leave you in the dark, my darling daughter, it said, and I could almost imagine her saying the words as I read them. Could almost feel her warm breath stirring the hair near my cheek. *But I was given little other choice. Besides, I saw my death long ago and knew it was the price I had to pay for having you. I never regretted my choice—not then, and most certainly not now, when that death is at my doorstep. Don't ever think I accepted my fate placidly. I didn't. But the cosmos could show me no way out that didn't also involve your death or Riley's. Or worse, both of you. In the end, it just had to be.*

Live long, love well, and I will see you in the next life. I love you always. Mom.

I closed my eyes against the sting of tears. Damn it, I wouldn't cry again. I *wouldn't*.

But my tear ducts weren't taking any notice.

I swiped at the moisture, then sat back on my heels. Oddly enough, I almost felt better. At least now I knew *why* she'd refused to tell me what was going on. She'd seen my death—and Riley's—if we'd intervened. And I would have intervened. I mean, she was my *mother*.

And as a result, I'd have died.

Her death still hurt—would always hurt—but a tiny weight seemed to have lifted from my soul.

I glanced down at the letter in my hand, smiling slightly as her scent spun around me, then folded it up again and tucked it into my pocket. That one piece of paper was worth more than anything else in her safe.

I scooped up the remainder of the jewels, but as I rose, awareness washed over me. Someone—or something—was in the house.

I was half werewolf, and my senses were keen. Though I hadn't actually locked the front door, I doubted any humans could have entered without me hearing. Humans tended to walk heavily, even when they were trying to sneak, and with the house almost empty the sound would have echoed. But this invader was as silent as a ghost. And it wasn't nonhuman, either, because in the midst of awareness came a wash of heat—not body heat, but rather the heat of a powerful presence.

An Aedh.

And he was in spirit form rather than physical.

My pulse skipped, then raced. The last time I'd felt something like this, I'd been in the presence of my father. Of course, that meeting had ended when two Aedh priests had gate-crashed the party in an effort to capture my father—who'd fled and left me to fight the priests off alone. Needless to say, the odds had been on their side, and I'd been taken and tortured for information. And while my father might not have led me into the trap, he still bore some responsibility for it. It was him they wanted, not me.

Hell, *everyone* wanted him. The Directorate of Other Races, the vampire council, and the reapers.

And they all were intent on using me to get to him.

Which pissed me off no end, but there wasn't a whole lot I could do about it. Especially given the deal I'd made with Madeline Hunter—the woman who was not only in charge of the Directorate, but also one of the highest-ranking members of the vampire council. Of course, she *had* managed to catch me at a vulnerable moment. She'd arrived uninvited as I said my final good-bye to Mom, had heard my vow for vengeance, and had all but blackmailed me into becoming an adviser to the council. In exchange, they would throw their full resources behind finding Mom's killer.

I hadn't walked away from the deal yet—not when finding Mom's killer might well depend on the information the council could give me. They might be using me to get to my dad, but I sure as hell intended to return the favor.

Not that they'd given me a whole lot so far, but then I hadn't done a whole lot for them, either.

Still, instinct said that would change quickly now that I'd set my sights on finding the killer.

Sometimes, having psychic skills like my mom totally sucked. Although I guess I had to be thankful that mine were nowhere near as strong as hers had been.

The sensation of power coming up from the floor below was growing stronger. Whoever it was, they were closing in fast. I needed help, and I needed it *now*. And the only person I could call on so quickly was the one person I was trying to avoid. Azriel—the reaper who was linked to my Chi. I hadn't heard or seen him since Mom's death, and part of me had been hoping to keep it that way.

I should have known fate would have other ideas.

Of course, Azriel wasn't just a reaper. He was a Mijai, a dark angel who hunted and killed the things that returned from the depths of hell—or the dark path, as the reapers preferred to call it—to steal from this world.

But what he hunted now wasn't a soul-stealer or even my soul.

He—like everyone else—was looking for my father.

And all because my father and his fellow Raziq— a secret subgroup of Aedh priests dedicated to finding a way of preventing demons from being summoned— had created three keys that would override the magic controlling the gates, allowing them to be permanently closed. And if the gates of hell were permanently locked, no souls would be able to move on and be reborn. A good percentage of the babies currently born into this world contained reborn souls, so it was a possibility that terrified me. Because without a soul, they would be little more than lumps of flesh, incapable of thought, emotion, or feeling.

Of course, what could be closed could also be permanently opened, and I had no doubt there were those who would also welcome the hordes of hell being set free.

The one *good* thing that had come out of this mess so far was the fact that my father had apparently come to his senses late in the development of the keys. He'd arranged for them to be stolen and hidden, but he'd been caught in the process and punished by his fellow Raziq, and the people who'd hidden the keys had offed themselves before they could tell anyone where they were.

Hence everyone's interest in me. I was currently the only link to my father and—according to my father— the only person capable of not only finding the keys, but also destroying them.

Although he had yet to explain just how.

Azriel, I thought silently, not wanting to alert who- ever was approaching that I was calling for help. I knew from past experience that Azriel could hear thoughts as well as spoken words. *If you're out there, come fast. There's an Aedh in the house and it could be my father.*

He didn't answer; nor did the heat of his presence sting the air. Either he *had* given up following me or something else was going on.

Which was typical. There was never a fucking reaper around when you wanted one. I took a deep breath that did little to calm the sudden flare of nerves, and said, "Whoever you are, reveal yourself."

"That, as I have said before, is impossible, as I can no longer attain flesh." The reply was measured, cul- tured, and very familiar.

Because it sounded like me. A male version of me.

My father.

"The last time you and I met, the Raziq came run- ning. And that was your fault, by the way, not mine." I crossed my arms and leaned back against the wall. The pose might appear casual, but every muscle quivered, ready to launch into action should the need arise. Not that I'd have any hope against a full Aedh—I knew *that* from experience.

"I have taken precautions this time." His cultured tones reverberated around the small room, and his presence—or rather the energy of it—was almost smothering. "They will not sense me in this house just yet."

"Why not? What have you done this time that's any different?"

He paused, as if considering his reply. "Because I was once a priest, I emit a certain type of energy. If I remain stationary for too long, they can trace me."

Facts I knew, thanks to Azriel. "That doesn't answer my question."

"Wards have been set. They not only give misinformation as to my whereabouts, but they will prevent any beings such as myself from entering."

Hence Azriel's failure to appear. Reapers were energy beings, the same as the Aedh.

I didn't bother asking how'd he'd actually set the wards when he couldn't interact with this world, simply because he'd undoubtedly had his slaves do it. Or rather, his Razan, as the Aedh tended to call them. "And are you sure these wards will work?"

"Yes. I have no wish for you to be captured a second time."

So he knew about that—and it meant he was keeping a closer eye on me than I'd assumed. "So why are you here? What do you want?"

"I want what I have always wanted—for you to find the keys."

"And destroy them?"

"That goes without saying."

Did it? I really wasn't so sure. "You haven't yet told me what will happen when the keys are destroyed, and I'd prefer to know that before I do anything rash." Like endanger the very fabric of my world.

The heat of him drew closer. It spun around me—an almost threatening presence that made my skin crawl. And it wasn't just the sheer sense of power he was exuding, but the lack of any sense of humanity. This was a being who'd worn flesh rarely even when he was capable of it, and who had no love or understanding for those of us who did.

Which made his desire to find and destroy the keys even more puzzling. Why would he care what would happen to this world if the keys were used? He *wouldn't*. Which meant something else was going on. Something he wasn't telling me.

Although I wasn't surprised that he was keeping secrets. That seemed to be par for the course for everyone searching for these damn keys.

"I am sure that when the keys are destroyed, everything will remain as it currently is."

"But aren't the keys now tuned to the power of the gates?"

Or the portals, as the reapers preferred to call them. Apparently there was only one gate into heaven or hell, with each gate consisting of three interlocked portals. Each portal had to be locked behind a soul before the next one opened. It was a system that prevented those in hell from escaping—although it wasn't infallible. Things still escaped when enough magic was used either in this world or the other.

"They are," my father said. "Destroying them should sever the link, and the gates should remain intact."

It was those *should*s that were worrying me. "You know," I said slowly, "it seems that it would be a whole lot safer for everyone if these keys were to remain as they are—indefinitely hidden."

Energy surged, making the hairs along my arms and the back of my neck rise. "Do you honestly think the Raziq will let matters lie?"

"Honestly? No. But they can't kill me if they need me to find the keys."

"Then what about your friends? Such a move could place them in peril."

"Not if I let the Raziq grab me. Once they realize I can't help them, I'm guessing they'll forget me and start concentrating on you again." After all, he might not know where the keys actually were, but he had some general knowledge of where they'd been sent, and he knew what they'd been disguised as.

Although admittedly, handing myself over to the Raziq wasn't at the top of my list. I'd barely survived their interrogation the last time.

The threat in the air was growing stronger. My father's energy was so sharp and strong that it hit with almost physical force. Part of me wanted to cower, but the more stubborn part refused to give in.

"You forget it is not just the Raziq who want the keys."

"The reapers aren't going to—"

"I am not talking about the reapers." His cultured tones had become soft, deadly. "I am talking about *me*."

The words were barely out of his nonexistent mouth when he hit me. Though he didn't have a flesh form, and though he'd told me he couldn't interact with things of this world, his energy wrapped around my body, thrusting me upward, squeezing so tightly it felt like every bone in my body would break. Then he flung me back to the floor, all but smothering me with the fierce, blanketing heat of his presence.

"How the hell did you—"

"You are my blood," he cut in, his voice a mere whisper that reverberated through my entire being. "It is the reason you can find the keys, and it is the reason I can do to you what I cannot to others."

Meaning he *couldn't* do this to Ilianna and Tao. But even as relief surged, he added, "But do not think your friends are any safer. I have Razan to do my bidding."

"If you touch them, you'll get nothing from me."

Amusement seemed to touch the fierce energy surrounding me. "Do you really think you have the strength and will to resist me? You might hold out for a little while, but in the end you *will* do what I want."

Not if I'm dead, I thought. And therein lay the crux of the matter. I didn't want to die. Not until I'd at least found Mom's killers.

"You *will* find those keys for me," he added.

"Go fuck—"

But I didn't get the rest of the sentence out, because he flung me violently across the room. I hit the shower doors sideways, tearing them off their hinges, and we fell in a tangled heap of shattered glass, twisted metal, and bruised limbs.

"You will get those keys for me," he said, "or what I do to you today I will have done to your friends tomorrow. Only my Razan will ensure they do not survive the experience."

Bastard, I wanted to say, but the words stuck somewhere in my throat, caught up in the desperate struggle to breathe.

"The information you need to find the first key is in the Dušan's book," he continued as his essence continued to bear down on me. My lungs were beginning to burn and panic surged, making it even harder to breathe. "Only one of my blood can read it, and only from the gray fields while the book lies here. But it must be retrieved from the Raziq first. They have it concealed. And again, only one of my blood will be able to find or see it."

"Why—" the words came out croaky, barely audible thanks to my lack of air. I licked my lips and tried again. "Why not simply tell me everything you know?"

"Because if I only feed you small pieces of the puzzle, you are still almost useless to the Raziq if they capture you."

I guess that made sense, even if the rest of it didn't.

"You still have the locker key," he continued. "Go there today at one PM, and you will find further instructions."

"Why not just give them to me now?"

"Because my Razan foolishly set the wards for a brief window, and I am out of time." The smothering energy evaporated, and suddenly I could breathe again. "And the less I am close to you, the less likely the Raziq are to use you to come after me."

Yeah, right. There was more to these fucking games of his than just a need to keep his distance.

"And what happens once I get the book?" I asked instead.

He didn't answer immediately, and his retreating energy became more distant.

"I must go."

"Wait!"

But he didn't. I drew a shaky breath and slowly picked myself up from the shattered remains of the shower doors.

"Are you all right?"

The words emerged from the silence even as the heat of Azriel's presence washed over me. Reapers, like the Aedh, were creatures of light and shadows, with an energy so fierce their mere presence burned the very air around them. And while they weren't true flesh-and-blood beings, they could attain that form if they wished.

Which is how I'd come about. My father had spent one night in flesh form with my mother and, in the process, created me—a half-breed mix of werewolf and Aedh who was lucky enough to mostly get the best bits of both and few of the downsides.

"Do I look all right?" I said, trying to extract myself from the remains of the shower door.

Azriel appeared in front of me, taking my arm and holding me steady as my foot caught on an edge and I stumbled. His fingers were warm against my skin— warm and disturbing.

While reapers were basically shapeshifters, able to take on any form that would comfort the dying on their final journey, they did possess one "true" shape.

And while the combination of my Aedh blood and my psychic skills usually allowed me to see whatever form they used to claim their soul, for some weird reason I saw Azriel's real form rather than whatever shape he decided to take on. And that shape was compellingly attractive.

His face was chiseled, almost classical in its beauty, and yet possessing a hard edge that spoke of a man who'd won more than his fair share of battles. He was shirtless, his skin a warm, suntanned brown, and his abs well defined. The leather strap that held his sword in place seemed to emphasize the width of his shoulders, and faded jeans clung to his legs, accentuating their lean strength. A stylized black tatt that resembled the left half of a wing swept around his ribs from underneath his arm, the tips brushing across the left side of his neck.

Only it wasn't a tatt. It was a Dušan—a darker, more stylized brother to the one that had crawled onto my left arm and now resided within my flesh. They were designed to protect us when we walked the gray fields. We'd been sent them by person or persons unknown, although Azriel suspected it was probably my father's doing. He was one of the few left in this world—or the next—who had the power to make them.

Azriel's gaze met mine, his blue eyes—one as vivid and bright as a sapphire, the other almost navy, and as dark as a storm-driven sea—giving little away.

"I have seen you in worse condition," he commented. His voice was mellow and rich, and on any other man it would have been sexy. But this *wasn't* a man. He merely held that form. And if I reminded myself of that enough, then maybe that tiny, insane part of me that was attracted to this reaper would move on. "What happened?"

"My fucking father." I pulled my arm from his grip and tried to ignore the warmth lingering on my skin as I thrust a hand through my sweaty hair. "And his spell prevented you from answering my call, didn't it?"

He nodded, and I leaned a shoulder against the nearest wall. My legs were as shaky as hell, and my stomach was still doing unsteady flip-flops.

"What did your father want?"

"Aside from beating me up and threatening to kill my friends, you mean? He wants me to find the keys, and he got rather irked when I suggested that the damn things would probably be better where they are."

He frowned. "Why would you want to leave them as they are?"

"Because if no one can find them, then they can't endanger the fabric of my world."

"But that is foolishness. If they are out there, they will eventually be found. The Raziq will never give up looking."

"And my father won't let me give it up, either." I sighed again and walked unsteadily across the room to scoop up the scattered jewelry and photo disks. "He's directed me back to the locker at the railway station. Apparently, he's had further instructions left there."

"If he was here, why did he not simply tell you?"

"He claimed he was out of time," I said irritably.

"But who knows? It's not like anyone is actually confiding in me."

Azriel studied me for a moment, expression neutral even if a faint hint of annoyance flickered through the heated energy of his presence. "I tell you what I can."

"No, you tell me what you think I need to know. There is a difference."

He didn't dispute it. No surprise there, given it was the truth.

"The last time you followed your father's instructions, you ended up being captured by the Raziq."

"My father won't be anywhere near me this time, so he claims it shouldn't be a problem. Besides, if the Raziq wanted me, they could have come after me anytime they wished."

"I doubt it. The wards that Ilianna has set around your apartment are as strong as those at the Brindle. They would make it difficult for the Raziq to enter."

The Brindle was the witch depository, and few outside the covens even knew of its existence. "We were told that the magic surrounding the Brindle wouldn't keep the Aedh out, so it's unlikely to keep them out of our apartment."

"Granted, but they also now know that I guard you, and they could not be certain whether there would be one or more Mijai waiting for them if they *did* attempt it. The Raziq are single-minded when it comes to their goals, but they are not stupid."

"So why haven't they snatched me outside the apartment? And why don't the wards make it difficult for you?"

"I am attuned to your Chi, so any magic that allows you to pass should also allow me."

"And yet the wards my father set up *did* stop you?"

"Because those particular wards were designed to reject energy forms. Human wards are not, so even the strongest will not prevent the Raziq—or a reaper—from getting through."

"If the Raziq did come after me a second time," I asked, suddenly curious, "would you actually stop them?"

He raised an eyebrow. "Do you think I wouldn't?"

"To be honest, I have no idea what you'll do in *any* situation." Especially given how many times in the past he'd stated that he would not interfere in the daily events of my life. And in fact, he hadn't—not when I'd been attacked by humans who could somehow attain half-animal form, and not when the Raziq had captured me. Although he had, at least, saved me and Tao—one of my best friends—from the hellhounds.

But once again he changed the subject. "You are fortunate the Aedh can only form a permanent telepathic connection through sex. Otherwise, your trip to the railway station would now be compromised."

Did that mean that Lucian—the fallen Aedh who'd become my lover—had formed a telepathic connection with me? Or was that one of the skills that had been stripped from him when they'd ripped the wings from his flesh? I didn't know, but I suspected it might be wise to find out—even if I was positive Lucian was on no one's side but his own. Still, given what the priests had done to him, I had no doubt he'd kill them given the slightest opportunity. His punishment might have happened many centuries ago, but the anger still burned in him.

I frowned at Azriel. "The priests rifled through my thoughts when they held me captive, and they certainly *didn't* do that via sex."

He nodded. "Aedh—like reapers—can read thoughts when in the same room as a person, but unlike human telepaths we are incapable of doing so from any great distance."

Thank God for small mercies. Although I did wish my rebellious hormones would remember more often that, when I was in his presence, he knew exactly what I was thinking. "Then you'd better be vigilant. If the Raziq get their hands on me, any information we get from the locker will be theirs."

Because I certainly wouldn't be able to resist them. I might be psychic, but my skills were on a more ethereal level. And as I'd already discovered, me fighting the Raziq was like a leaf fighting a gale.

"When it comes to you, I have learned to be *very* vigilant."

"And just what is *that* supposed to mean?"

"Nothing more than it says." But a glint in his eyes belied his words.

Despite the fact that reapers were generally about as emotional as a plank of wood, *this* one definitely had a sense of humor—even if it was a very odd one.

I headed back into Mom's room. The main safe was in the study, just across from my old bedroom. As in all the other rooms, the furnishings here were minimal. A desk, a couple of chairs, and the colorful painting that hid the wall safe. But sunlight streamed in through the double windows, lending the space a warmth that many of the others lacked.

Azriel followed me in, a powerful presence who was quickly becoming a permanent—if often distant—fixture in my life.

"I'm not believing a word of that statement, Azriel."

"Allowing you to fall into Raziq hands again would not be the wisest move. Not when they already have the book." His soft voice held little inflection, but I still had the odd feeling that he was amused. "And especially when they are the very people we are trying to stop."

"You could stop them by just killing them."

"I cannot do that unless they actually succeed in this plan, simply because there is nothing concrete connecting them to the portal's unauthorized opening."

"You may not have proof, but you know they've made keys and you know my father was involved. I thought that would have been enough, given that life as we know it hangs in the balance."

He shook his head. "It is not within the rules."

"Whose rules?"

"The rules we must live by."

I glanced over my shoulder. "And who made the rules?"

He shrugged—a small movement that was oddly elegant. "I do not know and I do not care. I just obey."

"Because a world without rules is a world in chaos."

"And that chaos is called earth," he commented.

I swung around in surprise. "Did you just try to be funny?"

"Reapers are many things, but we are never funny."

But that twinkle was stronger in his eyes, and I felt an answering smile tugging at my lips. "You lie, reaper."

"I never lie."

"You might not tell *outright* lies," I said, walking around the desk to the wall safe, "but you certainly don't always tell the absolute truth."

"No, I just don't always say everything I know. There is a difference."

I snorted softly. "Only by a matter of degrees, Azriel, and you know it."

"In my world, degrees can mean the difference between life and death."

That was true in mine, too, but I resisted the comment and instead pressed my palm against the reader, then let it scan my retinas. When the scans had registered and the first lock released, I spun numbers on the old-fashioned dial and unlocked the safe. Inside was a stack of papers—nothing vital, I guessed, because Mike already had all the necessary legal stuff for Mom's companies, insurance, and whatnot.

I left the door open and turned off the alarm. The new owners could reset it when the place finally sold. After gathering everything together, I turned around and faced Azriel, only he was no longer paying any attention to me. His head was cocked to one side, as if he was listening to something. And Valdis—the sword strapped to his back, which held a life force of her own—was beginning to flicker with blue fire.

Tension slammed into me and my pulse ratcheted up. Valdis only ever reacted to two things—evil and danger.

Whatever it was, it wasn't my father; I would have

felt his return. I licked suddenly dry lips and breathed deep, trying to keep the fear at bay as I listened. I couldn't hear anything—couldn't smell anything—and as a half-wolf, I would have. But there were things in both this world and the others that had neither scent nor smell nor form, and it wasn't out of the question for one of those things to be hunting me. The Aedh could traverse the gray fields—the unseen lands that divide this world from the next—as easily as the reapers, and those who'd trained as priests could also control the magic of the gates. The Raziq were rogue priests. It wouldn't be beyond them to free something from the dark path and fling it after me.

Although I couldn't actually imagine them doing that when they still needed me to find the keys.

Valdis grew brighter, sending flashes of electric blue light across the pale walls. Azriel silently drew her from the sheath at his back and held her at the ready. The blade hummed with every movement. "Someone comes."

"I gathered that." I dropped the papers and the items I'd gathered from the two safes onto the desk, then looked around for some sort of weapon. But with the house cleaned for sale, there really wasn't anything left. Not that Mom had ever had weapons in the house, anyway.

Which meant I'd have to rely on my own fighting skills, damn it. Because while I *could* fight, I preferred not to.

It wasn't cowardice, merely practicality. I'd learned the hard way that I was never going to be as good as a guardian, despite the fact that I'd been trained by two of the best.

I flexed my fingers, then said, "What is it?"

"Vampire."

I blinked in surprise. "A vampire? Really?"

He nodded, glancing at me. "You sound relieved."

"I am. I mean, vampires *can* be nasty, but I wouldn't put them in the same league as something that's crawled from the gates of hell."

"Oh, I don't know," an-all-too-familiar voice said from the hallway. "I could name quite a few people who would consider me far worse than any nightmare hell has ever produced."

I closed my eyes and swore softly. This day was *definitely* going from bad to worse. Because the vampire out in the hall was the one and only Madeline Hunter, queen bee of the Directorate, major vampire supremo, and a woman deadlier than almost anything on the planet.

She sauntered through the doorway, her light steps leaving little trace in the thick carpet. She was a small, slender woman with longish dark hair and startling green eyes, but those eyes were as icy and as remote as her near perfect features.

"I never knew you and Mom were friends." I crossed my arms and watched her warily. I might have agreed to work with this woman—or at least the council she represented—but that didn't mean I had to trust her.

And Valdis's reaction emphasized just how accurate my gut reaction was.

"We weren't. But she, at least, had some manners." Which was a not-too-subtle dig at the fact that I'd refused her entry into my apartment a couple of months ago. "Mom gave up teaching me manners when I was a teenager. And I can tell you right now, they're not about to improve anytime soon."

Not where she was concerned, anyway. I had a bad feeling I was going to need my bolt-hole, and Hollywood had at least gotten the whole threshold-and-vampires thing right.

Amusement touched the corners of her lips but never cracked the ice in her eyes. Her gaze flicked to the warm presence beside me. "I gather this is your reaper?"

"This is Azriel, yes." I didn't bother pointing out that he wasn't actually mine, simply because no one seemed to listen. "Azriel, this is—"

"Madeline Hunter," he finished, and bowed slightly. "You walk a dark path, vampire. Beware of overstepping your own boundaries."

She raised a dark eyebrow. "And would that be advice or warning, reaper?"

"Both." He sheathed a still-glowing Valdis and glanced at me. "I shall leave."

If you need me, call. The words were unsaid, but I heard them nonetheless. I nodded, and he winked out of existence.

Hunter's gaze returned to mine. Her scent—a faint mix of jasmine, bergamot, and sandalwood—was surprisingly pleasant. But it sent a chill down my spine, because nothing about this woman was ever pleasant.

"Why would my mother invite you into her home?" She'd *hated* Hunter. Hated and feared her. I never really knew why, although maybe it was as simple as sensing that my destiny would be tied to hers.

"Because, technically, she was in my employ, just as you are." Hunter pulled back one of the visitors chairs near the front of the desk and sat down, crossing her legs elegantly. "In fact, your mother and I had many a pleasant discussion in this very room."

Yeah, I believed *that* about as much as I believed in the Easter bunny. "About what?"

Again that eyebrow winged upward. I suspected amusement, although it was hard to tell given her emotionless demeanor. "About you. About her debt to the Directorate and what she might do to repay it."

"She helped the guardians bring down more than her fair share of criminals."

Hunter picked a piece of lint off her pants with long pink fingernails and flicked it idly away. I had a sudden image of her doing the same to me, and a brief smile touched her lips, then drifted away.

The bitch was reading my thoughts.

"If you wish your thoughts to remain unheard, then kindly keep them to yourself," she commented. "You've already asked your friend Stane to acquire some nanowires, have you not?"

Stane was Stane Neale, Tao's cousin. He wasn't only a computer whiz, but a major black-market trader. And if she'd overheard me asking Tao to get the wires, then she either had super-hearing or there were bugs in our apartment. "Yes, but I suspect even the strongest wire available won't be able to stop you."

"Oh, it won't," she acknowledged. "But they require a little more effort on my part, and therefore would afford you some of your much-relished privacy. It might even stop the reaper from following your thoughts."

Given that the wires were designed to work against those who wore flesh on a permanent basis, I doubted it would affect Azriel. And I wasn't as worried about him catching my thoughts anyway.

"You could show a little restraint in the meantime," I said.

"I could," she agreed, and flicked away another piece of lint.

An imaginary one this time, I suspected, because I certainly wasn't seeing anything on her pants.

Again that ghostly smile crossed her pale lips before she added, "But I am not here to discuss your mother."

I leaned back against the desk, my stance casual even though both of us knew that was far from the truth. "I never thought you were."

She nodded and leaned back in her chair. "We have a problem."

"*We* as in the Directorate, or the council?"

"The council, of course. You will never be on the Directorate's books."

"Odd, given that the Directorate approached me several years ago about becoming a guardian."

"Yes, but my brother has since been informed of my plans for you."

Meaning he'd made the approach without her approval? Somehow I doubted that. I knew enough about Jack and the guardian division to know that while he might have autonomy over the day-to-day running of the division, there weren't many decisions that didn't go through Hunter first.

"And just what, exactly, are your plans for me?"

She made a casual movement with her hand. "Nothing more than what you've already agreed to."

What I'd agreed to was being a consultant to the council, but her statement had sounded a whole lot more comprehensive.

"Besides," she added, "I believe you have an aunt and uncle who would strenuously object to you becoming a guardian. And right now, the Directorate can't afford to lose either of them."

Riley and Rhoan would do more than object—they'd lock me in a small room and throw away the key. And then they'd storm Hunter's citadel and demand my release from Directorate duty.

Thankfully, they had no idea I'd agreed to work for someone even more dangerous than the Directorate, and I fully intended to keep it that way. Right now I didn't need any more grief in my life.

"Why can't the Cazadors handle your problem?" Cazadors were the council's vampire assassins. They were highly trained, extremely deadly, and they got the job done no matter who or what got in their way.

Uncle Quinn—Riley's mate, and the half-Aedh who'd taught me how to use my own Aedh skills—had been one many centuries ago. He was also one of the few Cazadors to not only survive the experience, but walk away virtually unscarred. And to me, that only emphasized just how deadly *he* could be.

"I have no doubt they could handle it—if we had any idea just who or what the problem is."

"Then how do you know it's a problem?"

"Because we have a councilor who is dying, and the cause seems to be a sudden onset of age."

That surprised me. Vampires didn't ever age—and when they turned from human to vampire, they stayed at whatever age they'd been when they'd undergone the vampire ceremony. Which meant that if they were twenty when the ceremony was performed, but ninety when they died, they reverted to how they'd looked at twenty. The human population had been trying to uncover the scientific reasons for this switchback for years, but so far with little success.

Of course, there *were* psychic vampires who could drain the life force of their victims, thereby causing the sudden onset of age or even death, but surely Hunter and the Cazadors would have been able to track one of those without my help. "How would one vampire get that close to another without alerting them to their presence?"

Vampires might not be entirely human, but they were still flesh-and-blood beings with a heart and circulatory system. And *all* vampires—even the freshly turned—were extremely sensitive to the sound of blood pumping through veins. Which was no surprise given that their survival depended on a regular supply of the stuff.

"It's not another vampire."

Which also suggested it was something *other* than a flesh being—hence Hunter's sudden reappearance in my life. And while there were plenty of mythical creatures who existed by feeding off the energy of the living—whether that feeding consisted of blood, energy, or even souls—we certainly weren't talking about an ordinary victim here. This was a councilor—although she hadn't said whether it was the local vampire council or the high council that ruled them all—but you didn't generally rise to that level without a few hundred years under your belt. Which meant most of them were not only extremely dangerous, but more than a little knowledgeable about the darker things that haunted this world.

"I can't imagine anyone—human, nonhuman, or even a creature from hell itself—being able to feed from a councilor without him knowing about it."

"You and me both."

She tapped her bright fingernails against the desk, but it was a sign of anger rather than frustration. Those nails were almost long enough to be weapons, and I had an odd feeling she was imagining them ripping through someone's neck. Possibly mine, if I didn't come up with an answer.

"Whatever this is," she continued, "it attacked during the day, when Pierre was asleep. It wasn't a physical attack, as such. He would have been aware of that. This is more abstract. His energy was drained, but he remained unaware."

My frown deepened. As much as I hated to admit it, I was intrigued. Of course, anything game enough to take on a councilor and get away with it wasn't exactly something I wanted to get involved with.

But it wasn't like I had a choice, and she wasn't actually asking me to *kill* it. I was only the hunter, and I intended to do my damnedest to keep it that way.

"So if Pierre isn't sensing anything or anyone, how can you be sure this is an actual attack?"

She reached into her purse—which I hadn't actually noticed until now, and that said a whole lot about the state this woman got me into—and withdrew her phone. She pressed a button, then turned it around for me to see. "This was Pierre Boulanger two weeks ago."

He had dark hair, dark eyes, an imposing nose, and seemed to possess the sort of distant arrogance often found in those of royal blood.

"And this," Hunter continued, "was Boulanger when I saw him not two hours ago."

It didn't even look the same man. In this photo, he was stooped over and could barely manage to look at the camera. It was as if the weight of his head were too much for his neck. His black hair was shot with gray, and his unlined face was now seamed and littered with age spots. And his eyes were the eyes of a madman.

I met Hunter's gaze again. *Her* green eyes were assessing. I wasn't entirely sure why, because she was the one who'd all but blackmailed me into helping the vampire council hunt down the prey that eluded the Cazadors. If she didn't think I was up to helping, why even come here? "So you're dealing with some sort of succubus?"

Hunter shook her head. "I spoke to Pierre when this attack first happened, a week ago. He could not remember sexual dreams."

"And now?"

"He is, as you guessed, lost to madness. He remembers nothing."

"I think the key word here is *remember*. I don't know much about succubi, but I imagine that if one decided to target a member of the vampire council, then maybe it's also decided to cover its tracks."

"A succubus would not have the strength to erase Pierre's memories; nor do they drive their victims mad. A succubus is *not* at fault."

"Then what *do* you think it is?"

"If I knew, the Cazadors would already be on the job." She reached into her pocket and withdrew a business card. "You have an appointment with Catherine Alston at eleven o'clock."

I accepted the business card. It was one of Hunter's, and on the back she'd scrawled an address. It was a city address—a penthouse apartment in the Green Tower, which was the latest of the government backed eco-building projects, and it had a price tag to match its credentials. But most old vamps also tended to be obscenely rich. I suppose it was one of the benefits of living so long.

I shoved the card into my pocket. "So why am I going to see Catherine Alston when Pierre Boulanger was attacked?"

"Because Catherine woke up this morning with a head of gray hair and an old woman's face. Whatever is attacking Pierre is now after Catherine."

"And you wish to stop this before Alston goes the way of Boulanger?"

"Catherine can wither and die, for all I care." Mirth briefly touched Hunter's lips but did little to crack the ice in her eyes. "She is not the reason I wish to see this matter resolved quickly."

"Then what is?"

She studied me in a way that had fear curling through my limbs. This *wasn't* about the need to stop a killer finding more victims. This was about *me*.

And her next words confirmed that. "There are some on the high council who think it would be better for us all if you were dead. I am trying to convince them that you might be useful for more than just finding the keys."

I swallowed heavily. "So this is a test?"

"And you had better pass if you value your life."

Chapter Two

"If they kill me," I said eventually, my throat so dry it felt like the words were being scraped out, "they won't ever find the keys."

"That," she said coolly, "is precisely the point."

"But—" I paused, my thoughts filled with panic and going a dozen different ways. "I thought the reason the council recruited me in the first place was to find the keys so that they could use them?"

"It was. It is."

The rhythm of her nails on the desk suddenly stopped, and something flickered in her eyes. Something dark and very deadly. A chill hit me and the sick sensation of fear ratcheted up several notches—though up until that point I hadn't thought that was possible.

Because, in that brief instant, I'd seen death. Not my death—not yet, anyway. But someone else's, someone who'd had the stupidity to cross her path.

"Only a very small fraction have decided it would be better to keep the keys unfound," she continued. "Unfortunately, all voices on the council must be heard, and efforts to persuade them otherwise have so far proven ineffective. Which means it is up to you to prove your worth to them."

I licked my lips and said, "So this councilor who's dying—is it possible that one of the lesser members of the council has decided he or she needs to be higher on the ladder?"

"It is always possible, but there are easier ways to do that."

I was curious despite the fear twisting my insides. After all, it wasn't often you got the chance to hear about the inner workings of the local vamp council. They were a secretive lot at the best of times. Hell, most people didn't even know there was both a local council and the overall high council, situated in Melbourne. "Like how?"

Her shrug was oddly graceful. "There is always the blood challenge."

"Which I'm gathering is a physical challenge of some sort?"

"Of some sort, yes." This time, amusement touched not only her lips but also her eyes, and it was a fearsome sight. "The winner wins the right to drain the blood of the loser."

"Killing them?"

"No. Under most circumstances, it merely weakens them."

I wondered about the exception to that rule, but didn't say anything. Instead I asked, "Yet vamps do kill one another to gain position on the hierarchical ladder, do they not?"

"Of course. But that is different."

I couldn't actually see how, but then, vampires didn't always think with human—or, in my case, nonhuman—sensibilities.

"So where are Boulanger and Alston on the hierarchical ladder?"

"It does not matter, as I doubt ascension is the cause."

"Why? If both die, all those vampires below them automatically step up a couple of rungs, don't they?"

"It is not that simple. There are levels rather than rungs. The kill and the killer must be acknowledged and confirmed before he or she can move up to the next classification."

Which sounded a whole lot more formal and complicated than I'd expected. "It's still something that should be investigated."

"There are Cazadors examining that situation as we speak." She pushed to her feet. "I wish an update once you talk to Catherine. I need to keep the council informed as to your progress."

"And what if there isn't any?"

"I still wish an update."

Her expression made me gulp. No progress was *not* an option if I valued my life. "Is it possible to get a list of anyone who might have held a grudge against Alston and Boulanger?"

"That could be a very long list."

"Meaning you'll arrange it?"

"The list is being prepared as we speak," she said, a cool smile teasing her lips again. "But it is an encouraging sign that you've asked. You might yet survive this little task of ours."

She turned and walked out of the room, but her scent and her presence lingered, casting darkness through the sunlit room.

As soon as she'd vanished, Azriel reappeared. Valdis lay quiet across his back. "She does not linger. She has left the house."

Tension slithered from my limbs, and I blew out a breath. "Do you have any idea what might be attacking the councilors?"

He shrugged. "There are many things—both in the gray fields and beyond—capable of such acts."

"But surely most of them would have enough sense not to attack a councilor."

"Most of them," he corrected, "would only do so if ordered. Those who break through the dark gates under their own power are generally not so selective with their targets."

Probably because they knew the Mijai would be on their tails, and that, if they were caught, their fate would be eternal death, not eternal hell. "Has anything like that broken through recently?"

He shrugged. "Things break though all the time."

In other words, either he had no idea or he wasn't going to tell me. I squashed the flare of irritation and glanced at my watch. It was nearly ten thirty, so I had to get going if I wanted to make my appointment with Catherine Alston. Given that she was a high councilor—and generally you had to have a few hundred years under your belt to even be considered for the local council—I suspected it would be a bad move to be late. I met Azriel's gaze again. "Are you going to be present at the interview?"

"Do you wish me to be?"

I hesitated, then nodded. "We both know you're going to be listening in anyway, and I think I'd feel safer if you were an actual, physical presence."

"Meaning you do not trust this vampire?"

"Right now, I'm not much into trusting anyone."

He studied me for a moment, his face as impassive as ever even if I felt an odd sense of fierceness emanating from him. "Even me?"

Especially you, I wanted to say, but that wasn't entirely true. "I wouldn't be asking you to watch my back if I didn't trust you to do it."

"Which does not entirely answer the question."

"No, it does not."

I gathered my things from the table then brushed past him and headed down the stairs. No footsteps followed me, but I felt his presence nonetheless. And this time, annoyance seemed to mingle with the fierce heat of him.

Although why he'd be annoyed I wasn't entirely sure. At least I was being honest—which was a lot more than I could say about *him*.

My phone rang as I neared the front door. I tucked everything under my arm, then dug the phone out of my pocket with my other hand.

"Tao," I said, as his handsome features appeared on the vid-phone's screen. "What's up? Is there a problem at the café?"

Tao, Illiana, and I weren't only best friends who shared an apartment together, we also co-owned RYT's—a café situated right in the heart of Lygon Street's famed restaurant and club district. We had a prime position near the Blue Moon, and had been so busy lately that all of us had been working extra shifts. Not that I particularly minded; the more I worked, the less time I had to think about Mom. But it also meant I had less free time to spend with Lucian, who'd come to my rescue a couple of months ago and had quickly become my lover. He'd never be anything more than that, because—like Reapers—Aedh were unemotional creatures. Lucian might be a sexual being, but he didn't want or need anything more. Which was okay by me. Having suffered the heartbreak of one broken romance, I wasn't ready to step into another. Sex for the fun of it was all I wanted right now. And with Lucian, fun was *always* guaranteed.

Tao laughed, the warm sound jarring against the cold stillness of the house. "Can't I call my best friend without her expecting something to be up?"

"Tao," I said, a touch impatiently as I slammed the front door shut and coded the alarm, "it's your day off and it's only ten thirty in the morning. So there *has* to be a problem if you're already out of bed."

His warm brown eyes were twinkling, which meant the problem—if there was one—wasn't major. "Hey, maybe I just never got *into* bed."

"Oh, you were in bed," I said wryly, "but whose is the million-dollar question. And if you say Candy, I will kill you."

"Then I won't say Candy."

"Tao! She's the best waitress we've got, and she's not a wolf."

"So?"

"So you know humans take sex more seriously than wolves, and she's just going to quit like all the others when she realizes that you're never going to be anything more than casual."

"And if Candy herself doesn't want or need anything more than casual?"

"How many times have you heard humans say that, and how many times has it actually been true?" I said impatiently. "Damn it, Tao, we have a hands-off policy for a reason."

The humor in his eyes faded at the testiness in my voice. "I know, and honestly, I didn't seek this out. Quite the reverse."

"You should still know better."

He snorted. "Why? Because I'm a man? Why should it always fall on the male of the species when it comes to self-control?"

"It shouldn't," I agreed. "But you're the *boss* and you shouldn't be fucking around with employees. Literally *or* figuratively."

He muttered something under his breath, then said, "Stane gave me a call this morning. He's finally picked up the nanowires we asked for. He needs us to drop by his place ASAP so he can fit them."

"Fit them?" I said, frowning. "Don't you just click them on like a necklace?"

"Not these, apparently. We did say cost was no object, so he's gone for the latest technology."

I grunted. Cost *wasn't* an object—not when we had vampires like Hunter to deal with. "I've got a couple of appointments I have to deal with first, so I won't get there till midafternoon at the earliest."

"He'll be there." He hesitated, then added in a softer tone, "Are you okay?"

I smiled at the concern so evident in both his voice and his expression. We might be long-time friends and past lovers, but that didn't really do justice to the depth of our relationship. We weren't soul mates, but I couldn't ever imagine living without Tao—and Ilianna.

"Yes," I said. And, for the first time in weeks, almost meant it.

"Good," he said. "I'll see you tonight, then."

"Wait!" I said. Then as he paused, I added, "Can get you get Stane to sweep our apartment for bugs? I've got a feeling either the council or the Directorate is listening in."

"Why the hell would they want to do that?"

"Because they're after information about my father, just like everyone else."

He grunted. "You'd think they'd realize by now that we know jack-shit, but I'll ask."

"Thanks. See you tonight."

I hung up, then shoved the phone back into my pocket and walked across to my bike. Once I'd tucked everything into the under-seat storage, I pulled on my helmet, then glanced at the house one final time. *Good-bye*, I thought. *May you bring the next family better luck.*

"A house is an inanimate object," Azriel commented, suddenly appearing beside me. "It can bring neither good luck nor bad."

"I really wish you'd keep out of my head!"

"I would, except for the fact you sometimes have very interesting thoughts."

I glanced at him, bemused despite my annoyance. "Only sometimes?"

He nodded, his expression impassive but with that

almost devilish glint back in his eyes. "It's more than can be said about most humans."

"As I've noted before, I'm not human."

He bowed slightly in acknowledgment. "And for that, I am extremely grateful. My task might otherwise be extremely tedious."

Then he winked out of existence again, leaving me wavering between amusement and surprise. "Well, at least someone's having a good time," I muttered, climbing onto my old silver Ducati. She fired up quickly, the hydrogen engine making little noise as we cruised out the gates and down the street.

The Green Tower was located in the Docklands precinct of Melbourne, and the building itself was something of an enigma. While most of the towers close by were the standard straight-up-and-down glass buildings, the Green Tower was spiral in design. From a distance, it almost looked like a twisting tree trunk. Recycled wooden louvers—which were apparently powered by the photovoltaic arrays that lined its rooftop and provided much of the building's power—lined its sides and tracked the position of the sun even as they sheltered the building from the worst of the heat.

The underground parking lot was for residents only, so I found street parking, then walked back. Azriel appeared beside me as I entered the lobby.

The balding guard glanced up and gave us a cool smile. I wondered what he was seeing Azriel as, because it obviously wasn't his half-naked, sword-carrying self. "May I help you?" he said.

"I'm Risa Jones. I have an appointment with Catherine Alston."

"One moment please and I'll check with her." He turned away and made his call, and a few moments later returned with a far warmer attitude.

"She's sent down the penthouse elevator. Just head left—it's the last of five, in the separated section."

"Thank you." I followed his directions and found the appropriate elevator.

"A businessman," Azriel said as the doors closed and the elevator whisked us silently upward.

I glanced at him. "What?"

"You wondered what the guard saw me as. I answered."

"Why would a guard see you as a businessman?"

He shrugged. "Perhaps he has high expectations of death."

I snorted softly. "*I* have high expectations of death, but he continually disappoints me."

"Then don't have expectations," he said, either ignoring the jibe or not getting it. He was staring at the floor indicator like he'd never seen one before. "I speak with experience when I say it's easier that way. And what I've never seen before is the type of magic that protects this elevator."

I blinked. "It's protected by magic?"

He nodded. "A fairly old spell, by the feel of it. And very powerful."

I glanced at our chrome-and-glass surrounds but couldn't see anything out of the ordinary. Then again, I wasn't usually sensitive to magic, so that really wasn't surprising. "What's the difference between a new spell and an older one?"

He glanced at me. "The age of the practitioner?"

Laughter bubbled through me. "Oh my God, you just made a *joke*! I can't believe it."

"I merely told the truth." But that twinkle was back in his eyes.

Was my reaper getting more human, or was I merely getting more used to him? And why was I even wondering that when the man was obviously following my thoughts? "Can you tell what it's designed to do?"

He shrugged. "It's some sort of protection spell. More than that, though, I can't say."

I frowned. "But if she's got protection spells here, then she's probably got them in her apartment, too. So how was she attacked?"

"Ask her. I am by no means an expert on magic."

"Meaning there are Mijai who are?"

He nodded. "I am a simple warrior, but there are some who specialize in more specific areas."

"There's nothing simple about you, Azriel."

"On the contrary," he replied. "I work and I live. That is the existence of a reaper, and I am no different from any of my brethren."

"What about playing? Loving? Having families, stuff like that?"

"I live in a family unit, if that is what you mean."

I glanced at the floor indicator, suddenly wishing it would slow down. Azriel wasn't usually this chatty when it came to himself, and I really wanted to make the most of it.

"Family unit as in mom, dad, and siblings, or family unit as in wife and kids?"

"We do not pair up in the manner that you do here."

"Which doesn't answer the actual question."

His smile briefly touched the corners of his eyes. "Indeed, it does not."

"In other words, mind my own business," I said, mentally swatting at hormones dancing about in the lingering warmth of that smile, with little effect. "Which, I may point out, is not entirely fair, given you've got access to my life *and* my thoughts."

"I agree, it isn't fair. But for the moment, that is how it has to be."

"Oh yeah, got to maintain the status quo," I said, the mirth in my voice giving way to a deeper edge of annoyance. "The one where you know everything and I know nothing."

The elevator slid to a smooth stop and the doors dinged open, revealing dark marble and warm, subtle lighting. Unlike most penthouse elevators that I'd seen, this one opened into a small foyer area rather than the apartment itself. Dark glass doors dominated the three walls, all of them closed.

"If I knew everything, I would not be here," he said all too reasonably as he followed me out of the elevator.

"And if you told me everything you knew, then maybe you could get out of here sooner," I bit back, stopping in the middle of the foyer and wondering what the hell I was supposed to do now.

"Knowing whether I have what you would term a mate has no bearing on this case or on what we seek to do."

"I know." No one appeared to be coming for us, and I was half tempted to just get back into the elevator. It was only the knowledge that the high council wanted results or death that kept me standing there. "Forget I mentioned it."

I could feel his gaze on my back—a weight that, oddly, seemed to demand that I turn around and look at him. I ignored the urge, listening intently. Somewhere in the silence of the rooms beyond, someone was moving. But whether they were actually coming to fetch us, I couldn't tell.

"I do not," Azriel said quietly.

Something inside me unclenched, and I finally looked over my shoulder and met his gaze.

"I am Mijai," he continued. "It is not practical for us to consider a Caomh."

I raised my eyebrows. "I gather *Caomh* means 'mate'? And since when does practicality ever come into it?"

"Caomh is a whole lot more than merely a mate," he said, his gaze moving past me. "A thrall comes."

Surprise flitted through me—as much for the fact that I hadn't sensed the approach as for the fact that Catherine Alston had created a long-lived servant. From what I understood, it was considered bad form for vampires to have thralls. But maybe Alston simply didn't care. And maybe other vampires *did* have them, but they just hid their existence better.

The middle door opened. The man who stood there was brown-haired and brown-eyed, with a pleasant, open expression. He wasn't a man who'd stand out in a crowd or linger in the mind, and he looked to be in his mid-twenties.

Except he *smelled* older than that.

Much older.

He was also armed. There was a slight bulge under his right arm, and if the prickly heat crawling across my skin was anything to go by, it was loaded with silver bullets.

"May I help you?" he said, his voice low and cultured.

"I'm Risa Jones. I have an appointment to see Catherine Alston."

He nodded, but his gaze was on Azriel. "He may not enter."

"He's my partner."

"He is death," the thrall said. "And death shall go no farther than this foyer."

"Azriel is not here to collect your mistress," I said impatiently, at the same time wondering what the hell the thrall thought he could do to stop Azriel. "He's here to help."

The brown gaze met mine. "You'll swear your life on this?"

"Yes."

"Be aware that I will shoot you the minute I suspect ill intent from *either* of you."

Oh, fucking great. A trigger-happy thrall was just what we needed right now. "As I said, we are here by request. Neither of us means your mistress any harm."

He stepped to one side. "Proceed, then. It is the third door on the right."

The hallway was wide but far from airy. Darkness lingered, and the air so thick with the scent of roses that it made my stomach twist.

Each door was lit solely by a small tea light. I wondered if Catherine had a thing against electrical lighting, or whether it was done for effect. After all, most vamps weren't beyond the occasional attempt to terrify their guests.

"I am not trying to terrify you, young woman." The voice was rich, cultured, and almost plummy—the sort of voice that sounded as if it came from royal stock.

"That is because I *am* of royal stock," she said, then added, almost impatiently, "Come inside where I can see you."

I walked through the doorway. This room, like the hallway, had only a couple of candles providing light. But at least the overly sweet air stirred here, meaning either that there was an open window nearby or the air-conditioning was on.

Catherine Alston rose from her chaise lounge as we entered. She was a tall, thin woman with a regal nose, sharp brows, and black eyes, and she reminded me of a crow. It was an impression somewhat enhanced by her sweeping black dress with its long, almost wing-like sleeves.

"You are not what I expected, Risa Jones." She held out her hand, forcing me to reciprocate. Her skin felt like old parchment. "From our would-be dictator's description, I was waiting for someone far more . . . homely."

Not being homely wouldn't usually be considered an insult but, somehow, this woman made it so. "Two barbs in one sentence. That's pretty impressive."

Her grin was fierce and toothy. "And not afraid to voice an opinion. I like that. Why do you bring death into my presence?"

"He's my insurance policy."

"Ah. You do not trust me?"

"Not you, and certainly not Hunter."

She laughed, but it held an edge that was not alto-gether sane. Concern flicked through me. If the attack had sent Pierre Boulanger mad, then it more than likely would affect Catherine Alston the same way. And the last thing I needed was an insane vampire—even if I had Azriel watching my back.

"I am *not* about to attack you," Catherine snapped. She sat back on her chaise lounge again and crossed her legs elegantly. "It took a week for Pierre to be fully affected. I have six days left, and Hunter assures me you will have tracked this thing down by then."

Her tone implied it was already too late for Pierre. Did that mean he was now dead? I very much sus-pected it. Neither council was likely to let a madman survive very long. "So tell me what happened."

"If I knew that, you wouldn't be here."

I bit back a rush of irritation and wondered what the hell I'd done to deserve being surrounded by so many question-phobic people. "When did you realize you were also being attacked?"

"Yesterday evening, and I rang that dark-haired bitch straightaway. It took you long enough to get here."

I ignored the impulse to point out I'd only just been told, and said, "So you woke up at dusk and then what?"

"I looked in the mirror and saw this, of course." She waved a hand toward her face—a face that was still relatively free of wrinkles. And her dark hair had little in the way of gray.

"If you don't mind me saying, I can't actually see much of anything."

"Well, of course not," she said crisply. "Do you think I'm about to advertise the fact that I'm being attacked? Makeup and hair dye were invented for a reason, young woman."

I guessed so. "Then how bad is the aging?"

"There are crow's-feet and lines around my mouth, and my hair is salt and pepper. I can live with both, but I do not wish it to get any worse. You *will* stop it."

It was imperiously said, and amusement played about my mouth. While I had no doubt that Alston was every bit as dangerous as Hunter, she didn't emit anywhere near the same level of scary.

"Where did the attack take place?"

"In the bedroom, of course. Where else does one sleep away the tiresome daylight hours?"

"I shall check it out," Azriel said, and winked out of existence.

"And where has your dark defender gone?" she said. Maybe she was a little hard of hearing, because Azriel hadn't whispered. "If he steals anything, there will be hell to pay."

"Reapers don't steal," I said patiently. "And he's gone to see if your attacker has left any sort of scent trail in your bedroom."

She harrumphed. "I'll check, you know."

"Check away," I said, rather rashly, then added, as her gaze narrowed a little, "And nothing disturbed your sleep? You had no unusual dreams, felt nothing odd, have no strange marks or bruising on your body?"

"No. I did get Bryson to check when I realized what had happened, but neither of us could find anything."

"Bryson being the armed fellow who is standing behind me?"

"No, that's Ignatius. Bryson is my butler."

Which was another word for "dresser, lover, and food source," if her slight smile was anything to go by.

I cleared my throat, oddly sickened by the thought that this woman had spent centuries loving and feeding off her men. I mean, what sort of life was that for them?

"A good one," she snapped, more angrily this time. "And mind your thoughts, young woman. It is possible to push me too far."

I smothered my instinctive curse—if only because swearing wouldn't actually get me anywhere—and said, "What about the magic that protects your elevator and apartment?"

Her surprise rippled through the air. "You felt that?"

"Azriel did, although he could not tell what sort of protection spell it was."

"It is designed to guard against ill intent."

"So why didn't it work against whatever is responsible for these attacks?"

"Because it is flesh-sensitive. If what is attacking doesn't wear flesh, then it will not stop them."

Which didn't really narrow the field all that much. We'd already guessed this thing wasn't a flesh being— both Alston and Boulanger would have sensed such an approach. "Did you set the spell?"

"Do I look like a magic user, young woman?"

Her tartness had my grin rising again. "I didn't realize magic users had a specific look."

"Well, they do. And obviously, I am not one of them. I hired a woman to set the spell when I purchased this place."

"Her name?"

"Adeline Greenfield. She came highly recommended."

It wasn't a name I was familiar with, but Ilianna might know her. Either way, she was worth talking to, if only to uncover the extent of the spell.

"The fact you're the second councilor to be attacked suggests this might have something to do with the council itself. Has there been a decision or action taken recently that was met with opposition?"

She waved a dismissive hand. "Council decisions are always controversial. There's rarely one hundred percent agreement in the vampire community at large, let alone on either of the councils."

That's because the vampire community as a whole is—

I stopped the thought cold when her gaze narrowed again. The sooner I got to Stane's and had those damn nanowires fitted, the better. "So there's no one decision that sticks out as worse than the rest?"

"Not to my knowledge, no."

"Then why do you think you and Boulanger have been targeted this way?"

She shrugged—a movement that emphasized the thinness of her shoulders. "The two of us are council elders—there are three in all—and therefore have the controlling votes, but I cannot think of anything we've overruled recently that would merit any sort of retribution."

"Meaning there's been stuff in the past that might?"

"It is possible. We are not angels."

I snorted softly. That *surely* had to be the understatement of the year. "I don't suppose you could write a list of people who might hold a grudge against the two of you? It would give us something to work with."

"Such a list would only be useful if Boulanger were able to write one. He cannot."

It was interesting that she continued to avoid referring to Pierre in past tense. "Maybe not, but I've asked Hunter to see what she can come up with."

"Oh, I can just imagine how well she took *that*." She chuckled softly. "Still, it will be interesting to see if we come up with the same names."

If they did, then those vampires had to be next in line for questioning. And if I was going to be the one doing the questioning, then Azriel was going to be watching my back. Not that he was doing such a good job of it right at this moment.

"On the contrary," he said softly, suddenly appearing beside me. His gaze met mine, oddly full of censure. "I am aware of everything that is going on in this place. Do not doubt *that,* even if you doubt me in general."

I frowned. "Did you discover anything?"

"Yes." He glanced at Alston. "The thing that attacked you is a Maniae."

"And that is?"

"The Maniae are the spirits of madness and death.

They are related to the Erinyes, the deities of vengeance."

Holy cow, I thought, blinking. We weren't just dealing with ordinary, everyday bad guys here, but old Greek gods!

Could the day get any fucking worse?

Chapter Three

"Yes, it could," Azriel murmured, amusement crinkling the corners of his eyes, "because they cannot be killed."

"Oh, fabulous." I raked a hand through my hair. Hunter was *not* going to be pleased.

"Could someone please explain what the hell a Maniae is?" Alston said irritably.

He glanced at her, expression noncommittal. "As I said, the Maniae are spirits—daemones—of madness or death. They, like the Erinyes, can be summoned by those seeking vengeance for crimes against the natural order."

She glanced at me. "Does death always speak in riddles?"

"For as long as I've known him," I said, and felt amusement swirl through him.

"Crimes against the natural order can mean anything from murder to unfilial conduct," he said. "And usually the only way to stop the attack is by uncovering the perpetrator of the curse and having them either perform a rite of forgiveness and purification, or complete of some task assigned for atonement."

Her snort was less than regal, and really said all that needed to be said. "Unfilial conduct? I am an old vampire and my maker is long dead. I hardly think it would matter to anyone else if I was an undutiful daughter."

"That would depend on whether the term is used strictly or loosely," Azriel commented. "Maybe it is simply a matter of engaging in conduct unbecoming a vampire."

"All vampires engage in conduct unbecoming," she snapped, "It is the nature of the beast."

I'm glad *she* said that, because if I'd pointed it out, she'd have gotten pissed. "Conduct unbecoming wasn't the only point mentioned, Catherine."

Her gaze flicked to me, her eyes steely black. And I'd been wrong before: Alston could do scary every bit as well as Hunter if she wanted to. "I have not murdered anyone in a very long time, young woman. Although right now I will admit the itch is rising."

"Murdering me isn't going to help catch your attacker," I replied calmly enough—though she no doubt noted my accelerated heart rate.

"No," she agreed. "Although Hunter would not be pleased, and that in itself would almost be worth the cost. Perhaps it is just as well you have your dark guard here."

And why Azriel would be by my side the next time I had to visit her. I was beginning to trust this woman even less than Hunter.

"I would suggest that you avoid sleeping for the next couple of days, as that seems to be when the attacks occur."

"And why do you think I am here rather than lying wrapped in Bryson's warmth?"

"You don't need to sleep to enjoy Bryson's warmth,"

I couldn't help pointing out. "Nor do you need a bed."

"I am not a young woman," she remarked haughtily. "And I tend to be old-fashioned when it comes to sex. You, obviously, are not."

I certainly wasn't—and thank the gods for that. The real spice of life—and sex—was variety. I restrained the urge to smile and said, "Please call me when you have the list compiled."

"Ignatius will call you. Better yet, I shall have him deliver it." Her gaze flicked to Azriel. "The less I see of *him*, the better I shall feel. Good-bye, young woman."

Summarily dismissed, I turned and walked out. Ignatius was back at the glass door, waiting for us. It was almost as if they couldn't wait to get rid of us. Even the elevator was waiting.

Once the doors had closed and the elevator was on the way back down, I said, "Did you find anything in the bedroom?"

"A reaper."

My head snapped around. "*What*?"

The corners of his lips quirked, and I had a sudden suspicion that he liked surprising me. "Catherine Alston is slated for death, and nothing we do can stop it."

"When will she die?"

He shrugged. "Soon."

"From the Maniae, or through something else?"

"The Maniae will attack again, because she will forget your warning and sleep. That attack will weaken her greatly. She will fall onto some furniture, break it, and in the process stake herself through the heart with a stray piece of wood."

I reached for the STOP button, but Azriel caught my hand. His grip was gentle, yet steel lay underneath it, ready to react should I fight. "Even if Alston heeds your warning, she will still die. Sometimes you can save them, Risa. This is not one of those times."

"But we can at least try—"

"Then try with someone worthy of salvation. Catherine Alston is not."

"Many vampires are not," I said irritably, ripping my hand from his. Warmth lingered where his fingers had rested. "But that doesn't mean we should just give them up to fate."

"Fate does not like being thwarted too often, and she exacts consequences if she is. Alston's death will be quick. If we change the timing, her next one may be long and painful." He hesitated, then added softly, "Your mother knew that."

"Don't you *dare* bring my mom into this!" I snapped, clenching my fists against the sudden rush of anger and futility.

The elevator reached the ground floor and the doors opened. I stormed out, desperate to get away from Azriel. Desperate to ignore the confirmation of what Mom had already told me, and what I knew deep down to be true. Because it didn't make me feel any better right now to know she couldn't have been saved no matter what I'd done. Which was totally irrational given that the same knowledge *had* made me feel better earlier.

But I guess it was an irrational sort of day.

By the time I'd gotten back to my bike, I'd calmed down a little. I took a deep breath, released it slowly, then said softly, "I'm sorry, Azriel. I shouldn't have jumped down your throat like that."

He reappeared beside me, one dark eyebrow raised. "Jumping down someone's throat is a difficult task at the best of times. I certainly would have noticed if you'd done it to me."

I chuckled softly and shook my head. "Two funnies in one day? Be careful, Azriel, or I might just begin to think you're not as emotionless as you let on."

"Just because I am not created the same way as you doesn't mean I am emotionless," he said, with a hint of censure in his voice. "We are not the Aedh."

No, he certainly was not. Although Lucian—the full blooded Aedh I was spending time with—not only had a somewhat wicked sense of humor, but he could and *did* enjoy sex with humans. Then again, he'd spent a whole lot of time—centuries of it, in fact—trapped here on earth. Which must have knocked some of the emotionless edges off him.

Reapers didn't have that sort of interaction with us, however, and I couldn't ever imagine them thinking about sex, let alone doing—

The thought stalled as his eyebrow lifted again. Heat seeped into my cheeks. Damn it, I really was going to have to watch what I was thinking around *this* particular reaper—especially when my thoughts headed in *that* direction.

I shoved on my helmet and said, "I'm heading home to get the locker key, then into Melbourne to check out the locker. You'd better keep your distance, just in case my father changes his mind and decides to turn up."

"You will call if he does?"

"Trust me, I have no desire to be thrown about like an old rag a second time."

"As you wish, then."

He winked out of existence. I climbed onto my bike, then headed home. Our place was a square, two-story brick building situated in the heart of Richmond, and its somewhat bland gray exterior belied the beauty of its internal space. Ilianna, Tao, and I had purchased it fresh from college and had renovated every inch of it, filling it with the latest and greatest in technology and design. And that included the latest in security, although it wouldn't keep me safe from a determined Raziq.

After parking in our garage, I ran up the stairs to the thick alloy door that was both fire- and bullet-proof and looked into the little security scanner beside it. Red light swept across my eyes, and a second later the locks tumbled and the door slid silently open.

The huge industrial fans that dominated the vaulted ceiling were on full, creating such a breeze that it whipped my hair out of its ponytail—although it didn't do a lot to erase the two voices harmonizing, or the sharp scent of roses, honey, and rum.

I knew that scent and stopped cold. Ilianna and Mirri were making love potions in the kitchen again, and there were certain moments in the creation of such potions that you really *didn't* want to walk in on. Not unless you wanted to fall hard for the next male—or female, if your tastes ran that way—that you met.

Although a lot of people might still mock anything connected to witches and magic, Ilianna's potions and charms were extremely popular simply because the damn things worked. Ilianna was a witch in the truest sense of the word, and she'd been trained in magic since she was very young. I might not have tried a love potion—and had never actually wanted to—but I'd always relied heavily on the charms she made to keep me safe while walking the gray fields.

Of course, these days I supposedly had the Dušan to do that, but the dragon had so far been untested. And even if it *had* been proven, I think I'd still wear Ilianna's charms. In my opinion, you could never have enough protection when walking a place as potentially dangerous as the fields between life and death.

Even now the simple charm—which consisted of a piece of petrified wood to connect me to the earth, and small pieces of agate and serpentine for protection— was nestled between my breasts. And right beside it was the gold filigree droplet that my father had given to my mother on the night of my conception. It was shaped like two wings, and very much represented my heritage.

"Hey, ladies," I yelled. "Is it safe for me to come in?"

Mirri's head popped into view as she leaned around the kitchen doorway. "Totally," she said, her smile bright against the richness of her skin. "Or at least, it is for you. We're brewing potions aimed at men seeking men."

"I didn't know you could make gender-specific potions, let alone preference-specific." My boots echoed on the wooden floors as I walked toward the kitchen. "And I hope you've forewarned Tao. He'll be totally pissed if he gets caught in the backlash."

Mirri made a face then disappeared, her voice floating back to me from the depths of the kitchen. "I doubt there's a potion alive that would turn *him* away from the ladies."

I laughed and leaned a shoulder against the door frame; the rich scents were just too strong to go any farther.

"So," Ilianna said, her green gaze meeting mine as she glanced over her shoulder. Like Mirri, she was a horse shifter, but she was a rich palomino where Mirri was a mahogany bay. "How'd it go today?"

"Good and bad." I updated them briefly on my father's visit and Hunter's mission. Mirri frowned. "If your father wishes your cooperation, why would he do that to you?"

Ilianna studied me for a moment, then said, "Because you refused, didn't you?"

"Well, yeah. Kinda."

She snorted softly. "So he resorted to violence. And then, undoubtedly, threats."

She was good, there was no doubt about that. "Against you and Tao, yes."

"The man is a bastard," Mirri muttered.

"Yes, except he's not a man. He's something far worse."

"So we can't do anything about him, right?" I nodded when she looked at me. "But why would you even consider undertaking a mission like that for the vampire council?"

"Because Hunter was a bitch and caught her in a moment of weakness, and now she can't get out of the deal," Ilianna commented tartly, then grimaced as she glanced at me. "And I suppose you're going to this locker even though the last time you followed one of your father's orders the Raziq used it as an opportunity to capture you?"

"I don't have a choice, Ilianna." Not about this, and not about helping Hunter. "And Azriel will be there."

"He'd better be." She glanced past me. "Hear that, reaper? Be there. Protect her."

"Trust me, it's in his best interests to keep me alive and functioning."

"His version of functioning might well be different from ours, remember."

Maybe, but in this case, at least, he needed me not only alive, but able to walk and talk. At least until I'd found the keys. "I'm heading there now. If I don't call by one thirty, marshal the troops."

She snorted. "Like that's going to help."

She was right—it probably wouldn't. But if I didn't at least have a backup plan, Aunt Riley would kick my ass. Although she was going to kick it anyway for going to the locker again after what had happened previously.

"Listen, have you heard of an Adeline Greenfield?"

Ilianna raised a pale eyebrow. "Sure. She's a practitioner and is renowned for her protection spells. Why?"

"Because the vamp I just talked to had some of

Adeline's spells protecting her apartment, but something is getting past them." I hesitated, then added, "And of course, this is all a secret. Hunter would be incandescent if this got out."

"And Hunter is not someone I want to piss off," she said. "Protection spells aren't infallible. How well they work very much depends on how comprehensive the spell is."

"Which is why I want to talk to Adeline. Do you know her well enough to get me in to see her?"

"I don't, but I'm sure Mom does."

I smiled. "Wouldn't asking your mom involve finally being forced to meet your potential stallion mate?"

"You know, as far as stallions go, he's not actually that bad," Mirri commented. Both of us glanced at her in surprise, and heat crept into her cheeks. "What can I say? I was bored one weekend and he happened to be around. And it was before you and I were an item, just in case you were wondering."

Ilianna smiled and squeezed Mirri's arm gently. "I wasn't. Although if Mom *does* insist on that dinner, then maybe we can kill two birds with one stone. Introduce you, and get the rotten dinner date with Carwyn over with."

Mirri's response was quick and joyous. She'd been angling to meet Ilianna's parents for almost as long as they'd been an item, and while we both knew Ilianna wasn't ready to come out of the closet, this would at least be a step in the right direction.

"That would me fabulous," Mirri said, stepping forward and dropping a quick kiss on Ilianna's cheek. "And as I said, Carwyn isn't really that bad."

"Maybe," Ilianna said, her smile almost a grimace. "But if he starts coming on too strong, I expect you to run interference."

"Your parents might not be too pleased . . ."

"He's a stallion," Ilianna said. "They wouldn't give two hoots about you capturing his attention as long as *I* did as well."

"True," Mirri said with a laugh, then glanced at me. "Are you going to be home for dinner tonight? We're making vegetarian lasagna, because Tao will be out with his new lady love."

"Whom I really hope *isn't* Candy," I said, and pushed away from the door. "And no, I won't be. If Lucian doesn't call, then I'm heading over to Franklin's." Which was an upmarket wolf club specializing in clients who preferred—and could afford to pay for—discretion.

Ilianna gaped. "Why are you waiting for him to call? Call him, for heaven's sake!"

I grinned. "I would, except he had to go interstate for business reasons, and wasn't sure whether he'd be back tonight or tomorrow."

I turned away, then paused. "While I remember, my father set up wards at Mom's place that were capable of preventing both the Aedh and reapers from either detecting his presence or being able to enter. Is there any chance you could retrieve them and figure out how he did it? The magic in them dissipated after a set time, but something like that would be handy here."

"They would have to contain some pretty heavy-duty magic to achieve something like that."

"But do you think you could work out the spell?"

"If there aren't any remnants of it left, probably not. But I can't say for sure until I've looked at the wards themselves."

I tossed her Mom's house keys. "Your prints are still registered in the system. It might be worth checking out."

"If it means making our apartment an Aedh-free zone, then I'll make it a priority."

"Thanks, Ilianna."

I headed for my bedroom. Then, after picking up the locker key, I walked back down the stairs and drove into the city.

Of course, Melbourne was a bitch of a place to find any decent parking in—and had been since they'd introduced the car-free zone. Most of the underground parking lots were filled with rush-hour travelers, forcing the rest of us to park outside the city limits and either walk back or catch public transport. And *that* was as unreliable as ever. One of these days a politician was actually going to keep an election promise and fix the system, and the whole damn city would keel over in shock.

I jogged back into the city. Southern Cross Station, with its undulating roofline that always reminded me of mounds of snow, came into view. Lots of people were exiting, meaning several trains must have just pulled in. I picked my way through the crowd, heading for the locker area situated in the middle of the station.

Like before, there were a handful of people hanging about, either collecting or depositing goods, but no one seemed overly interested in what I was doing. But then, if someone was watching, it was in their best interests to be discreet.

I shoved the key into locker 97 and opened the door. Inside sat a solitary envelope.

I plucked it free, closed the locker, and shoved the key in my pocket. And at that precise instant I became aware that the atmosphere in the room had suddenly sharpened.

I glanced up quickly and saw a familiar face.

It was the cat shifter who'd been part of the attack on me in the parking garage when this madness had first started. And once again, he hadn't come alone.

Chapter Four

"WELL, WELL, WELL," HE ALL BUT PURRED. "Imagine meeting you again."

"Yeah, just imagine." I shoved the note into the back pocket of my jeans, then flexed my fingers. He wasn't alone. I could smell a second man trying to creep around the lockers, obviously hoping to come up behind me. "Where are the rest of your friends? Oh, that's right. Two are dead, and the other is in the hands of the Directorate. Are you *sure* you want to do this a second time?"

Several people scurried out of the locker room. Obviously, the guy attempting to creep around the back had spooked them. Such brave souls, leaving a woman to tackle two men alone. Of course, I wasn't exactly defenseless, but they wouldn't know that.

His quick smile was all teeth—not vampire teeth, but razor-sharp feline teeth. He might not be a full shifter, and he might not be able to take on full feline form, but he had extraordinary control over the bits he *could* change. Like his teeth, and the nails that were even now elongating into claws.

But as I watched him closely, waiting for his first move, anger surged—an anger so thick and deep that it stole my breath. It was all I could do *not* to flow into Aedh form and rip him apart.

I took a deep, quivering breath that did little to tame the fury.

It was scary, that rage. Really, *really* scary.

He made a motion with his claws. "Hand that letter over right now, and we'll leave you in peace."

I clenched my fingers against the urge to leap for his throat, aware that the second man was getting closer.

"Sorry," I said, barely keeping my voice even, "but I had a nice little chat with the man who ended up in the Directorate's clutches, and I know for a fact that's *not* true."

He smiled. It wasn't a pleasant sight. "Orders can change, you know."

"Whether they've changed is not the point." Heat swirled across my skin. Azriel had taken form on the other side of the lockers. Was he taking care of the second man or at least running interference? I hoped so. I said to the first man, "And I'm hardly going to hand you a note I haven't even read yet."

"That," he said softly, "is unfortunate."

And with that, he sprang. His leap was high, graceful, and *fast*. I threw myself out of the way, twisted around, then lashed out with a booted foot. The blow missed by inches, catching the end of his foot and little else.

I brushed my fingertips against the concrete, steadying myself as he leapt a second time. But the rage surged again, becoming a haze of heat that would not be denied.

This time I held my ground until the last possible moment. And when he lashed out, I let the blow hit me, his claws cutting through my jacket and into flesh. But the anger inside was burning so bright that I didn't feel it, even though blood pulsed, rich and warm, down my side. I grabbed his arm, wrenched his claws free, then twisted him around, flinging him as hard as I could into the lockers on the far side of the room.

There was no response for the second man. Azriel *had* to have stopped him.

The first man hit with a resounding crash, denting metal as he fell. As he scrambled to his feet, I launched at him, twisting around in the air so that I hit him feetfirst, knocking him back into the lockers again. When I hit the ground, I lunged forward, shoving one hand against his throat to hold him in place as I kneed him hard in the balls. He wheezed in pain and tried to double over; it was only my grip on his neck that kept him upright. And my fingers were shaking with the urge to squeeze harder, deeper . . .

Fuck, where is this coming from?

"Tell me who you're working for." My voice was edged with the madness within, my face mere inches from his. His scent clawed at my throat, stale and unpleasant.

He took several gasping breaths then wheezed, "Handberry. It was Handberry."

"Handberry's *dead*." My grip tightened on his neck, and it was all I could do not to keep on squeezing. God, I *so* wanted to wring the life from him, and I think it was only the fear of that need that kept it in check. "So tell me the truth."

"Fuck! I don't *know*," he spat out. "We got a call from a guy saying he was our new handler, and he told us to come here and wait for you to collect the letter. We've been waiting for fucking *weeks*."

I hadn't expected that. "When did you get that call?"

"A month ago."

"And he hasn't contacted you since?"

"No. He just said to keep watch and to call when we retrieved whatever was in the locker."

"If all you wanted was the note, why didn't you just break in and get it?"

"Because it wasn't in there, was it? We checked yesterday."

"So how did the new handler know something would be there?"

"He's getting orders from someone, isn't he? Why can't it be the same someone as Handberry?"

Why not indeed? I guess it was lucky they'd checked last night rather than this morning, because my father must have had it placed there after he'd talked to me. "If you've been stationed here for weeks, why didn't you sense the Razan who delivered the note?"

"Because we haven't seen another Razan for weeks. I told you, we've been stationed here."

So how did the note get into the locker? "What about an Aedh?"

He snorted softly. "An Aedh doing his own dirty work? *That's* likely."

For a man who was all but a slave to an Aedh, he was pretty damn critical of them. "Do you have a contact number for this new handler of yours?"

He nodded as well as he could with my hand pressed against his throat. "On my phone, in my top pocket."

I reached into his jacket pocket, pulled out his cell

phone, and shoved it into mine. "What name is your handler under?"

"Handberry. I figured it was as good as any."

Fair enough, I thought, and then hit him, as hard as I could, with my free hand, knocking him out. Then I let him drop to the floor.

For several seconds I did nothing more than stand there staring at him, my fists clenched and body shaking. Then, gradually, the rage eased and I dropped down beside him, hugging my knees to my chest as I squeezed my eyes shut and fought the urge to cry.

Goddamn it, what had just happened?

Warmth surrounded me, then strong hands caught mine and squeezed them gently. "Risa," Azriel said softly. "Look at me."

I didn't want to. I really didn't, but there was a note of command in his voice that I couldn't ignore. I opened my eyes and stared into the blue of his. Saw the understanding there, the compassion.

It shook me almost as much as the rage.

"The events of the last few months have not only threatened your physical well-being," he said softly, "but also damaged your emotional safety and security. It is natural that, sooner or later, you will experience trauma-induced incidents such as this."

"But I was moving on, I was *coping*. Why would the rage hit *now* and not before, when it all first happened?"

"Because you did not seek help for—or even talk about—the events. You bottled it up inside and forced yourself to go on as normal—"

"But I *didn't*. I was useless to everyone for weeks—"

He squeezed my hands again, his gaze searching

mine—and, I suspected, seeing far more than anyone else ever had. "That was grief, and natural given what had happened. But we are connected through our chi, and I know the fury, self-loathing, and uselessness that burn inside you, even now."

Tears tracked their way down my cheeks, cold against my skin. I didn't dispute his words, though. How could I, when they were true?

I hadn't dealt with the anger at *all*. I'd merely pushed it down, pushed it away, and tried to function as normally as I could.

"The rage had no outlet until these men—who may or may not be involved with your mother's killer—reentered your life." He released one hand and touched my cheek lightly, and I closed my eyes against the compassion in his eyes and the sense of caring in his touch.

He was a reaper. He *couldn't* care.

It was dangerous to even think that, because he was only here for the same reason as everyone else—to find my father.

"Yes," he agreed softly, "but that doesn't mean I don't understand what you are going through, or sympathize with the rage. I have felt such rage myself."

I opened my eyes again. "But you're a reaper—"

"I'm a Mijai," he corrected. "And as a warrior, I have experienced more than my fair share of loss."

My gaze searched his. "Someone close to you?"

"A friend," he said, then released my hand and rose.

The compassion and understanding disappeared in an instant, and I knew I'd get little more out of him.

But that didn't stop me from asking, "So what did you do?"

He raised an eyebrow. "I did exactly what you are attempting. I tracked down and killed those responsible."

"And did it make anything any better? Did it make *you* feel any better?"

His mouth twisted bitterly. "No. But at least I could rest easier with the knowledge that they would not be able to destroy anyone else."

And that's what I wanted. While it was undoubtedly true that I wanted vengeance so badly I could almost taste it, I also wanted to stop these people from doing to someone else what they'd done to my mom.

He studied me for a heartbeat, then said, "You're bleeding."

As if his words were a trigger, the pain hit, rolling through me in heated waves. I unzipped my coat and peeled it away from my side. The shirt underneath was torn and covered in blood, but the wound itself wasn't really that deep. It hurt like a bitch, but then shallow wounds were often more painful than the deep ones.

"That is a debatable point," Azriel commented.

"You've obviously never experienced a paper cut." I pulled off the remnants of my shirt and used the unbloodied bits to stanch the wounds. There were benefits to being half wolf, but quick healing was one of those things I didn't quite get enough of. I healed much faster than a human, but my inability to shift into wolf shape meant I couldn't get the almost instantaneous restoration that most wolves enjoyed.

"Why do you not heal yourself in Aedh form?" Azriel said.

I wrinkled my nose and zipped my jacket back up. "Shifting into Aedh saps my strength badly, so I can imagine what trying to heal myself while changing form would do."

"So you've never actually tried?"

"I've never even really thought about it."

There was censure in Azriel's gaze, but he simply nodded toward the panther. "Are you going to call the Directorate about these two?"

"So you did run interference with the other one?"

"Yes. He had an unfortunate collision with a fist."

He said it so matter-of-factly that I actually stared at him for several seconds, wondering if I'd heard him right. But then his lips twitched, ever so slightly, and amusement bubbled through me—although I had a suspicion if I let it loose, it might hold a slightly hysterical edge.

"Wasn't there some sort of reaper rule that said you couldn't interfere in matters of the flesh?"

"No, I said I couldn't dispense *justice* to those wearing flesh unless they stepped into the realms of the gray fields, as the witch had. Which does not preclude the possibility of interaction with humans should the need arise."

"Well, I'm glad you decided to step in. I'm not really sure I could have coped with two of them myself."

He nodded in acknowledgment, then said, "I will guard the door and keep people out while you phone your uncle."

I watched him walk away, my gaze dropping from

the broadness of his shoulders to the stylized tattoos decorating his well-defined back. While the biggest of these was the Dušan, there were others. One was rose-like, another like an eye with a comet tail, and still others nothing more than random swirls. They were his tribal signatures, apparently, although I had no idea what that meant.

And I wasn't likely to find out anytime soon, I thought wryly, as I pushed to my knees and leaned over to feel the cat shifter's pulse.

It was steady enough, meaning I couldn't have done too much damage. I got my phone out, hit the VID-SCREEN button, and said, "Uncle Rhoan."

The screen went into psychedelic mode as the voice-recognition program swung into gear and dialed Rhoan's number. A couple of seconds later, he appeared. "Hey, Ris," he said, the corners of his gray eyes crinkling with warmth as he smiled. "How are you this morning?"

"Not as good as you, by the looks of it."

He laughed. "Liana and Ronan are home from the academy for the weekend. It's just nice to have the whole family in one place again."

Lianna and Ronan were the eldest of the Jenson children and had—against Riley's wishes—enlisted in the Victorian Police Force. "They're nearing gradua-tion soon, aren't they?"

From what they'd told me, the course ran for about six weeks; after that, there was a two-year probation-ary period.

"Yeah, only a couple of weeks to go. Riley's trying to convince them to go for a country posting. She reckons it will be safer."

I grinned. "Bad guys do make it into the country, you know."

"I know, but convincing her is another matter. What can I do for you, my sweet?"

"Well," I said, my smile fading a little, "you know those half-shifters that attacked me once before?"

His whole demeanor changed in an instant. Gone was the man I knew and loved. The countenance now on the screen was one of the best guardians the Directorate had ever produced.

"They've attacked again?"

"The other two have, yeah. They're both unconscious at the moment, but if you could get some help down here, I'd appreciate it."

"Where are you?"

I told him, and he nodded. "I'll be down in ten."

"Wait—"

He didn't, just clicked off. I swore softly. Riley was going to kill me. She didn't often have her entire family together for a weekend, and now I had to go spoil things by calling Rhoan away.

Although, to be fair, she'd always considered me part of her extended pack, and she would have killed me if I'd called anyone else.

A steady stream of curses began flowing from the far side of the lockers. Obviously, the other shifter was now awake. I checked the panther's pulse again, then rose, wincing a little and holding my side as I walked around to the back of the lockers. The second shifter lay on his stomach, and his hands and feet hog-tied behind his back. The rope used to bind him was nothing I'd ever seen before. It looked ethereal,

as if it had been pulled from the gray fields themselves.

He twisted his head around and glared up at me.
"This is fucking uncomfortable!"

"Good," I said, a little amused that he'd actually
think I'd care. "Who sent you?"

I'd already had the answer from the panther, but it
never hurt to double check.

"What's in it for me if I tell you?"

"I'll consider releasing you before the Directorate
gets here. Now answer the question."

He studied me for a moment, obviously weighing
his options.

"Handberry," he said eventually. "Or whoever it is
that has taken his place."

"Does that mean someone has taken over owner-
ship of the Phoenix?" The Phoenix was a down-
market bar situated on a street that just happened
to be at the intersection of several major ley lines.
We'd all but stopped the consortium that had been
attempting—through any means necessary—to buy
all the properties along the street in an effort to control the ley-intersection, but not all of the consortium's owners had been caught.

"Like I fucking know *or* care," he said. "Handberry was just using the Phoenix as a base of opera-
tions, as far as I knew. I doubt this new guy will even
go near the place. He sounds way too posh for that."

Posh or not, that didn't preclude the possibility that
he was there. It was certainly worth checking. "And
you've never seen the new handler?"

"Nah, he always has his vid-screen off, and we've
never met him in person."

"And you don't find this strange? I mean, Handberry worked alongside you, didn't he?"

"Yeah, but Handberry was one of us."

"Meaning a Razan, or a human twisted by magic?"

"Both."

"So which Aedh do you belong to?"

Something flickered in his eyes. "I can't say."

"Can't or won't?"

"Can't," he said. "The information was burned away when the magic happened."

And *that* sounded a little too convenient. "So who gave you the ability to shift shape?"

He shrugged. "We weren't allowed to see the practitioner."

I raised an eyebrow. "And how, pray tell, did they achieve that miracle?"

"We were knocked out. Apparently it would have been too painful otherwise."

Well, given the fact that the magic had twisted their beings at a cellular level, I'd guess that was something of an understatement. It was pointless asking where and when—apparently one of the benefits of being a Razan was a very long life, and though these men looked to be little more than midthirties, they could have been hundreds of years old. And I doubted the shifting ability was new. They were too good at controlling it for it to be a recent event.

Although it seemed odd that these Razan wouldn't have a stronger connection to their masters than just a telephone number.

But maybe the Razan ranks had levels. Maybe it was only the ones like Handberry who had a direct connection to their master. Maybe the grunts were kept ignorant for safety reasons.

"There's nothing else you can tell me about the ceremony or the people who performed it?"

"It was a man. Other than that, your guess is as good as mine. How about releasing me now? My arms are going fucking numb."

"Can't say I'm sorry about that, considering what you were intending to do to me." I swung around and left.

"Hey," he shouted after me. "You said you'd release me before the Directorate got here!"

"No, I said I'd consider it," I flung over my shoulder. "Which I have. Consider the request denied."

He swore, long and viciously, but I ignored him and walked around to check out my other prisoner. He was also beginning to wake. But I didn't really have anything to tie him up with, so I did the next best thing—I knocked him out again.

Rhoan appeared ten minutes later, and he wasn't alone. The man who accompanied him had dark hair and well-defined, handsome features. His eyes were the blue of the ocean, his shoulders broad, and his body lithe. He was also a werewolf. Vamps might not be able to traverse the daylight hours well, but other nasties certainly could, so it was logical for the Directorate to have more than just vamps on their team.

"Ris," Rhoan said, his gaze sweeping from me to the man at my feet and then back again. Humor glinted in the cool depths of his eyes, but died quickly as his nostrils flared. "You're hurt."

I shrugged. "It's a scratch."

He eyed me, demeanor disbelieving—undoubtedly because he could smell the blood. "This is Harris. Riley's threatened me with death if I spend more than an hour away, so Harris will ensure these two are taken back for questioning. And it doesn't smell like a scratch."

"Honestly, it's okay. I'm okay."

If my reply sounded halfhearted, it was only because I was racking my brains trying to remember where I'd heard Harris's name before. Then it hit me—Harris was the cop who'd helped Aunt Riley out the time she'd been kidnapped and brainwashed.

The man in question nodded my way, then continued on past us, heading for the other side of the lockers, moving with an economy that spoke of both grace and understated power. As he disappeared around the corner, the shifter's swearing abruptly ceased.

I glanced at Rhoan. "I asked the other man who his maker was, but he said the information had been burned from his mind. Can you check that out?"

Rhoan nodded. "What did they want?"

"The letter my father left in the locker."

His gaze narrowed. "Why would your father leave a letter in a locker in the middle of a train station?"

"Because that's just the way he does things."

"What does it say?"

I shrugged. "It's instructions on how to read the Dušan's book, which is pretty useless given the Aedh have the book, not me."

He grunted, accepting the half lie. "*That* could be a good thing. If you don't have the book, you can't chase keys. And that means Hunter might just leave you alone."

Given Hunter was all that stood between me and the high vampire council, I was actually hoping she didn't. And I had hell's chance of the Aedh giving up. But I didn't say that. I simply shrugged.

He eyed me for a moment, obviously suspecting there was a reason behind my silence, but thankfully Harris chose that moment to reappear. He was dragging the second man along behind him by the ethereal webbing.

"A very interesting rope you've got here," he said, his gaze meeting mine. The blue depths were cool and distant—not a man who trusted easily, I thought. "What is it made of?"

"I couldn't say, because it isn't my rope."

He raised a dark eyebrow. "Whose rope is it? And can you remove it?"

"It's Azriel's. And yes, he probably can."

"Who's Azriel? The cop at the door?" Harris asked.

"That's no cop," Rhoan said. "*That* is a reaper."

"*He* is a reaper," I corrected gently.

Rhoan glanced at me, bemusement crinkling the corners of his eyes, but all he said was, "Can he remove it so that transporting our prisoner is a little easier?"

Even as he made the request, the webbing disintegrated. The shifter groaned when his legs and arms were released, but it was a sound that became another curse as Harris quickly replaced the webbing with cuffs.

"Thanks, Azriel," Rhoan said, then frowned.

"Have you been the victim of any other recent attacks that you haven't told us about?"

I shook my head and lied. "This is the first."

"If there are any more, you *will* tell us, won't you?"

"Of course." It would have been stupid to do say anything else.

He relaxed a little, bending to cuff the shifter at my feet before glancing at Harris. "Let me know how the questioning goes."

Harris nodded, then dragged the second shifter to his feet. He shoved him forward, then looked at me. "You okay there while I get this bit of scum out to the van?"

"Of course."

"Good. I won't be long."

As he headed out, Rhoan kissed my cheek. "Be careful. And if you're free tomorrow night, come around for dinner. The twins would love to see you."

"I'll try, but the café's fully booked and it could be a long night."

"I'll let them know. They might even drop by on the way to the Blue Moon."

"Tell them drinks are on me if they do."

Rhoan snorted. "You could regret that."

I grinned. Ronan—the older of the twins by a mere three minutes—and I had a long history of trying to drink each other under the table. Of course, both of us had nonhuman constitutions, so getting drunk took not only a long time, but a whole lot of patience *and* money.

"Take care of that wound, Ris, or Riley will have my hide." He touched my shoulder lightly then jogged out of the room. Harris returned soon after. I watched him drag the second shifter to his feet.

"I don't suppose you could let me know if you uncover anything about his employer?"

His gaze met mine, blue eyes glinting. "I don't suppose you've double-checked with your uncle first?"

I half smiled. "I don't suppose I have."

"Then I'll give him the information, and you can attempt to get it from him."

"Fair enough. Have fun with the interrogation."

"I always do," he said cheerfully, then swung the panther around and pushed him toward the exit.

Azriel appeared almost immediately. "What does the note actually say?"

"I don't know." I pulled it from my pocket and opened it up. I quickly scanned the spidery writing, then read it out loud. *"The Dušan's book is being held by the Raziq at the underground lair where they interrogated you. At one o'clock tonight, I will arrange a diversion and draw them out. Be there to get the book."* I snorted softly and looked up at Azriel. "Like it's going to be that easy."

"No," he said, obviously taking my words at face value, "it won't. Just because the Raziq have gone doesn't mean there won't be Razan. And I presume our window for getting in and out will be extremely small."

More than likely. I glanced down at the note again, then folded it up and shoved it back into my pocket. "I have no idea where the Raziq were holding me, so I hope you can find your way back there."

"I can."

I studied him for a moment, then said, "I'm a little

surprised that you haven't suggested you retrieve it while I remain behind."

He raised an eyebrow. "And what would that achieve? According to your father, the Raziq have the book veiled, and only one of the blood can see it. I am not of the blood."

"No, but you're Mijai, and surely if anyone would be able to see through a veil, it would be you."

"The veil could be magical rather than connected to the gray fields. And if it is, it would work on me as effectively as on anyone else."

"Really? You saw the spell on the elevator clearly."

"That was human magic. The Aedh are more adept at concealing their magic from us." He shrugged. "We will have little enough time as it is, and attempting to find something that I might or might not be able to see would be foolish."

Point taken. A glance at my watch revealed it was nearly two thirty. I wasn't going to make Stane's this afternoon, given I started work at three.

"Isn't the nanowire more important at this juncture?" Azriel commented.

"Yes, but I doubt Hunter is going to come waltzing into the restaurant anytime soon. Plus, we'd never get anyone to step in for me this late."

"Then what time do you finish this evening?"

"Eleven. Or thereabouts, depending on how busy we are. Why?"

"Because while you are working, I will scout out the tunnels the Raziq hide in."

"Won't they sense you?"

"Yes, but one of their Razan is allotted to die this evening. I will use that to our advantage."

Meaning he'd follow him around like a regular reaper until the moment his death occurred. As plans went, it was pretty good. At least we'd know the lay of the land before we went in. "But won't that piss off whatever reaper has already been assigned the job?"

He frowned. "*Piss off* means 'annoy,' does it not?" And when I nodded, he continued, "Why would you think it would annoy whoever was his previously al- lotted guide?"

"Well, you're usurping his position."

"That's not the way it works for us. And this inves- tigation would get priority even if it was."

"And here I was thinking you were stuck like glue to my ass until everything was done and dusted."

"Well, at least it *is* a most suitable ass to be follow- ing," he said, and winked out of existence.

Leaving me a little speechless. What sort of compli- ment was "suitable"? And why the hell was he even noticing my ass anyway? Especially given his stated disinterest in the human race as a whole, and the hu- man body in particular?

I shook my head, beginning to suspect I was never going to understand him. Then I left the locker room and made my way back to my bike, pausing only to place my promised call to Ilianna, assuring her all was okay.

The streets were crowded, so it took me longer than usual to get over to Lygon Street—and of course that meant I was late.

I jogged up the stairs to wash and change, thankful that I'd made a habit of keeping several changes of clothes at work. After grabbing an apron, I pitched in, taking orders, working the till, clearing tables—

basically, just being where I was needed the most. We were busy the entire shift, and my side wasn't the only thing aching by the time we neared the end. Of course, doing this job in stilettos was never a good idea, but the shoes were new and pretty, and sometimes that won out over sensible.

By the time Ilianna came in for her shift, we'd hit a lull and I was leaning a hip against the bar, one shoe off as I rubbed an aching heel.

"Here," she said, stopping at the other side of the bar and delving into her bag. "I brought you this."

She held out a little red bottle, and I grinned. Foot balm. "You're an angel."

She smiled. "I prefer goddess. Especially since you already have one angel in your life."

"A very dark angel."

"At least he's cute."

I raised my eyebrows. "And why are you even noticing something like that?"

"Hey, just because I bat for the other team doesn't mean I'm incapable of appreciating a good male form. Azriel is all that and more."

"Yeah," I said wryly. "The *more* being extremely dangerous, and only here for one reason."

She shrugged. "Which doesn't mean we can't appreciate the show while he's around. Did anything happen that I need to know about?"

It took me a moment to realize she was talking about the café. "Nope. We were running around like mad, though. We might have to think about hiring more people if this keeps up."

"Can't be sad about that," she said, and headed up to the changing room. I rubbed the oil into my poor feet. And then, feeling decidedly better, I counted the shift's take. Once I'd taken it up to the safe, I clocked out, changed into jeans, a sexy purple shirt, and more sensible shoes, then headed off.

The night was cool and fresh, and filled with music and the delicious aroma of wolves having fun. I paused on the sidewalk, looking a little wistfully toward the Blue Moon. There was a line out front. Even if I *was* tempted, I wasn't going to stand there for an hour or so to get in. Not after such a busy shift, and not when I was a member at Franklin's, which didn't have Jak Talbott—the wolf who'd used our relationship to get close to Mom and write an in-depth but somewhat fictitious story about her life—as one of their regular clients. Mom had sued the paper and him—and had won an out-of-court settlement as well as a retraction—but some mud always sticks.

I glanced at my watch and cursed softly. Given my one o'clock appointment, I really didn't have time to go enjoy myself at *any* club. Maybe another night. Of course, it would be better if Lucian got back to Melbourne. Maybe I needed to give him a call, just to remind him what he was missing out on.

The thought brought a smile to my lips. I grabbed my phone and said his name as I made my way around to the secure parking lot the café shared with several other business.

As the old gates screeched open, Lucian came online and a sigh escaped me. If ever there was a man who was perfectly formed in every way imaginable, then he was it. His face was truly beautiful, though he could never be considered effeminate—there was simply too much strength, too much . . . manliness.

Which was odd, because he wasn't a man, but an Aedh, an energy being. His hair was golden and his eyes were the most glorious jade green. They were also so full of power that, even through the phone's screen, it was almost impossible to look at them without flinching.

He had the look of an angel and in the past—before his golden wings had been torn off—he probably would have been mistaken for one. Because even though reapers were the true soul guides, it was the Aedh who had given rise to the angels seen in so many myths.

"Risa," he said, his deep voice reverberating with pleasure. "I was just thinking about you."

I grinned. "I hope you're alone. If not, your partner might be a bit miffed to hear that."

He laughed. "I am—unfortunately—quite alone. Yourself?"

"The same." I gave my sigh a wistful edge. "Which is unfortunate, as you said, because I happen to be horny as hell."

Something very primal sparked in the recesses of his eyes. "And is it your intent to torture me with this news?"

I laughed. "Totally. Either you get your butt back here, or I shall have to seek release elsewhere."

"It is lucky, then, that I'm currently waiting to board a plane, and that I'll be back in Melbourne by six tomorrow morning."

I made a tsking sound. "I'm not sure that's soon enough."

"But if you pick me up at the airport, we could both get our ease sooner rather than later."

"If you send me the flight details, I just might."

He smiled, and it was a hungry thing. Heat curled through my belly, and it was difficult not to hum in pleasure. "How's the trip been otherwise?"

"Business is always boring," he said, "but the client is an important one, so I do what I must."

Lucian was a financial adviser—a fairly high-profile and wealthy one, from what I could see, even though he tended to play that down. "I take it this client didn't have any pretty secretaries?"

"Not a one," he said solemnly, though his bright eyes danced with mirth. "I had to fill my time making good on promises."

"Hmm," I said. "To whom?"

"To you, lovely lady."

"Me?" I said, surprised. "What promises have you made to me?"

"Well, I did say I'd attempt to see what I could un- cover about your father. While I've had no luck there, I managed to discover whom the Razan known as Handberry was supposed to meet the night he was killed by the soul stealer."

I frowned. I couldn't actually remember mention- ing Handberry to Lucian, but given everything that had happened over the past weeks, it wasn't out of the question that I'd simply forgotten I'd done it.

Either that, or he'd gleaned the knowledge from my mind during one of our many lovemaking sessions. That was always the risk with our relationship, but not one I was overly concerned with. After all, there weren't that many questions he could ask that I *wouldn't* answer.

Still, it made me wonder if the nanowire would work against him.

"How did you discover who Handberry was supposed to meet with?"

He smiled. "A good investigator never reveals his sources, but I will note that it cost me a crate of very expensive champagne."

My cheeks dimpled. "I shall repay in kind, if you like."

"Oh," he said, his voice suddenly lower *and* a whole lot sexier, "I intend to extract their worth in another way entirely."

That curl of heat in my belly got stronger. I grinned. "That could take more time than *either* of us has in our schedule."

"Which only makes the thought all the more delectable."

The man was incorrigible. *And* insatiable. Not that I was quibbling about either. "So who was he?"

"His name is Ike Forman. According to my source, he's a thug with pretensions. He has a very upper-class attitude, but he fights dirty."

Upper-class . . .

Excitement rolled through me. It sounded very much like the man the panther had described.

Meaning I more than likely had a name for the next person up the ladder—and was one step closer to discovering who the hell was sending these things after me.

Chapter Five

"I TAKE IT FROM YOUR EXPRESSION THAT THE name means something to you?" Lucian said.

"The name, no. It's just that one of the half-shifters used very similar terms to describe their new handler. I'm betting it's not a coincidence."

"More than likely not," he agreed. "I gather this means the half-shifters have attacked you again?"

"Yes. Did your source say anything else about Forman?"

"Not really. I simply asked if he knew anything about Handberry, as he represents the sort of clients that Handberry would associate with. Forman was the only name he could suggest."

"If Forman has upper-class pretensions, why would he associate with someone like Handberry?"

"That's a question you'll have to ask Forman when you find him."

"So you couldn't get an address for the man?"

"No, but I daresay you're resourceful enough to get that information yourself."

"I daresay I am." Or, at least, Stane was.

"They're calling my flight. I'll see you in the morning?"

"You will."

"And you'd better wear something you don't value," he warned, his eyes glowing, "because I have every intention of tearing it off you the minute we are alone."

"I like the sound of that."

He laughed, blew a kiss, and hung up, leaving me grinning like a fool as I fired up my bike and drove over to Stane's.

I parked on a side street off West Street, away from Stane's computer shop and well out of sight of any foot traffic coming from the Phoenix. Given the condition of Stane's storefront, it was obvious that the club's patrons didn't mind doing a bit of damage as they stumbled home.

As I took off my helmet, the noise hit—the music a heavy beat that pounded through the air and rattled the nearby windows. Underneath it ran the sound of raucous voices—men *and* women. I could only be thankful I didn't have to go there. I didn't mind loud music, but I liked to be able to dance to it. This seemed little more than noise.

I set the bike's alarm, then made my way around to Stane's shop. Thick grates covered the front windows, but a lot of the bars were bent—the work of drunken nonhumans, most likely, since humans would never be able to budge metal that thick without assistance.

I pushed the front door open and a tiny bell rang cheerily. The camera above the doorway buzzed into action, tracking me as I entered the shop—not that I could go too far in. Stane had a containment field around the entrance, and no one was getting into the inner sanctum without his permission.

"Stane, it's Risa, reporting in as ordered."

"I believe you were supposed to report some ten hours ago," he said, his voice dry even over the speakers.

"Something came up."

"An event that occurs quite often around you, I've discovered." The slight shimmer that was the containment field disappeared. "Come on up."

I headed for the stairs at the back of the shop. This area was small and smelled of dust and mold. There were shelves everywhere, all packed with boxes, old and new computer parts, and ancient-looking monitors of varying sizes.

Of course, mold and dust weren't exactly good for computers, but I had it on good authority—Tao's—that this area was little more than a ruse. The expensive items were all kept upstairs.

And up there, you stepped into another world—one that was clean, shiny, and filled with the latest in computer technology. In fact, Stane's system dominated the main living space and wouldn't have looked out of place on a spaceship.

It was a stark contrast with Stane himself, who could only be described as a mess with his unkempt brown hair, thick ill-fitting black sweater, and wrinkled jeans. He certainly didn't look like someone who'd put up any sort of fight—until you actually gazed into his honey-colored eyes. Stane, like Tao, was smarter and tougher than he looked.

He gave me a bright, warm smile as he rose and kissed me on the cheek. "So this thing that came up . . . ," he said cheerfully. "I don't suppose there's anything I can do to help?"

A grin teased my lips. "What, the black market not exciting enough for you these days?"

"It's not that." He sat down and pushed a second chair my way. "It's more the challenge. You task me with the impossible and just presume I'll come through. I like that."

I laughed. "Well, I do have an information hunt, but I don't think it's going to tax you or your system too much."

"I have complete faith in the fact that, now that you're back chasing otherworld crap, my tasks will only get harder." Anticipation mingled with humor in his eyes. "So hit me with this first one, and don't be too long with the rest."

I shook my head as I said, "I need any and all information you have on an Ike Forman. Apparently, he's the man Handberry went to meet the night he was killed, and he might also be the half-shifters' new handler."

Stane frowned. "Forman? That name rings a bell. Hang on a sec." He twisted around and touched one of the light screens on his circular "bridge." "Here, listen to this."

A harsh voice suddenly shouted, "Fuck it, Forman, I'm not going to waste more good men like this. It's not worth it."

The voice belonged to Handberry, and the conversation had obviously been going for a while. But given that Handberry had stormed out not long after I'd released the listening bug into his office, I guess we'd been lucky to get anything at all.

The voice on the other side was muffled, but the tone was definitely urbane.

"I don't fucking care what Harlen said," Handberry ranted in response. "These are my fucking men, not his. There must be a better—"

Forman obviously cut Handberry off, because he fell silent for several heartbeats. Then he swore loudly and said, "Tell the bastard to meet me at home. I'll be there in twenty."

With that, he hung up. Footsteps retreated and the door slammed. That's when Tao and I had witnessed him storming out of the club like some great black thundercloud. And twenty minutes later he was dead.

Stane pressed the screen again, preventing the recording from looping and replaying. "I tried to enhance the other end of the conversation, but could only get snatches of words. I think the other guy was using some sort of scrambler to hamper recording."

Which meant he was not only urbane, but also smart *and* careful. "What about the name Handberry mentioned? Harlen?"

"I did do a search for both Harlen and Forman, but without knowing their full names, it was pretty useless. Still, there's no Forman or Harlen connected to either the club or the consortium that was buying up the properties around here."

I frowned. "What happened to the third man connected to the consortium, John Nadler? The one we never found?"

Stane shrugged. "Whoever he really is, he's got his tracks covered. I've tried just about every search I can think of, and I'm coming up with nothing."

Which was undoubtedly frustrating to someone like Stane, who prided himself on being able to go anywhere, and find anything, along the Net's super-highway. "Meaning he's probably using a fake ID."

"Actually, I think it probably means he's living two separate lives. Fake ID will only get you so far in this day and age."

"But even if he was living two lives, wouldn't one of those still require a fake ID?"

"Not if he simply stepped into the life of another man."

"But that's not possible—"

"Really?" he interrupted, eyebrow raised. "Do you think you're the only face shifter on the planet?"

Face shifters were able to make basic structural changes to their faces—hair, eyes, and shape. Most could only hold the new form for limited amounts of time, but I'd inherited my shifting ability from my mom, and her genes had been enhanced in the laboratories of a madman. It took a lot of effort for me to change, but once I was there, I could hold it for a long time. "Well, of course not. But it would mean he's a Helki werewolf, and that *would* impact both identities. Moon heat isn't exactly something you can hide."

"Why would he have to be a werewolf? I know for a fact that the military has face shifters, and they aren't all werewolves."

I stared at him for a moment. "Just how do you know all this stuff?"

He shrugged. "I told you, I get bored. It's amazing what risks you'll take when you're bored."

I snorted softly. "And what happened to all the land the consortium purchased?"

"It's still all owned by the consortium, which is now run solely by Nadler. But James Trilby and Garvin Appleby's heirs are suing the consortium and Nadler for a bigger piece of the pie."

Trilby and Appleby were the other two men we'd linked to the consortium. They were dead, just as the witch who'd been in their employ was dead—killed by Azriel after she'd sent a soul stealer after a little girl. "Does that mean the two men didn't leave wills, or did they simply not leave their heirs enough money?"

"The latter." He grimaced. "See, this is where pack mentality wins out. In the event of my death, everything either goes entirely to the pack, or it's split seventy–thirty between my heirs and the pack. Everyone understands the situation, and everyone wins."

I grinned. "You don't have any heirs, so your pack wins big time."

"Hey," he said, voice offended but eyes dancing. "I might not have heirs yet, but that doesn't mean I'm not looking for a suitable lady."

I snorted softly. "It's a little hard to find said lady if you never actually leave your house."

"I leave," he said. "And ladies *do* occasionally come into the shop."

"Yeah, and then run screaming when they see the mess downstairs," I said drily.

"That, unfortunately, is more true than not. Hence the reason I don't invite many lovelies back." He paused, then wiggled his eyebrows outrageously. "Of course, there is *one* lady who's not afraid to brave the mess. I don't suppose you'd consider taking another lover?"

"One lover is *more* than enough for me at the moment."

"And you call yourself a werewolf?" he said, pretending outrage.

I laughed. "Half-werewolf. There is a difference." At least, there was with me. Apparently my Aedh heritage had toned down what society generally considered the "worst" aspect of being a werewolf—that is, the moon heat, which forced us to seek sex or go mad during the full moon phase. And—unlike every other werewolf—I wasn't forced to shift shape on the night of the full moon. In fact, I couldn't attain wolf form *anytime*.

But I *did* have a wolf's keen senses and high sex drive, as well as the attitude that sex was something to be celebrated. Which came in handy when I had a lover like Lucian.

"So if the consortium is being sued, doesn't that mean Nadler will have to appear in court?"

"Not necessarily. The case has gone into arbitration. And from what I've seen, his lawyers are handling it."

"But isn't getting the two combatants to face each other across the table the whole point of arbitration?"

"Yes, unless one of them has money and friends in high places, as is the case here, apparently." He shrugged. "I'm keeping an electronic eye on the situation. If anything new comes up, I'll let you know."

"Speaking of electronic eyes, did Tao ask you to do a sweep of our apartment?"

He nodded. "I won't get there until tomorrow, though. I've got several deals going down tonight."

I wondered if they were legit or black market, then decided I really *didn't* want to know. "This nanowire you're supposedly fitting—care to explain just what that involves?"

"Ah," he said, his expression becoming decidedly smug. "These things are real gems."

He walked over to a storage shelf on the far side of the room and picked up what looked to be a small plastic container. "This," he said, holding it out so I could see, "is the very latest development in nano-technology. Not even the Directorate has these little beauties yet."

The little beauties in question were no bigger than a pin head and copper in color. "And they're going to stop vampires from invading my mind?" I demanded. "It's not that I don't believe you, it's just that they don't look powerful enough to stop an inquisitive gnat, let alone a vampire with any real telepathic abil-ity."

He laughed softly. "Trust me, these work. I got them hot off the military supply chain."

"I do *not* want to know that," I said. "Just install the things, then hit me with the price."

He did the latter first, and I just about fell off my chair. Still, we'd said price was no object, and if they actually worked, then it would be worth it.

He handed me the container, then headed for the small kitchen tucked into the corner of the room. He retrieved a weird-looking syringe-type device from a drawer and then came back.

"You keep syringes with your knives?" I asked, eye-ing the massive thing dubiously. "I really *don't* want to know where you're going to insert *that*."

"Nowhere interesting, unfortunately," he said wryly. "One microcell goes into your right heel, the other into your left ear."

"You are not shoving something that large into my ear!"

"Don't be a baby. Both Ilianna and Tao lived through it. You will, too."

"Well, I hope you've at least sterilized the needle," I muttered, almost mutinously. I hated needles nearly as much as I hated spiders.

"Of course. Now take your right shoe off and give me your foot."

I blew out a breath and did as he asked. He took a tube of cream out of his sweater pocket and rubbed some of it on my heel, then pulled on some gloves. After a minute, he hit a button on the syringe and plucked out one of the microcells; a second later the thing was in my heel. I didn't even feel it.

"See," he said, grinning up at me. "All that worry for nothing."

"You haven't gotten to my ear yet," I grouched, more for the sake of it than anything else.

He repeated the process on my ear, then said, "That's it."

I put my shoe back on. "So how is it supposed to work?"

He held up his hand and looked at his watch. After a couple of minutes, he dropped his hand. "Okay," he said. "The microcells have now been warmed by your body and will have started doing their job. However, it'll take twenty-four hours before they're working at full capacity."

I frowned. "But how are they supposed to work when they're not even connected?"

I knew the basics of nanowires—like cells, they were powered by the heat of the body. But for the wires to be active, both ends had to be connected, so that a circuit was formed. They also gave off an extremely faint electronic tingle when in use, whereas these things didn't.

"Think of these as yin and yang—constantly interacting, yet never existing in absolute stasis."

I blinked. "That made a whole lot of sense." *Not.*

He grinned. "Okay, simpler terms. They are polar or contradictory forces that interact once put in a certain environment. In this case, the body. Once they are fully activated, the push–pull of their interaction provides a shield that is ten times stronger than any wire ever created."

"Whoa," I said, stunned. While even *that* might not be enough to stop the likes of Hunter, it *would* stop the majority of vampires out there. And surely something that strong would at least hamper Hunter. "How can something so tiny be that strong?"

"Science these days is amazing," he said, sounding like a kid peering though a candy store window. "Trust me, you won't believe some of the things both the military and private research labs are developing right now."

"Well, given your love of acquiring such objects, I daresay we'll see them sooner rather than later."

"I'd love to agree, but I do have to be cautious. Or rather my sources do. We wouldn't want to start any nasty investigations, would we?"

"No, we wouldn't."

"Too right," he said, dumping the gloves and the syringe into a tray near his desk. They were promptly sucked away to God knew where.

"Risa, it's time to go," a familiar voice behind me said.

Both Stane and I jumped, and I turned. Azriel was standing behind me, arms crossed as he studied us both. He seemed amused, even if his expression was its usual blank slate.

"Damn it," Stane said. "For the sake of my nerves, let alone my heart, you *really* need to learn to knock or something."

"Wouldn't a knock coming out of nowhere alarm you almost as much?"

"Not nearly as much as hearing a voice come out of nowhere, then looking up to see a man-mountain," Stane commented.

Stane, like nearly everyone else, couldn't see Azriel's natural form. He saw the form most likely to give him comfort and make him feel safe. In this case, it was the image of a deceased relative. Interestingly, Tao saw the same image.

Azriel shrugged. "I cannot alter the manner in which I appear. I am either here or I am not."

Which wasn't exactly true, because he could be here and not be visible. He'd done that more than a few times.

"How did your scouting trip go?" I asked.

"There were six Razan in the tunnel. But there are now five, thanks to one taking a rather careless step into the street without looking first."

"And his soul?"

"Guided down the dark path, as was his lot."

"By you?"

He nodded. "Why do you seem surprised? I told you before that was my intention."

"Yeah, but I wasn't sure if you meant actually guiding the soul as well. I mean, you're a Mijai, not a reaper."

"I was a reaper long before I was a Mijai."

"So becoming a Mijai is a promotion?"

His smile held a slightly bitter edge. "No, it is not. We are merely the warriors, the dark angels. Reapers are the soul guides, and that is truly an honored position."

"All reapers are guides, but not all reapers can become Mijai, so why would the former be more honored than the latter? Both do important tasks."

"Yes, but we are called dark angels for a reason. We really must go."

"Not without telling me the reason for the moniker."

"Later," he said, and winked out of existence.

I swore softly, then looked over at Stane. "I guess I have to go."

"Sounds like it," he said, amused. "Good luck with getting that information. Personally, I think it'd be simpler getting blood from a stone."

"You could be right. And don't forget to send me your account details so I can flash over the money."

He leaned sideways and pressed a couple of buttons. A second later my phone beeped. "Ta," I said, and waved a sketchy good-bye.

The containment field went down as I neared the door. I walked around to my Ducati and was relieved to see she was still in one piece. I pulled on the helmet, jumped on the bike, and headed home.

Azriel appeared as I drove into our garage. "We really must be going," he said, a slight edge of impatience in his voice. "It is nearly one."

"Fine, but I paid an absolute fortune for this bike when I was younger, and I do *not* want her damaged."

"You are rich, are you not? You could buy another."

"Yes, I'm rich, and yes, I could buy another, but that is *not* the point. I bought her with my own money, not with anything Mom had invested for me." I stowed the helmet and pocketed the keys. "How do I follow you in Aedh form?"

"You don't." He stepped forward and wrapped his arms around me. Before I could even register surprise, power surged, running through every muscle, every fiber, until my whole body sang with it. Until it felt like there was no me and no him, just the sum of us— energy beings with no flesh to hold us in place.

Then the garage winked out of existence and we were on the gray fields. Only it wasn't the gray fields that I saw—to me, they were usually little more than the real world covered by thick veils and shadows, where things not sighted on the living plane gained substance. But in Azriel's arms, the fields were vast and beautiful, filled with airy, intricate structures and sun-bright pulses of life that teased the imagination.

Then the fields were gone, replaced by darkness that smelled of earth, mold, and disuse. The old sewer tunnels the Aedh were apparently using for their lair.

Azriel released me the minute we were solid. I

stepped back, my body still humming from the energy he'd released—not to mention our closeness.

"We are down the far end of the tunnels from where the Razan are," he said softly. "They are apparently not using this section."

"So why are we here?" I asked, attempting to shake off the effects of his touch.

"Is it not best to start at one end rather than the middle?"

I guess it did make more sense. I swung around and studied the darkness behind us. "Have the Raziq all gone?"

"Yes."

"Then let's get this over with."

I walked forward, my footsteps soft yet echoing faintly in the darkness. I kept close to the damp brick wall, using its presence as a guide, because I sure as hell couldn't see. It wasn't long before we reached the first puddle of light and I paused, recognizing the small room to the left. It was where the Razan guards had been the night I'd escaped my prison. This time the TV was off, and the air was free of the scent of men.

"Should we check it?" I said, pausing near the doorway.

"Given that the book is hidden by veils, it would be wise."

"My father said I'd feel its presence. I don't." But then, I hadn't "felt" it when it first arrived, either. Of course, that could have been because I'd been too busy trying to avoid the lilac-colored dragon that had exploded from it—a dragon that now decorated my left arm.

I stepped inside and made a cursory circuit of the room, avoiding the take-out and drink containers that littered the floor. I didn't feel anything more than the chill in the air.

We continued on down the tunnel. After a while, more doors came into view, and as my gaze went to the first one, I shivered. This was the cell where I'd been kept. The cell where I'd been tortured.

I reached for the door handle—my fingers shaking and my stomach flip-flopping—and opened it up. The room inside was small, dark, and yet familiar, even if the glass embedded into the concrete floor was barely visible and there was little sign of the energy field that had hampered my ability to shift into Aedh form. I stepped to the edge of the glass and wondered if the remnants of my jeans still lay in the middle of the circle.

"Risa." Azriel touched my elbow lightly, making me jump. "We cannot linger."

"Okay." I couldn't sense the book in the cell, anyway, so I closed the door and tried the other two, with the same result.

The tunnel swept slowly around to the right and sounds began to invade the darkness. The slight drip of water, the murmur of conversation, the stir of heat through the air.

I glanced at Azriel, and he held up three fingers. I guess I had to be grateful that he hadn't indicated that all five were present, although that did raise the question of where the other two were.

I walked on more cautiously, but no matter how much I tried to be quiet, my footsteps couldn't help but echo in these shoes. I should have taken them off

and walked barefoot, but given the Raziq's penchant
for laying glass into their floors . . .

"What's that?" a voice ahead said.

I stopped, my fists clenched. After a moment, another man said, "We're in a fucking disused tunnel.
It's probably the goddamn rats again."

"No, I heard something else. Something bigger."

"Well, go investigate then," the other man retorted.
"I'm not leaving the fire."

The other man swore, then said, "Frank, come with
me."

Heavy footsteps echoed, then light suddenly swept
the wall inches from where I stood. I pressed my back
against the bricks and held my breath. The light
jumped away and scanned the other wall before disappearing again.

I blew out a breath, but the relief came too soon as
the two men began walking toward us. The flashlight's beam bobbed across the walls. I ducked, but
not quickly enough, and the man swore again.

"Just saw someone," he said, and stopped. I
couldn't see either man, only the brightness of their
flashlight, but I could smell them. They were human—
although from what I understood, most Razan were.
They just enjoyed an extraordinarily long life thanks
to their Aedh masters.

"Are you sure?" the other man said, his deep voice
uncertain. "I sure as hell didn't."

"It was just a quick movement on the edge of the
light, but it was there."

"Then you yakking about it is a good way of letting
them know we saw them."

Azriel touched my shoulder lightly; when I looked

up, he motioned me to stay low. I nodded and he winked out of existence. A second later the sound of footsteps running up the tunnel—away from where I was hunkered down—echoed.

"Shit, after him," the first man said. The two of them disappeared after Azriel, leaving me with only the man in the room up ahead. And I couldn't avoid dealing with him—not when I had to check the room he was in.

I rose and crept forward. A warm flickering light began to infuse the darkness, and the air was decidedly warmer. I crept forward, listening intently but unable to hear anything beyond the soft murmur of conversation. TV, I decided, and wondered how the hell they got power down here, let alone reception. I pressed my back against the bricks and peered cautiously around the doorway.

He was sitting in a tattered red armchair in front of a metal barrel that had been cut in half and now had a fire burning in it. The smoke rose and fanned out, hanging like a shroud from the ceiling—a good way to die if there was no cross-ventilation, and I couldn't actually see any. Obviously, these Razan weren't too bright.

I reached for the Aedh, but a hand grabbed mine and it was all I could do to stop myself from screaming. But only because the wash of heat told me who it was.

I glanced at Azriel, who shook his head. *Do not,* he said, his voice crystal clear inside my mind. Obviously, the microcells weren't an impediment to *him* reading my thoughts. *They are attuned to the Aedh and will sense it.*

Well, fuck. Why couldn't something just be easy for a change?

I flexed my fingers, then took off my shoes and left them near the doorway. I crept forward, the old brick flooring icy under my toes. The man stirred and reached for another piece of wood, tossing it into the barrel with a clunk. I froze. The flames flared and sparks bloomed upward, briefly illuminating the ceiling before the smoke closed in again.

He settled back down and, after a moment, I crept on.

But somehow, he sensed me.

In one swift movement, he rose and swung around, a gun rising in his left hand. I dove forward, grabbed the top of the chair for balance and twisted around in midair, aiming my feet at his midriff. He jumped back, firing the gun as he did so. My feet missed his belly, but his aim was better. The bullet skimmed my left leg before tearing a chunk of flesh from my thigh. Pain curled through me but I ignored it and let go of the chair, landing in a crouch, the gun following my movements. I threw myself sideways, realized too late just how close I was to the barrel, and hit it hard. As the barrel and I spilled to the floor, Azriel took shape behind the man and grabbed the weapon. I jerked away from the fire and pushed to my feet, only to see the man flying through the air and hitting the wall with enough force to break bones. He slid down to the floor and was still.

I glanced across at Azriel, who calmly handed me the weapon. I slipped the safety into place, shoved it into the waistband of my jeans, then said, "You're breaking the rules again, aren't you?"

"As I said," he replied, his expression impassive, "my quest comes first. If that man had succeeded in killing you, it would have created serious problems. How is your leg?"

I blinked at the sudden change of topic, and looked down. The bullet had torn a hole in my jeans, and blood was pulsing down my leg. Of course, the minute I became aware of it, the bloody thing began to throb like hell. I swore softly and wished—for the hundredth time in my life—that I could shift shape to heal myself. Unlike my side wound, this one wasn't about to heal in an hour or two. I was stuck with trying to stem the flow of blood until that happened. I guess I just had to be thankful that these men were human rather than shifter or wolf. Otherwise, the damage might have been greater.

I limped around the chair and over to the Razan. After checking his pulse, I stripped off his shirt, tore it into strips, then wrapped them tightly around my thigh. Not exactly hygienic, but better than nothing.

"The guard will be out for about eight minutes," Azriel said. "The others will be back before then. We must find the book quickly."

"Which would be a whole lot easier if the fucking thing weren't hidden by veils." I paused, looking around the room, trying to find something—anything—that sparked a reaction in me. There was nothing.

I sighed in frustration, then put my shoes back on and limped out of the room. The tunnel curved on, and in the distance I could hear the footsteps of the other two men. They were heading back already. All hell would break lose once they'd found their companion. We were running out of time.

The tunnel split into three. I paused, peering into each branch intently, trying to figure out which way to go. The one to my immediate left echoed with the sound of footsteps, so there was no way I was heading down there if it could be avoided. The one straight ahead smelled stale and old, but the air in the one to the right stirred gently, and held the freshness of rain. There was an exit down there somewhere.

My gaze went back to the middle tunnel and, after a moment, I walked on. I don't know why; it just felt right.

The tunnel's old brick walls ran with slime, and the floor was slick with moisture. I couldn't see it because the darkness had closed in once again, but I sure as hell could smell it—and it was *nasty*. Thankfully I wasn't wearing my pretty new shoes, but even these older ones weren't going to be wearable after this. If I'd had half a brain, I would have changed into boots when I'd gotten home.

Any further delay would not have been wise, Azriel commented.

"Stop reading my goddamn thoughts," I muttered.

No.

I glared at him. "Why the hell not?"

Because you do not tell me everything you know or suspect.

Which seemed a bit hypocritical to me, given he was guilty of the same crime, but I knew it wasn't about to change anytime soon. "Then will you at least do one thing for me?"

If it means you will stop risking exposure with all this talking, I will seriously consider it.

"All I'm asking is that you keep your distance whenever I'm with Lucian. That is *my* time, and it has absolutely *nothing* to do with your goddamn mission."

He looked at me, his eyes glowing with an unearthly energy. "Trust me when I say that I have absolutely *no* desire to watch your liaison with the Aedh."

The edge in his voice made my eyebrows rise. "You don't like him, do you?"

"I do not trust him." His gaze slid from mine. The edge in his voice had receded a little, but it still spoke of something more than distrust.

Which was curious. "Why?"

"Because he is Aedh."

"A fallen Aedh."

"Exactly. The Aedh do not tear wings off lightly."

"He's already explained that. He hunted down and killed the people responsible for his sister's murder."

His gaze flicked to mine once more. "And you believe him?"

"Why shouldn't I?"

"Because full Aedh do not live in familial groups or feel love."

"Which doesn't mean it can't be true."

He studied me for a moment, then shrugged. Oddly enough, it seemed more an angry gesture than a casual one. "I shall bow to your judgment, as I have no knowledge of this Aedh." And didn't really want any, from the sound of it. "Now can we keep quiet and concentrate on finding this book before the priests return?"

I shut my mouth and walked on, my footsteps deadened by the slimy concrete. The air became fouler, clogging my lungs with its putrid stench. "God," I murmured, raising a hand to my nose and pinching it shut. It didn't help a whole lot—the smell still clawed at my throat and seared my lungs. "It smells like something massive has died down here."

Azriel didn't say anything. Maybe he was hoping I would follow suit. The tunnel widened slightly and my steps slowed as a sense of greater space hit me. But the darkness was still intense, and I couldn't see any farther than my hand.

But I didn't need to, because I could feel something. It was a presence—an energy—that tingled across my skin like fire and made the dragon on my arm stir and writhe within my flesh. It was a weird sensation.

"I think it's here," I said softly.

Azriel drew his sword and Valdis flared to life, blue flames caressing her razor-sharp sides before spreading out across the darkness.

Dark shapes scurried away from the light, and the source of the smell soon became obvious. A body lay in the center of what once must have been a wastewater junction. I couldn't immediately tell if it was old or young, because most of its features had been eaten away by the rats. Its clothes were in tatters, but the remnants looked old and worn, and its hair—or what remained of it—was shot with gray.

A vagrant, I thought, continuing to hold my nose as I walked forward. The closer I got, the more the dragon writhed, and the more my stomach turned. The rats had been feasting on the vagrant's body for a while, because intestines had spilled out over the

old brickwork, gleaming like sausages in Valdis's unearthly light.

"Do you still feel the presence of the book?" Azriel
said softly.

I thrust up my arm so he could see the Dušan. She
moved serpent-like around my arm, her eyes gleaming with an eerie lilac light.

"Interesting," he said. "The Dušan do not usually
react to stimuli outside the gray fields."

I didn't reply, concentrating on the Dušan as I held
out my arm and swung around in a slow circle. Her
twisting became more intense as I pointed to the right
wall. I stepped over the vagrant's legs and walked on.
The Dušan's reaction became stronger and stronger,
until my flesh burned with her energy.

I stopped. The only thing in front of me was a
wall . . . or was it? My father had said the book was
veiled, but that didn't necessarily mean it was cloaked
in shadows. I ran my hand over the wet stained wall,
searching for any unusual markings in the cold bricks.
My fingers brushed against a perfectly round indenta-
tion and the Dušan's head swung around, staring
at it.

That had to be it.

I stuck a finger into the hole. Something sharp
pricked my finger and I instinctively jerked back. A
droplet of blood beaded the tip, but it didn't actually
look as if anything had bitten me. I frowned, remembering my father's words. *Only one of the blood will
be able to find or see it.* I shoved the finger back into
the hole. After a heartbeat, there was a soft clicking
noise and a small rectangular section of the wall receded, revealing a small chamber. In it sat the book.

I reached inside and picked it up, but the minute I did, there was a huge whooshing sound and three metal gates dropped down from the ceiling, forming a very solid cage.

The bastards had set a trap, and I'd just sprung it.

Chapter Six

As soon as the thick metal bars had clanged home, a rainbow shimmer flared up around them, quickly encasing us on all four sides as well as above. I knew that shimmer—it had been present in the cell, too. It was a veil of magic that prevented me from reaching for the Aedh. To do so would only send me crashing to the floor in writhing agony—or so I'd discovered the last time they had me trapped.

"You have to get us out of here," I said, turning quickly to Azriel. "I can't shift shape when that veil is in place."

"And I can't transport you out of here when it is present," he said, his expression grim. "So let's hope this works."

He raised Valdis and swept her across the nearest barrier. The sword screamed as she bit through the air, the blue flames incandescent by the time metal hit metal. Sparks flew and Azriel's arms jerked as the sword's speed slowed abruptly. Still, bit by bit, Valdis was cutting through the bars, hissing and screaming every inch of the way. Metal melted, running like water down the bars to pool at their base.

The sound of running steps began to echo from the

tunnel we'd just left. The Razan were coming. The Raziq were probably on their way, too. I licked my lips, my heart racing as Azriel withdrew the sword and started cutting again lower.

Valdis's screaming continued to fill the air, her fire flicking across the darkness, sending blue shadows dancing up the slick brick walls. When the second cut was as long as the first, Azriel withdrew the sword, raised a foot, and kicked at the metal. The bars went flying, clattering noisily against the opposite wall. A shout came from one of the men in the tunnel and the sound of their steps grew faster.

"Go," Azriel said, turning to face me. Sweat beaded on his forehead and ran down the edge of his face.

I shoved the book down the front of my top, then grabbed the bars above the cut and swung through feetfirst. My wounded leg brushed one edge and pain rolled through me. Gasping, I stumbled forward, going down on one knee, my hands disappearing into the thick slime lining the floor as I tried to stop my fall.

"Don't move!" a voice said from the tunnel doorway.

I looked up and saw a blond Razan burst into the main tunnel. I saw the gun in his hands, already raised. I saw him pull the trigger.

I threw myself sideways, but it was too late. Far too late . . . only suddenly I was jerked roughly to the right and there was a body standing between me and that bullet.

As Azriel's arms wrapped around me, I felt him jerk. Then energy surged and we were on the gray fields. This time the trip was short and sharp, and darkness still encased us when we reappeared.

We hit the ground together and sprawled forward, landing with some force against a surface that was hard and cold. For several seconds neither of us moved. Azriel's weight pressed me against the cold concrete, making it difficult to breathe. Not that I really cared; I was too busy listening to the silence, smelling the damp and the cold, and wondering where the hell we were.

"Not clear yet," Azriel stated as his weight lifted off me.

There was an edge in his voice that made me frown. "Meaning we're still in the tunnels?"

"Yes." He pushed upright. "Are you all right?"

"I'll survive." I rolled onto my back and accepted his offered hand. His warm flesh was slick—not with moisture or slime, but with blood.

"You've been shot?" I said, watching the blood pour from his wounded shoulder as he hauled me up. "How the hell can a reaper get shot?"

"When I'm in flesh form, I can be damaged." He shrugged.

"Meaning you can also be killed?"

"We are not immortal, Risa. If death is our fate, it will find us—whatever the form."

"But you're more vulnerable in flesh form?" The blood pouring down his arm dripped from our twined fingers—an indication of just how serious the wound was even if he didn't appear to be worrying. Hell, did reapers even feel pain?

"Yes," he said softly. "We are not Aedh. We live and love and hurt."

"So why the hell are we just standing here? Let's zap ourselves away."

"The bullet is silver. With it still in my flesh, I am prevented from doing anything more than short jumps into the gray fields."

"Then let's get the fucking thing out." I hesitated, and frowned. "Wait—they used *silver*?"

That didn't make sense. The Razan had aimed for my head, but the Raziq *needed* me alive. But it also meant that Azriel had saved my life by stepping in front of me and taking the bullet.

"I suspect the bullet was meant for me all along," he said. "The Raziq would have felt my presence the first time I rescued you. They'd know I'd do so again should you be captured a second time. By shooting me with silver, they are giving themselves extra time to find us."

"Then let *me* shift the two of us so we can get the hell out of here." The only problem was, I'd only ever shifted to Aedh form with another person in my arms once, and only then because we'd had no other option. But I knew Tao almost as well as I knew myself, and I'd been lucky. I suspected that would not be the case with Azriel. Hell, I didn't even know if I could reassemble the damn *book* after a shift.

"Which is why we cannot take that option," he said softly. "We cannot risk the book, and you cannot disassemble or reassemble me as you did Tao. I am an energy being, and my makeup is unlike anything you could ever imagine."

And yet, here he was, bleeding like a regular person. "Then let's damn well run! Anything is better than standing here."

He ignored my outburst, his expression as calm as ever. "You cannot go home. That is the first place they will look."

"Then where will we go?"

"Not we. *You.*"

I frowned at him. "I'm not leaving without you—"

"You must," he said. "The Raziq have arrived back in the tunnels. They will be here soon. Go, before they find us."

"But they can track me, can't they?"

"If you remain here, yes they can. If you flee, if you get as far away from this tunnel as you can and don't go back to your apartment, you will be safe."

I eyed him doubtfully, torn between not wanting to get caught by the Aedh again and not wanting to leave the man who'd just saved my life. "But if I remove the bullet—"

"We do not have the time. There is a small manhole above us. Use that to escape."

"Fuck it, I *can't*—"

Anger surged—a brief flare of energy that stung my skin and rushed through my mind. Then it was gone, and he released my hand, pushing me back from him. "*Go.* I will be fine."

I swore again, then shoved the book at him and said, "You'd better be, reaper."

I slid a hand into my pocket and wrapped my fingers around my keys and wallet, then reached into that place inside that wasn't wolf, that was something far more powerful and dangerous. My Aedh half surged to life and flared through my body—a blaze of heat and energy that numbed pain and dulled sensation as it invaded every muscle, every cell, breaking them down and tearing them apart, until my flesh no longer existed and I became one with the shadows, one with the air. Until I held no substance, no form, and could not be seen or heard or felt by anyone or anything.

Except reapers and undoubtedly the Aedh, if they were close enough.

I glanced at Azriel, but he'd already gone, zapped away to God knew where. I swirled upward, found the manhole, and slipped through the small opening in the center of the cover.

And found myself in the middle of Swanston Street. A tram rattled by inches from my smoky form, stirring rubbish and sending a breeze through my particles.

Don't go home, Azriel had said. So where the hell should I go? I couldn't go to Stane's, simply because I didn't want to place him in danger. Azriel might suspect that the Raziq couldn't find me unless I was close, but until we knew that for certain, I was better off keeping well away from those I cared about.

It also meant I'd better get the hell away from this manhole. I fled, swirling randomly through the city streets, the chill night air seeming to seep into my particles, making them feel heavy, as if ice had settled somewhere deep inside. I flowed out of the city and followed the Tullamarine Freeway into the suburbs— more out of habit than necessity, because in Aedh form I wasn't restricted to using regular roads and pathways.

I ended up at the airport. I had to meet Lucian here

later, anyway, and it was certainly the last place anyone would think to look for me.

I re-formed in a dark corner within the parking lot,
releasing my grip on my phone and wallet as I dropped
inelegantly to the concrete floor. My body shook and
my head spun, and for several minutes I could do
nothing more than simply lie there, my lungs burning
as I dragged in thick, ragged breaths.

Becoming Aedh had its price for those of us who
weren't full-blooded—and for me it meant a complete
inability to do anything other than battle for breath
for several minutes after re-formation.

When the debilitation finally started to ease, I
pushed upright and cautiously rocked back on my
heels. Several more minutes passed, and the stabbing
pain in my head settled to a more durable ache behind my left eye. An ache that matched the one in my
leg.

The other bad thing about becoming Aedh was its
effect on my clothes. They disintegrated just fine, but
re-forming them was trickier, as the magic didn't always delineate bits of me from the other particles.
Which meant I often ended up with a dust-like sheen
covering my skin rather than fully formed pieces of
clothing. Thankfully, my jeans had come out of the
change almost intact, showing only a small patch just
under my right knee. My underwear and bra hadn't
fared as well, hanging on in barely there strips that
tickled my skin. My leather jacket, like my jeans, had
a patch missing from the right elbow and was a little
tatty around the bottom hem, but otherwise had
come through in one piece for a change.

It was probably just as well that I'd left Azriel with the book. And that I hadn't attempted to shift shape with him in tow.

I climbed carefully to my feet. The pain remained, constant yet bearable. The bullet wound had finally stopped bleeding, so I unwound the bloodstained bandage and tossed the scraps into the corner. Thankfully, my jeans were dark, so the blood wasn't really noticeable.

I reached into my pocket and pulled out my phone. Metal and plastic weren't affected by the shift into—or back out of—particle form, but unless they were touching skin, they wouldn't actually change. Which is why I'd wrapped my hand around my phone and keys before I'd shifted. I knew from experience that there was nothing worse than metal and plastic stuck in the middle of your particle form.

"Hunter," I said into the phone. The voice recognition swirled into action, its screen flaring with a vivid mosaic of color as I limped toward the elevators.

Her face appeared on the screen and she did not look happy. "This is *not* what I call immediately."

Well, suck it up princess, I wanted to snap, *because it's the best I could do*. I wisely didn't say it, though, and was grateful she wasn't here in person. Pissing her off wouldn't be the wisest move right now, given she was all that stood between me and an extermination order.

I simply said, "Sorry, but something important came up," then updated her on what had happened at Alston's house, as well as what Azriel had said about both the creature and Alston.

"So," Hunter responded, her voice a purr that was pure satisfaction. "Catherine is slated to die regardless of what we do. And in a manner that most becomes the bitch."

"Yeah, she loves you, too," I said.

Hunter laughed. It was not a pleasant sound, sending chills down my flesh. "I'm sure she does. Did you ask her to write up a list?"

"Yes. She said she'd get one of her thralls to deliver it."

"Good. It will be interesting to see if there are any similarities to my own."

"And if there are? Do you want me to pursue those leads or will you?"

"That will depend on which names we agree on," she said, leaving me a little up in the air as to how to proceed. "What do you plan next?"

"I'm going to talk to Adeline Greenfield. She apparently set the protection wards Alston has in her home."

"And you think the wards are faulty?"

"No. I'm just covering bases."

"Excellent." She paused, and darkness seemed to creep into her eyes. "It's in your best interest to remember what you risk with the task, Risa. Keep me updated, or pay the price."

I resisted the urge to gulp and said, "I will."

The phone went blank. I blew out a breath, a little relieved to have gotten off so lightly, and said, "Tao." Once again the phone sprang into action.

"Hey," Tao said, as he came online. I could hear pots clanging in the background, which meant he was either at work or cooking up a storm at home. I was betting on the former. "What's happening?"

"I wanted to ask you not to go home tonight."

"I wasn't planning to, but why? What's happened?"

"Azriel and I stole the Dušan book back. I suspect the Raziq just might be a little aggravated about it."

"Oh yeah, I imagine they would be," he said drily. "I'm gathering everything went okay? You didn't get hurt?"

"I'm fine," I said, hoping he'd ignore the fact my voice ached with tiredness. And I was really glad he couldn't see the state I was in.

"Ilianna's here at the restaurant, so I'll warn her as well. She can stay at Mirri's until you give us the all clear."

"It'll probably be just for tonight." Once the Raziq discovered the book wasn't at our apartment, we'd be good to return home—I hoped. "How come you're at the café tonight?"

"Hanna called in sick and we couldn't find a temp." He gave me a decidedly wicked grin. "It's just as well I have legendary stamina, given I'm also on for the morning shift."

I smiled back, even though what he said was true. He *did* have fantastic stamina, in the bedroom and out—a fact I knew because we'd once been lovers.

"I daresay you already have some luscious lady on standby to massage your poor tired self afterward."

"I daresay I have," he said cheerfully, then his expression sobered. "Keep in touch, or I'll be contacting Riley."

"I will." Riley had given both Tao and Ilianna stern orders to get in touch the minute they even *suspected*

I was in trouble. And Aunt Riley could be pretty damn scary when she wanted to be. "But I'm meeting Lucian at six, so don't expect to hear anything from me until midday, at least."

"Oh, thank *God*," he replied, voice fervent but a twinkle in his eyes. "Do you know how grouchy you've been lately?"

"Says the man who has never experienced sexual frustration in his entire life?"

"And who has no *intention* of ever experiencing it," he replied. "Take care of yourself."

"Will do." I hung up, then caught the elevator down and walked across the ramp over the road and into the airport. I desperately needed to sleep, but I wasn't about to walk into the nearby Hilton looking like something the cat had coughed up. Thankfully, there were showers in the airport, and the stores were open twenty-four seven. I ignored the curious looks my bedraggled appearance was prompting and bought a week's worth of clothes, simply because I had no idea when I was going to be able to head back home. Then, keeping Lucian's promise to rip anything I was wearing right off again in mind, I found a sexy but inexpensive dress and headed to the nearest bathroom to shower and change.

Only to find someone waiting for me on the other side of the door when I opened it. I instinctively jumped back before I realized it was Azriel.

"For fuck's sake," I said, my gaze sweeping him and noting with relief that both the blood and the bullet wound had disappeared. "You could have at least warned me you were here."

He crossed his arms and leaned his butt back against one of the sinks. "Do you not usually sense when I'm near?"

"Sometimes," I muttered, feeling all that warm heat wash over my skin and stir things that had no right to be stirring. "But not always. How did you get the bullet out?"

"Once I was sure the Raziq were not following me, I called for help."

"There are reaper field medics?"

His amusement stirred all around me, further fueling the fires. I resisted the urge to pat my face with cold water as I washed my hands.

"There are no field medics. I called a friend."

I studied him for a moment, wondering if that friend was male or female. Wondering why I even cared. "What about the Dušan's book?"

"For the moment, it is safely hidden in the gray fields."

"It can't stay there." For me to read it, it had to be here on earth while I was on the gray fields, not the other way around.

He nodded. "But I suspect that the Raziq might have put some sort of locator spell on it. The minute we bring it out of the gray fields, they will be able to trace it."

I frowned. "And you can't undo the spell?"

"No. As I've said, reapers are not magic users. We can sense its presence, and we can sometimes—with care—manipulate it, as we did with the portals, but that is it."

"What about the Brindle witches? Do you think they'd have a shot?"

"No. The Aedh priests have forgotten more magic than your witches will ever know."

Oh fab. *Not.* I studied him for a moment, then said, "Well, I'm not going to attempt to read the book now. I need some sleep before I meet Lucian in a few hours."

Something frosty crept into the air. He stood upright and gave me a slight bow. "I shall leave you in peace, then."

With that he winked out of existence, making me wonder what the hell was happening. Or was he the same as ever, and it was me who was the problem? Or rather, my habit of reading far more into his words and actions than was intended?

I sighed, then dried my hands and headed across to the Hilton, taking a room for the night. Then, once inside, stripped off and slept the sleep of the dead— for a whole three hours. It wasn't anywhere near enough, but at least it took the edge off my exhaustion.

I freshened up again, then pulled on my dress, smoothing its silky sides over my curves so that they clung like a second skin. I didn't bother with underclothes—I might have bought them, but they were too nice to sacrifice if Lucian did go through with his threat.

Anticipation throbbed in a low-down ache as I left the room and walked—limped, given my leg was only half healed and still sore—across to the airport.

Naturally, his plane was late. I grabbed some breakfast—deciding on pancakes smothered with bananas and caramel sauce, simply because I figured I'd need the calories in the hours to come—and munched on it while I watched the screens and wondered if it were actually possible to burst with frustration.

His plane finally pulled in thirty-five minutes late. I leaned against a concrete pillar, scanning the disembarking passengers, my limbs trembling with anticipation. Damn, this was *bad*. The next time he went away, I needed to get to Franklin's at least once.

Eventually, I saw him. He towered over those nearest him, his hair gleaming like finely spun gold in the airport's harsh overhead lighting. His gaze scanned the waiting crowd and—when his green eyes met mine—a bright smile lit his face.

I pushed away from the pillar and walked across to him, loving the way he moved—like a sleek cat that had its quarry in sight. He dropped his bag onto the floor next to me, wrapped his arms around my waist, then kissed me.

It was heat and passion and desire, but his kisses also transcended all that, becoming something far more powerful and unearthly. Electricity surged between us, swirling around our flesh, *through* our flesh, until it seemed our flesh had disappeared and we were nothing more than night and air and energy. It was amazing. Truly amazing. And it was all I could do not to beg him to take me here and now.

When we finally parted, I could barely breathe and my legs felt like water.

He smiled as his hands slid from my waist. "I did so miss your lips."

I arched an eyebrow and said teasingly, "Just my lips?"

"And your neck, and your breasts, and your waist, and your—" He paused as his hands slid over my rump, and a fierce light flared in his eyes as he pulled me even closer. His erection, thick and hard, pressed against my belly, making me wish there weren't several layers of clothing separating us. His lips brushed my ear as he murmured, "Is it too much to hope that you've reserved a room at the Hilton? Otherwise, I might just be tempted to cause a major scene."

I laughed, cupped his face with my hands, and kissed him fiercely but quickly. "Luckily for everyone in the terminal, I *did* have such foresight. Do you have any luggage to collect?"

"No," he said, grabbing my hand as he bent to pick up his bag with the other. "Shall we go?"

"Let's."

We all but ran through the terminal and over the footbridge to the Hilton. The elevator doors hadn't fully closed before he was stalking toward me, a heated look in his eyes.

I grinned as my back hit the wall. "So," he said softly, stopping so close that all I could feel was the heat of his desire, and all I could smell was the raw scent of eager, hungry male. "I do believe I threatened to tear the clothes off your body the minute I saw you."

"The elevator is hardly an appropriate place," I murmured, resisting the urge to arch toward him. To encourage him with the press of my body, the heat of my need.

"It *is* likely to get us arrested if anyone happens to be monitoring the cameras." He raised his hands, his fingers teasing the top edges of the dress and causing my already hard nipples to ache with even greater intensity.

I flicked my gaze to the camera in question, then glanced at the floor indicator. My room was on the hotel's top floor, and the elevator was moving at a glacial pace.

"What would your clients think if you were arrested for indecent behavior in an airport hotel elevator?" I asked, pressing just a little into his touch as his hands skimmed down my body then moved back up again.

"They would think I'm a lucky man." And with that, he gripped the edges of my dress and tore it open. "A fucking lucky man," he repeated, his gaze sweeping down my fully exposed flesh.

Then he pressed against me, his lips claiming mine, his kiss like fire and his body trembling with the force of his desire. He kissed my chin, my throat, my shoulder blades. I gasped and climbed up his body, wrapping my legs around his waist, cursing the material that still separated us.

The elevator tinged and the doors opened. His grip slid down to my butt, supporting me as he swung us both around. "What room?" he growled, in between kisses.

"Nine-ten," I gasped, throwing my head back as his tongue teased the base of my neck.

We reached my room. I somehow swiped the key through the scanner and pushed it open. Lucian kicked the door closed but didn't step any farther into the room, pressing me back against the door instead.

"I need you," he said, his voice a rough, urgent vibration that ran through every part of me. "So badly, right now."

"Then take me," I muttered, the need to feel him inside of me so fierce that it was becoming hard to breathe.

He shifted his grip, supporting me one-handed while he undid his pants with the other. I tore open his shirt and ran my hands across the hard, golden planes of his chest. Then I gasped again as he plunged inside me, going as deep as it was possible to go. Pleasure spiraled through me, as fast and as furious as his movements. This wasn't lovemaking, this was fucking, pure and simple. And oh, it was *so* glorious. The tightness built up inside me, radiating out in fierce waves to the very tips of my toes and fingers, until it felt as if my body was ready to explode.

Then everything *did* explode, and I was shuddering and shaking with the force of my orgasm. A heartbeat later he came—an animal roar torn from his throat and echoing through the hush of the room.

For several seconds afterward, neither of us moved. He rested his forehead against mine, his rapid breaths fanning my lips, stirring the embers of barely sated desire. He was still semi-hard inside me, and anticipation of what was yet to come zinged through me. An Aedh's lovemaking might never live up to the promise of his kisses—mainly because an Aedh's kiss was designed solely to gain compliance for the act that followed—but it sure as hell blew everyone else I'd ever had out of the water.

"That was not a bad starter," he murmured after a while. He raised his head, his wicked smile creasing the corners of his bright eyes. "You realize, of course, that after not having sex for well over a week, I have an almost unquenchable desire to lose myself in your flesh for the next week or so?"

I touched his cheek then ran my fingers down to his lips. He caught one finger, sucking on it lightly. A tremor ran through me. "I'm afraid I can't manage a week. I can, however, promise you the next eight hours."

Which would mean I'd have to go straight to work from here—but right then, I wasn't caring.

"Only eight?" He clicked his tongue as he swung us both around and walked across to the king-sized bed. "That's hardly enough to take the edge off."

I laughed as he lowered us both to the bed, somehow managing not to break our intimate connection. "Then what about if I also promise to give you as much free time as I can manage over the next week?"

"That," he murmured, as he began to move inside me again, "will just have to do. Now, shall we get down to business?"

"Let's," I agreed, and we did.

I relaxed against the back of the large bath and lightly played with the bubbles floating around my toes. Lucian walked in and offered me a glass of champagne, then sat down on the edge of the bath and studied me with a smile.

"If you don't get out of that water soon, you'll prune up."

If I didn't get out soon, I'd be horribly late for work. I sighed wistfully and took a sip of bubbly. "I know. I'm just all languid and content. Moving would spoil the moment."

He laughed softly and clinked his glass against mine. "My job has been done, then."

"For a while, at least," I agreed. Which didn't mean I'd offer too many protests if he decided he wanted another round. Even if it meant I'd be late.

"So how did the book hunting go?" he asked after a moment.

I blinked. "So it's true. You *can* invade my thoughts."

"I wouldn't really call it invading," he said, amusement teasing the lips I'd kissed so often this morning. "Nor is it truly telepathy. There are only a few relatively minor areas of your thoughts open to me. Unlike most, you seem to have more than your fair share of secret compartments."

"Well, good," I said, a little tartly. "A girl does like to keep her secrets, you know."

"Then have no fear. I can only read what is foremost in your mind, and the Dušan book appears to be your biggest concern."

I sipped my champagne and studied him over the rim. Was he telling the truth? For some odd reason, I suspected not—even though I wasn't seeing any of the usual signs of deception. But maybe he wasn't. Maybe I was just being overly suspicious thanks to everything that had happened to me over the last few months.

But if he knew about the Dušan book, then he undoubtedly knew we'd appropriated it from the Raziq. And why.

"It's supposed to tell us what form the keys take," I said eventually.

"Supposed?" he said. "You haven't tried to read it yet?"

I shook my head. "Azriel suspects the book may have a locator on it."

"Azriel being your guardian reaper?"

"Stalker," I corrected, even though he'd saved my life that very morning. "Azriel wants what everyone else wants—my father."

Lucian grinned and dipped a hand into the water, running his fingers lightly up my leg. "I don't want your father. I'd much rather have the luscious, wanton female lying naked in my bath."

My skin tingled where he touched and my hormones shifted from languid satisfaction to eager anticipation. I ignored them and said teasingly, "I vaguely recall you stating that you've indulged in more than your fair share of threesomes and orgies over the centuries. Are you saying that not one of those involved a male?"

"No, I am not," he murmured, his fingers caressing higher up my thigh, making my breath grow ragged. "And I'm always more than happy to share some loving with several females and males. Now, however, the idea of a regular, one-on-one coupling has taken my fancy. Did you get this wound when you were retrieving the book?"

I nodded. The bullet wound was still raised and nasty looking, but at least the ache had eased. In a day or so, it probably wouldn't even be noticeable. Which didn't stop me wishing yet again that I'd gotten a higher percentage of a werewolf's natural healing ability, because I had a bad feeling I was going to need it over the coming weeks.

"I hope our athletic escapades haven't caused you any discomfort."

"You would have heard me complaining if they had."

He raised an eyebrow. "So you would have no objections if we continued said escapades in the bath?"

"Why would you want to do that when I apparently resemble a prune?"

He grinned. "Did I ever mention that I'm rather fond of prunes?"

I laughed and held his glass as he stepped into the bath and sat down at the opposite end, his long legs stretching out to either side of mine. I handed him back his champagne, and he took a sip.

"What," he said, his eyes twinkling with devilry, "would you give me if I said I knew of a way to block whatever tracer magic the Raziq have placed on that book?"

"Ah," I said, putting my glass down on the bath ledge. "For that, I might just be willing to be late for work."

"How late?" he asked, the devilry vying with desire.

I shifted position and slid up his wet, warm body, my hands on either side of him. "Very, very late," I murmured, as my lips met his.

For the longest time there was no more talking, only enjoying. When I finally straddled him, pushing him slowly—teasingly—deep into my body, we both groaned in delight. I began to move, slowly at first, then with mounting urgency, until desire burned, and all I wanted to do was reach that peak and shatter into a million pieces.

Then I did, and he did, and it was glorious. Oh, so glorious.

I rested my head against his shoulder for several minutes, breathing heavily and feeling completely—wonderfully—boneless.

Then he sighed, took my face between his palms, and kissed me gently. "You need to construct a void."

I blinked. "What?"

"For the book," he said patiently. "You will need to construct a magical void. It's a zone that can be built around an object to render any outsourced magic emanating from that object useless."

"How the hell am I supposed to do that?"

"You can't, but Ilianna could. She is more powerful than you suspect."

I looked at him. "You've only met her once, and then only for a couple of minutes."

"Which is more than enough time to get a sense of her capabilities." He paused. "Where is the book now?"

"Somewhere safe," I said, frowning at his questions. For someone who professed to have no interest in the book, he sure wanted to know a lot about it.

He smiled and tucked a damp strand of hair behind my ear. "As much as I hate to say this, if you get out of this bath right now, you might still make it to work on time."

"Only if I don't take you home first. And I thought that was the whole point of me meeting you at the airport."

"No, the whole point of you meeting me at the airport was me wanting to ravish you. And now I have."

He gave me another one of those devilish grins. "Of course, I wouldn't complain if you *did* escort me home, but I rather suspect I'd drag you upstairs and make you even later."

"A tempting prospect, but one I suspect would piss off Tao and Ilianna."

"And Ilianna is not a woman I would like pissed off at me," he agreed.

I laughed, kissed him quickly, then grabbed a towel and headed off to dry and dress.

I caught a cab to work, calling Ilianna in the process to ask if she'd drop in sometime during the shift. As it turned out, I *was* late for work, but only by a few minutes. The place was packed, so I slipped upstairs to dump my spare clothes and change into my work gear, then headed back down to once again help out where I was needed. By six the crowd had eased somewhat, so I headed up to the office to catch up on the paperwork.

Azriel found me there.

"The Raziq may know of this place," he said, his arms crossed and his expression as stony as I'd ever seen it. "It is not wise to remain here for long."

I leaned back in my chair and rubbed my temples wearily. Staring at the computer screen trying to make sense of the accounting was not a sensible thing to do after so little sleep. And the last thing I wanted was a confrontation with Azriel. "I can't turn my life around just because they may or may not know about this place. I won't go home, but I refuse to abandon everything and everyone in my life."

He didn't say anything. Just stared at me disapprovingly.

I sighed. "Look, if it's true that the Raziq have placed a tracer signal on the book, Lucian has told me a way of getting around it."

"How would he know?" Azriel's voice held an edge that sounded a hell of a lot like contempt. "He is neither a priest nor a magic user, and he was stripped of any Aedh powers a long time ago."

"He wasn't stripped of *all* of them." The annoyance surging through me hadn't yet reached my voice—but I suspected it wouldn't take that long. "And what does it matter whether he should or should not know? If it works, we'll be able to read the book without the Raziq dropping in on us."

"*If* it works," he said.

"If it *doesn't*, what have we lost?" I snapped my chair forward and leaned my forearms on the desk. "What the hell is your problem?"

He paused. "I have no—"

"Bullshit, Azriel," I interrupted. "Every time I mention Lucian's name you get all huffy and hostile."

He shrugged. "I do not trust him."

"But *why*? He's done nothing to prove he's untrustworthy."

"And he's done nothing to prove he *is*."

"Meaning you'll trust him if this idea of his works?"

"No."

I snorted softly. "Then you're just being unreasonable."

He didn't say anything. No surprise there. This reaper could make a clam seem chatty.

Footsteps clattered up the stairs, and I knew by the sound it was Ilianna. She might be fleet of foot, but she had a heavier step than most.

"Whoa," she said, stopping abruptly in the door-way and glancing between Azriel and myself. "Ten-sion, much?"

I grimaced. "It's just a disagreement about trust-worthiness. Nothing major."

Ilianna's gaze centered on Azriel. "So who don't you trust?"

"Lucian," he said, calmly.

"Why?"

"Good luck getting a real answer for *that* one," I muttered, at the same time that Azriel said, "Be-cause he is one of the fallen, and they should never be trusted."

"Is this experience talking, or merely word of mouth?" Ilianna asked.

"Lucian is *fallen*." He said it like that one word explained it all.

"One mistake does not mean the man is pure evil," Ilianna said reasonably, though it didn't look like it was having much impact on Azriel. "Are you sure there's no deeper reason?"

He lifted an eyebrow. "I do not understand the question."

Ilianna snorted. "Sure you don't." She glanced at me. "You wanted to see me?"

"Would you happen to know how to create a mag-ical void around an object?"

She blinked. "In theory, yes, although I've never ac-tually created one. Why?"

"Because—according to Lucian—that's the only way we can stop the locating spell the Raziq have more than likely placed on the book."

She grunted, frowning a little. "It may take a day or so. I'll have to brush up on the technique before I attempt it."

"Do it. We need to find and destroy these damn keys so my life can return to normal."

I glared at Azriel as I said it, but he returned it passively. And that was even more frustrating. Damn it, I wanted him to react, wanted him to . . . what? He was a reaper, for Christ's sake. I had to stop applying human sensibilities to him.

"It does mean I'll have to go back home," Ilianna said. If she still sensed the tension riding between me and Azriel, she didn't mention it. "Mirri doesn't have the texts or the equipment I'll need."

I frowned. "I don't like the thought of you going there alone . . ."

"I will accompany her," Azriel said abruptly. At my surprised look, he added, "If Ilianna were captured, you would drop everything to rescue her, would you not?"

"Yes."

"Then it is beneficial for my quest that she not get captured."

"So glad my safety came into consideration," Ilianna murmured with a wry grin at me. "Oh, and I've found Adeline Greenfield for you. She said to pop in after you've finished work. She'll be home all night."

"Good." I accepted the piece of paper she handed me and glanced briefly at the address. Toorak, not far from where Mom had lived. The protection-spell business was obviously booming. I tucked it into my jean pocket and added, "Where are you staying tonight? With Mirri?"

Ilianna nodded. "Although I miss the peace and quiet of our place. Her damn apartment always sounds like it's in the middle of a battlefield."

I snorted softly. Mirri lived in one of the old East Melbourne mansion blocks close to her work, and her apartment was on a middle floor, meaning it got noise from above and below. And the families living in the neighboring apartments had no qualms when it came to airing their grievances at the top of their lungs.

"Once we get the void in place around the book, it should be safer at home."

"Well, I'd better get my ass into gear then, as I really don't want to be at Mirri's too long."

If only, I thought with amusement, because Mirri didn't have the latest and greatest in security as we did. Mirri might not have lived in Melbourne for as long as Ilianna, but she was infinitely more secure about being here.

"So where are you going to be staying?" Ilianna added.

"I'm not sure yet." I flicked a glance at Azriel, and couldn't help adding, "Maybe with Lucian."

He didn't react. Not that I could see, anyway. But that chill in the air got suddenly stronger, and a shiver ran down my spine.

Ilianna clicked her tongue. "You, Risa Jones, are positively evil." She glanced at Azriel. "I'm heading home now. Are you coming?"

"Yes," he answered. "I shall wait downstairs for you."

He winked out of existence and, as far as I could tell, actually did leave the room.

"Ris, be careful," Ilianna said, her gaze coming back to me.

"Is that a general be careful, or a there's-shit-headed-your-way be careful?"

"General." She paused, frowning. "I have no sense that Lucian is evil or that he ever intends you harm, but I don't think you can entirely disregard Azriel's misgivings. He may have reasons other than what he's saying, but he's a warrior—and, like any good warrior, he relies on instinct."

"Lucian *isn't* evil, and he's shown absolutely *no* interest in the damn keys or my father." And for that alone I would trust him. "He's just an Aedh who's been bound to earth and is doing his best to survive."

She nodded. "I know, and I agree, but I've been wrong before and I'd hate for this to be one of those times. So just be careful."

"I will. I am." I gave her a crooked smile. "These days, the only people I truly trust are you, Tao, and the Jenson pack."

"Well, you can't go wrong there." She hesitated again, then drew a paper-wrapped package out of her pocket. "Here, I bought you this."

She offered me the package. Undoing it revealed a small, multipurpose hunting knife—the sort of knife that could cut wire as easily as it did throats. I glanced at her sharply. "You said you don't see specific trouble in my future, so why hand me a knife?"

She grimaced. "My foresight is being decidedly ambiguous at the moment. I just felt the need to buy this for you. I'm hoping you don't need it, but it's better to be safe than sorry."

"I guess." I tossed the knife lightly in my hand. It was very well balanced. "And at least it is small enough to keep hidden."

"That's the idea." Then she gave me a sketchy salute and headed back down the stairs.

I considered the knife for a few seconds longer, then tucked it into my jacket pocket and tried to get back to the paperwork. Unfortunately, the figures refused to compute. After twenty minutes I gave up and rang the Langham Hotel, booking a suite for a couple of nights. I wasn't able to go home, which gave me the perfect opportunity to indulge in a little pampering at one of my favorite five-star hotels. With that done, I headed back downstairs to help out until the end of my shift.

After grabbing something to eat from the kitchen, I caught a cab to the address Ilianna had given me. Adeline Greenfield lived in one of those beautiful old Victorian houses filled with character—the type of house all too often torn down and replaced by sterile concrete boxes. As the cab took off, I stood on the curb, admiring the graceful old elms that dominated her front lawn, and the thick carpet of moss growing across the tiled roof. There was an air of graceful age that hung over the place. And as I opened the old wrought-iron gate and walked through, it felt very welcoming.

The front garden was so lush with flowers that, even at night, they filled the air with a riot of perfume. And though it should have overwhelmed my olfactory senses, it didn't.

I climbed the red-tiled steps and walked across to the front door. A little gold bell sat on the right edge of the door frame, its cord swaying gently in the breeze. I rang it a couple of times, and the joyous sound leapt across the night, making me smile.

Footsteps echoed inside, then the door opened, revealing a short, gray haired woman with lined, leathery features and the brightest blue eyes I'd ever seen.

"You'd be Risa Jones?" she said, looking me up and down before her gaze went briefly past me. If her expression was anything to go by, I wasn't what she was expecting.

"Yes, I am. I hope I'm not too late. Ilianna did say to pop over after I finished work . . ."

"No, no, that's fine," she said, unlocking the security door then stepping aside for me to enter. "It's just that I wasn't expecting you to come alone."

I paused. "Why's that?"

"Ilianna mentioned you had a reaper following you about, but that I shouldn't worry about it." She snorted as she snipped the door closed then led the way down the long, shadow-filled hallway. The air smelled of ginger and some other spices I couldn't name. It was tantalizing and pleasant. "Not that I would. I've seen more than my fair share of them buggers, and they don't scare me."

She led the way into a cozy sitting room that was dominated by a log fire. Two well-padded armchairs sat in front of it and, in between them, a small coffee table on which sat a tea pot and two china cups.

"Would you like a cup?" she asked, motioning me to sit on the chair to the left.

"Thanks," I said, even though tea wasn't high on my must-have list. "So you can see the reapers?"

"Well, technically, no. Not like I see you, for instance. But sometimes when I'm dream walking, I cross their paths. As I said, they don't scare me. They seem to be mostly benevolent beings."

I supposed they generally were—even the moody ones who carried swords. I watched her pour the tea, then nodded when she mentioned the sugar. She stirred in several spoons, then offered me the cup. I took it gingerly—I was a mug girl at heart, and bone china always seemed too delicate for me. "By dream walking, do you mean astral traveling?"

She nodded. "I find it beneficial when it comes to dealing with some clients' problems. It is human nature not to be entirely honest, but there are no lies on the astral plane."

"So do you watch them go through their daily lives or do you walk through their dreams?"

"Mostly the latter. Dreams can be interesting—and sometimes dangerous—places." She studied me for a moment. "But you know that. You've walked the astral planes yourself."

"What you call the astral planes, I call the gray fields. But I've never walked through anyone's dreams."

"You could. You have many more of your mother's gifts than you think."

I did? That was certainly news. I took a sip of tea, then said, "Did Ilianna mention why I wanted to see you?"

She nodded. "Catherine Alston ordered the protection spell three years ago. She mentioned that there was some nasty business going down in the council, and she wanted to be sure she was safe at home."

I hadn't thought to ask Alston why she'd wanted such strong magic guarding her. "I guess she didn't clarify what the nasty business was?"

Adeline shook her head. "Vampires of her vintage usually work on a need-to-know basis. I didn't need to know. I just needed to make the spell work."

"So what sort of spell was it?"

She took a sip from her cup, then said, "Full protection. It should stop anything or anyone wearing flesh who intended her harm."

"What about Maniae?"

She peered at me. "What about them?"

"Well, they're considered spirits—or daemones. So should your spell have stopped them?"

"No, because Maniae don't wear flesh. They're also deities rather than spirits—a different type of being altogether. I don't think Alston ever imagined someone would hate her enough to raise a daemon against her, let alone the curse of the Maniae. And that makes her situation extremely tricky."

"Why?"

"Because the Maniae can usually be summoned only by great injustice. Alston must have cocked up pretty badly for the Maniae to be after her."

"Meaning the event three years ago is unlikely to be the cause, because the attacks have only just begun."

"Not necessarily. It could have simply taken that long to perform the summoning correctly. It is not a well-known spell, and it is not one that is well recorded."

"Would the Brindle have it within their archives?"

"Undoubtedly."

"Meaning it's the sort of spell that any witch could perform?"

"It's the type of spell *anyone* who feels they're the victim of a grave injustice could perform if they can find the full version. However, the only people who would get access to the spell are witches connected to the Brindle."

"So maybe all I have to do is go to the Brindle and ask who had access to that spell recently."

"It is worth a try, though I honestly doubt a witch would be involved in such a summoning—even if it is only to supply the text of the spell."

"Why?"

"Because of the threefold rule. And because one person's great injustice can be another's minor annoyance. It is a very gray area for a witch to be involved in."

I nodded and finished my tea, wincing a little at the almost bitter aftertaste. Give me Coke or coffee any day. Hell, even the cheapest instant was better than this.

"I don't suppose you've heard any whispers about this sort of summoning being performed, have you?"

She shook her head. "No, it is not my line of work. I protect, not destroy."

I said, "No witch destroys. That is against the laws, isn't it?"

Something gleamed in her eyes. Amusement, perhaps. Or pity. "Ask Ilianna that question. She could answer it more fully than me."

"Ilianna hasn't destroyed anything or anyone."

"I'm not saying she has."

"Then what are you saying?"

"Ask her."

Yeah, like that would do any good. When it came to talking about the Brindle and the brief time she'd spent there, Ilianna was decidedly mute. I pushed to my feet and held out my hand. "Thank you for your time."

She rose and clasped my hand. "Be careful, young woman. Evil nips at your heels, and that is not a good thing when your dark angel is not by your side."

"I can protect myself," I said. And tried to ignore the suspicion that I'd just tempted fate.

Adeline smiled. It was a knowing yet sad smile. "Yes, you can. Except in the areas where it perhaps matters the most."

I sighed. Why couldn't people just come out and say what they meant?

"Because," she said, a smile touching her thin lips, "speaking in riddles means we can never truly be wrong. It is merely a matter of interpretation."

I grinned despite the rather shocked realization that she could read my thoughts. Was I an open book to *everyone* these days? I hoped like hell the nano-implants worked better on vampires than they seemed to on Aedh, reapers, and witches. "You know, that's the most honest statement I think I've heard all day."

"And *that* is a sad state of affairs," she commented as she led the way back down the hall.

"I guess it is." I shivered a little as she opened the door and the wind whisked in, colder and stronger than it had been fifteen minutes ago. "Thanks for taking the time to see me."

She nodded and watched me leave, her gaze burning into my spine long after I'd left her house. I shivered again, then jumped as my phone rang loudly.

Lucian's cheery features came up instantly on the vid-screen. "Hey gorgeous," he said. "I'm missing you already."

I grinned. "No, I am *not* coming over to your place tonight. I'm tired. I need to sleep."

"And here I was thinking you had the stamina of a wolf."

"I do. It's just been one hell of a day."

He laughed. "Where are you at the moment?"

A yellow cab cruised down the street toward me. I waved a hand and was relieved to see it pull over. "On Chapel Street, just about to catch a cab."

I opened the door, hopped in, and told the driver the address.

"You're going to the Langham?" Lucian commented. "And you're not inviting me? I am offended!"

I laughed. "Yeah, right. Maybe tomorrow night."

"By tomorrow night I shall be mindless with need."

"Then go to Franklin's. You're a member there now."

"Ah yes, so I am." He sighed dramatically. "I suppose I shall just have to be satisfied with slaking my desire on a dozen or so of Franklin's most nubile offerings."

"Such a hardship," I said drily, then glanced up as the cabdriver swerved and swore dramatically.

"Problem?" I asked.

"Just some asshole coming out of a side street without looking," he replied. "Nothing to—"

The rest of his words were cut off as the cab—and the two of us—were flung hard sideways. Car engines roared, metal crumpled, and someone started scream-ing. The driver, I realized a little dazedly, feeling warmth trickling down the side of my face and not knowing how it had gotten there. Lucian was yelling, too, calling my name from what seemed a great dis-tance. Then the door on the opposite side was wrenched open, and something sharp hit my neck.

And everything went black.

Chapter Seven

WAKING WAS A SLOW AND UGLY PROCESS. MY head ached like a bitch, and every muscle in my body throbbed in sympathy. It felt like I'd been caught in some gigantic shaker and thrown about viciously.

Which I guess I had, I thought, suddenly remembering the accident.

That I was no longer in the cab was immediately obvious. The vinyl seat that had been pressed against my side had been replaced by cold concrete, and the air reeked of damp, rubbish, and excrement rather than orange freshener.

Which no doubt meant I was down in the goddamn sewer tunnels again. What the hell was it with these tunnels and bad guys? And why was I even here? Why hadn't Azriel come riding to the rescue?

No answer came out of the darkness and no half-naked, sword-wielding fury strode forward to rescue me. Obviously, for whatever reason, I was alone. Fear rose, but I thrust it aside and tried not to think about the last time I'd been trapped in the sewers by myself.

But I'd escaped that prison on my own, and I'd damn well escape this one, too.

As my eyes adjusted to the inky blackness, the

rough-hewn dirt walls and a high arched ceiling became evident. I frowned. This *wasn't* a sewer tunnel—although there had to be one close by given the stench in the air—and it certainly seemed a whole lot larger than the last cell I'd found myself in.

Not that it mattered what the hell this place actually was. All that *did* matter was getting the hell out of here before whoever had snatched me returned. I took a slow, steadying breath, and then reached for my Aedh form. But as the magic within me surged, a rainbow shimmer flared across the arched ceiling and pain—dark, familiar, and as sharp as a knife—speared into my flesh, right into my soul. I gasped and jackknifed into a fetal position, recognizing the magic, knowing what it could do. It was the magic the Aedh had used to stop the shift and break my connection with Azriel.

But *this* felt slightly different from that earlier version. It was darker. More bloody. Which didn't exactly make sense.

"Ah," a voice behind me said, just about giving me a heart attack in the process. "You're awake. Excellent."

I twisted around sharply—too sharply, if the needles of pain driving into my ribs were any indication—and saw him. Or rather, saw his outline, which appeared tall and wiry. The rest of him was difficult to make out, simply because he seemed to merge with the shadows, though I had no sense of a vampire. But I had no sense of humanity, either.

In fact, I still had no sense of *anything* living. It was as if he weren't even here.

I frowned and flared my nostrils, dragging in the foul air, sorting through the various stenches. There was definitely no indication that there was anyone else in this underground room besides myself.

So if he wasn't here, where the hell was he?

And just how well could he see me?

"Who the hell are you?" I asked, wincing a little at my loudness but, at the same time, glad the shakiness that still afflicted my muscles wasn't apparent in my voice.

"I actually believe you've been looking for me," he said, his voice jovial and plummy. "I'm—"

"Ike Forman," I finished for him as I scanned the walls again. I couldn't see any cameras or microphones anywhere in the room, and rather doubted he'd have access to the sort of nanotechnology that Stane would—or that he'd risk such expensive equipment in a place like this. So even if the figure in front of me *was* a projection rather than a reality, he still had to be somewhere close by. If only because most projections had distance limits. "You're the man who has taken over Handberry's team—not that there's any of them left right now."

"No," he said sadly, as if he really did regret losing them though I suspected quite the opposite. "They rather underestimated your capabilities. But rest assured that I will not."

Men had been underestimating me my entire life. I was hoping it wasn't going to stop now, despite Forman's statement. "What do you want with me?"

I pushed upright, only to discover my legs were tied together and my feet somewhat numb. I fell back down, my knees hitting the concrete so hard it jarred my already aching body.

I swore and his mirth swam around me. "Your legs are tied together with wire. I was tempted to use silver, but that might cause more damage than I wish just yet. We may need to leave this bolt-hole in a hurry if your dark protector breaks the outer barriers."

Meaning Azriel was somewhere close by? Part of me hoped so, and part of me refused to rely on that hope, preferring to depend on my own instincts and abilities.

Then the words *just yet* registered. I licked my lips and tried not to think about the underlying threat. I tried to think with some degree of clarity. It wasn't easy when my head felt like someone was trying to claw their way out of it.

So why *was* he using ordinary wire when silver was a much safer option for werewolves? If he knew enough about me to construct a barrier capable of preventing me becoming Aedh, then he'd obviously know I was also part were. What was he planning?

It was a thought that niggled as I said, "To repeat my earlier question, what the hell do you want with me?"

"I want what my predecessor wanted. The keys, or the book that tells us how to find them. I'm not fussed either way."

"But why do you want them? You're neither Aedh nor reaper, so gaining the keys to heaven or hell would be useless to you."

"Who said *I* wanted the keys?"

I carefully shifted position until I could see both him and the wire that was holding me hostage. It was a fine gray line that snaked away into deeper shadows. I had no idea what I was attached to, but I had no doubt it would be secure. I tested it anyway, and got the result I expected. No give, and no indication that it would readily pull free of whatever waited at the other end.

Interestingly, Forman didn't comment. Which maybe meant that, if I kept my actions small enough, he wouldn't see them.

"So it's Harlen who actually wants the keys?" I said.

He paused. "I don't know a Harlen."

"Well, you certainly did when you were talking to Handberry the night he died. In fact, Handberry was going to meet him. I guess it's lucky that Harlen didn't actually turn up, or he might have become the soul stealer's dessert."

I shifted back onto my butt and hugged my knees close to my chest. Fire ran up my bruised legs, but I ignored that. The position got me closer to the wire tying my legs together. But there was no knot to undo. The damn thing had been soldered on.

"Ah yes, I do recall that conversation now," he said, clearly amused if the note in his voice was anything to go by. "But Harlen is of no interest to either of us right now."

And yet his casual dismissal had instinct suggesting that the very opposite was true. "I hate to break this to you, but anyone involved in the attempted murder of my friends is of interest to me right now."

"Harlen didn't order any attacks on your friends."

"Indeed?" I shifted my arms a little so that they pressed against my sides. I still had my phone. I still had my knife. This man might not be underestimating me, but he sure as hell hadn't searched me very well. "Then Harlen isn't the man behind the buyout of premises on West Street?"

"No, he's not behind the buyout, although he will definitely benefit from it." Once again it sounded like it was all one big joke only he could understand. "You really must tell us your sources."

"The Directorate," I said, crossing my arms to hide my hands. Slowly, carefully, I grabbed my jacket and pulled it around until the pocket holding the knife was at the front of my body. "They did capture one of your boys and they do so enjoy the odd routine-breaking bit of interrogation . . . as you will experience yourself once I hand you over to them."

He laughed. "My dear, I'd start worrying about *your* future rather than mine."

I reached into the pocket and wrapped my hands around the hilt of the knife. "Look, I don't know where the goddamn book is. I don't know where my father is. Those facts cannot be changed, no matter how much you might wish otherwise."

"We shall see."

He moved, and his shadowy form wavered briefly— the first real indication that I was indeed watching a projection rather than a real person. I quickly scanned the wall behind his image, and for the first time noticed the faint outline of a doorway.

Then his image flicked a nonexistent switch—or at least it was nonexistent in *this* room—and something hit me with the force of a sledgehammer. I was thrown backward, my spine hitting a wall with bone-crunching force and my body shaking, trembling, and tingling. The assault stopped almost as soon as it had began, but the skin underneath the wire felt like it was burning, and my whole body felt weird. Numb, almost.

"Now that you've had a taste of what I can do, please answer the question."

I licked my lips and somehow croaked, "What fucking question?" God, there were spots dancing before my eyes, and my ears were ringing. What the hell had he done to me?

"Where is the book?"

"I don't *know*—"

I didn't get any further. The force hit again, and only the wall at my back prevented me from being thrown. But it didn't stop my limbs from shaking and dancing, and it didn't stop the energy that was flowing through me.

Electricity. He was using electricity on me. God, the *wire*. It was coming through the wire around my legs.

The energy snapped off again, leaving me a trembling, twitching mess. And yet my mind was suddenly clear. I had to get the wire off before he hit me a third time. *Had* to.

I closed my eyes and once again forced shaking fingers toward my pocket. The knife was still there. Relief surged.

"Answer the questions," Forman said, in that same dispassionate voice, "and the electrocution will stop."

I groaned in response and curled into a tight ball, my knees drawn up close to my chest. With my hands once again hidden, I slowly wrapped my fingers around the knife and drew it from the sheath.

"Risa," he said, an edge of sympathy in his voice. "I really have no desire to cause you such pain. All you have to do is answer my questions."

I slipped the knife from my pocket then flipped it back along my forearm so that it was hidden from view as I moved my arm down toward my curled-up legs.

"The book," I said, forcing my eyes open to watch for any indication that he realized what I was up to. Though what I would do if he *did* realize, I had no idea. I wasn't exactly in an ideal position right now. "It's on the gray fields."

He tsked. "That is most unfortunate, as neither I nor my employer has access to those fields."

His employer. Not Harlen, then; otherwise he would have simply said it. That was a name I already knew. Although maybe he simply thought I was fishing and was just being careful.

I flicked the knife around and caught the wire in the notch at the top of the blade. Slowly, carefully, I began to bend it back and forth.

"That," I said, my whole arm shaking with the effort to break the wire, "is not my problem."

"But I'm afraid it is," he said, "because it means you'll just have to fetch it for us."

Not on your fucking life. The wire snapped, and I quickly squeezed my calves together, stopping it from snaking away. If he flicked that switch now, I was still a goner, but that was a risk I had to take.

I sheathed the knife then reached down and caught the end of the wire, holding it gingerly.

Now what?

I glanced over to the silhouetted figure. I had to get up and over there fast. Really fast—because God knew what other traps he had waiting for me.

"Look," I said, keeping my voice croaky and weak—which wasn't really all that hard given I'd just been zapped. "I didn't hide the book on the gray fields. The reaper did. And *he* doesn't want the book found *or* used, trust me."

"Well, that is not helpful," he said. "I shall have to consult with my employer to see what he wants done." He paused, then added softly, "Please behave yourself. I am watching and—trust me—I can get to the switch far faster than you could ever hope to escape the wire or pull it free from the wall."

He turned away, giving me the only chance I was ever likely to get.

I released the wire. It made little sound as it snaked backward along the concrete. With my eyes on my captor's back, I pushed carefully upright. My limbs protested the movement and lights did a crazy dance in front of my eyes, but I bit my tongue, using one pain to ignore the others.

Then I ran—as hard and as fast as I could—for the door behind the figure.

He sensed me—he was always going to sense me—but I crashed through the projection of his body and then into the door, hitting it so hard I broke it off its hinges, sending me and the door spilling into the small room beyond.

He was already up and running. I scrambled to my feet and gave chase, launching myself at him as he fled through a second door. We both went down in a tangle of arms and legs, rolling along the concrete before we dropped off a ledge and splashed into some foul-smelling water.

Forman swore, his body twisting and bucking, his blows raining across my shoulders and back. It was all I could do to hold on. I didn't have the strength to fight back—not right now. Not when I was still suffering the aftereffects of both the electricity and the accident.

Then one of his knees hit my ribs and, for a moment, everything went red. I gasped and my grip loosened a fraction. He was up in an instant, and running yet again.

"Stop, or I'll shoot," a voice boomed out behind me. A voice I recognized but wasn't expecting.

Lucian.

Forman slowed and turned around. Surprise registered then his features disintegrated as the gun boomed and the bullet exploded his head, sending bits of blood and bone and brain matter splattering across the wet, slimy walls behind him.

As he slumped—lifeless and headless—to the ground, I battled the bile that rose up my throat. No reaper came to collect his soul, and that could only mean his death wasn't supposed to happen now.

I closed my eyes and attempted to keep my breathing even as footsteps approached. Then Lucian was bending over me, his warm fingers lightly brushing damp hair away from my face. "Are you okay?"

I nodded, swallowed again, then said, "Why the hell did you shoot to kill?"

"He had a gun."

"He did?" I hadn't felt it when I was grappling with him. And if he'd been armed, why didn't he just shoot me rather than running?

"Yes. Wait here."

He rose and walked forward. I took a deep, shuddering breath and regretted it almost instantly as the stench of the muck I was lying in made my already unstable stomach twist harder.

I pushed to my hands and knees and clambered from the water to the concrete walkway lining it. After a moment, Lucian returned. This time he was holding two guns.

"Told you," he said, handing me the smaller of the two.

I accepted it somewhat reluctantly. "And why would I want this?"

He offered me a hand. "Because I don't know who—or what—else might be down here, and another gun might come in handy."

I nodded and placed my hand in his. He pulled me up easily, but the minute I got close to him, his nose wrinkled. "You, my girl, stink to high heaven. Are you okay to walk, or do you need a shoulder to lean on?"

I let go of his hand. "I'm fine." Which was a total lie, but if there *were* other people down here, he needed to be able to react fast, and he couldn't do that if I was hanging off him. "How did you find me?"

"Remember that telepathic connection you were bitching about only this afternoon?"

I raised my eyebrows. "I would hardly call what I said bitching. I was just a little unimpressed that you were wandering through my mind uninvited."

"It is a by-product of sex," he said, "and can't be helped."

"I know." I stepped over Forman's body and tried not to look at him. Tried not to think that my ability to question him had been annihilated as thoroughly as his head. "But what does that have to do with finding me?"

Lucian glanced over his shoulder, his green eyes shining fiercely in the shadows of the tunnel. "I was on the phone with you when the accident happened, remember?"

"Sort of." I frowned and retrieved my phone from my pocket. It informed me that the connection had been severed. No surprise there, given the man I'd been talking to was now walking several feet in front of me. "So you used my phone to track me?"

"No," he said patiently, obviously realizing he was speaking to someone with a slightly addled brain. "I followed the connection sex has given us. I knew roughly where you were when the accident happened, so it was simply a matter of driving hell-for-leather down here and then walking around until I felt you."

"So the connection isn't a long-distance thing?"

"Yes and no." He shrugged. "Sometimes I do get tantalizing fragments, but it's really nothing clear or concise unless I'm close."

Which was a whole lot more than what he'd admitted earlier and made me wonder if this was actually the truth, or whether it was yet another misdirection.

"How did you get down here?"

"Sewer entrance. There should be another one coming up."

"And you didn't spot anyone else down here?"

"No." He glanced at me again. "Why?"

"I don't know." I paused. "It just seems odd. I mean, he was asking about the book, but surely if he were so desperate for it, he would have ensured that I was more secure."

"There was magic in the room. I could feel it even when I was standing outside the door."

"Yeah, I know. It prevented me from becoming Aedh—"

"*That* is some pretty serious magical mojo," Lucian interrupted grimly. "He may have thought that was all he needed."

Maybe. And yet, something still felt off to me. I couldn't explain it—particularly given that Forman had been pretty convincing in his desire to get the information out of me. It was just an odd, niggling feeling—and I'd long learned to listen to my feelings, no matter how weird they might seem.

"How long have I been missing?"

"Not long. A couple of hours." He shrugged. "I doubt anyone has even realized you're gone yet."

Azriel would have. He'd have felt it, even if—thanks to the magic barrier—he'd been incapable of doing anything about it.

As his name ran through my mind, I felt the heat of his presence surge across the foul-smelling darkness.

Lucian stopped abruptly. "I think your reaper just arrived."

"I think you might be right." I paused beside him. "Azriel?"

He stepped out of the shadows, Valdis held by his left side, her blade flickering with blue fire. The flames spun through the darkness like brief flashes of lightning.

His stormy gaze ran from me to Lucian then back again, but all he said was, "Are you all right?"

"No, actually, I feel like shit and I smell like it, too. Right now I just want to get somewhere safe and take a bath."

"I can take—"

"No," Lucian said forcibly. "*I* will take her to my apartment. She'll be safe—"

"I think it highly unlikely she would be safe with the likes of you," Azriel commented, his tone even but his grip on Valdis seeming to tighten. The fire along her blade flared.

"And yet it was *me* who rescued her, not you, reaper."

"Oh for God's sake, enough with this macho bullshit!" I all but exploded. "I'll fucking take care of myself, thank you very much."

Lucian swung around. "I did not mean that you couldn't—"

I placed a hand on his arm, stopping him. "I know, and thank you for both the concern and the rescue, but right now I need to be away from people I care about."

"I, like you, am more than able to take care of myself," he retorted. "And not just with a gun—"

"I know," I repeated, then rose up on my toes and kissed him lightly. "I'll see you tomorrow. Right now I think it's better I get the hell out of here, just in case Forman's boss decides to come investigate."

"Then perhaps," he said slowly, "I should remain here, just in case. At the very least, I can study the magic and see if there's a clue as to its origin."

I frowned. "I really don't think you should be putting yourself in danger like that—"

"Danger?" he snorted softly. "Trust me, one lone practitioner does not represent a danger to *me*."

"But—"

He briefly placed a finger against my lips. "I will be fine. Besides, it's a good chance to flex some muscle. The life of an accountant is somewhat boring."

I chuckled softly, then kissed him again. This time his arm snaked around my waist, and he kissed me more fully. It hurt my ribs but, right then, I couldn't have cared less.

"You still stink," he said eventually.

I grinned. "I promise I won't tomorrow."

"Hey, as long as you're warm, willing, and able, I honestly won't care what you smell like."

I laughed, touched a hand to his cheek, then wrapped my hands around my phone and wallet, avoiding Azriel's steely gaze as I called to the Aedh. Her energy surged through my body, numbing sensation as it broke down every muscle, every cell, until my flesh no longer existed and I became one with the air.

In that form, I fled down the tunnel until I found a storm drain and was able to escape into the cold night

air. I had no idea where Azriel was—he couldn't follow me when I was in this form—and half wondered
if I should have warned him to leave Lucian alone. If
Valdis was—as I was beginning to suspect—something
of an indicator of her master's emotions, then Azriel
had *not* been happy to discover Lucian beside me.

But had he been angry enough to attack?

I doubted it, if only because Azriel seemed to oper-
ate off some grand master plan. And if Lucian's death
had been part of that plan, then it would have happened long ago.

I whisked along the city streets, heading for the
café. While I could slide into the Langham unseen in
this form, my clothes were rank and there was no
way I was stepping back into them after a shower. I
still couldn't go home, so the week's worth of clothes
I'd left in my locker at the café was the next best option. I certainly couldn't go shopping in this state.

The place was relatively quiet for a change. Tao
was in the kitchen, humming happily as he worked,
and several waitresses were clearing tables, readying
for the next rush of people. I flowed up the stairs and
into the changing room, ensuring no one was about
before I shifted back to human shape. I released my
grip on my phone and purse a second before I hit the
tiled floor, then stayed there for several minutes, battling for breath and waiting for the pain in my head
and the shaking in my body to ease. It had been one
hell of a night, and I just had to hope the surprises
were done with. I really couldn't take much more
right now.

"You need to eat," a soft voice said behind me.

I jumped instinctively, then swore as I recognized the familiar wash of heat when he stepped into existence.

"Damn it, Azriel," I said, pushing up onto my knees. The pain in my head sharpened briefly then eased off, but the ache in my ribs remained at a barely bearable level. "You really have to stop scaring me like that."

"And if you'd been more attuned to your instincts, you'd have felt me coming long before I actually arrived."

And if any other man had said that, I might have been tempted to grin and tease him about double meanings. But Azriel wasn't any other man.

His legs appeared in front of me. I glanced up the length of him, unable to help admiring his lean, muscular body, then met his gaze. His expression was as neutral as ever, but his eyes, like the sword strapped to his back, were filled with energy. I sighed. "Azriel, I'm really not up to an argument about Lucian right now."

Surprise flickered briefly across his face before neutrality clamped in again. "I wasn't looking for an argument."

He offered me a hand and I accepted it gratefully, allowing him to pull me to my feet.

"And the Aedh is right," he added, not releasing me immediately. "You stink."

"Thanks." I glanced down at our hands and he took the hint, letting go. I flexed my fingers, unable to escape the warmth of his touch, and tried to ignore the feeling that he'd wanted to say more than he had.

I stepped back. "Did you and Lucian investigate the room I'd been held in?"

"The Aedh did. I examined the body in the sewer."

I turned around and began stripping off as I walked toward the shower. Azriel's gaze was a weight that pressed against my spine, and despite the fact that I was werewolf—and more than used to parading around naked before all and sundry—embarrassment began to swirl through me.

Because he *wasn't* all and sundry.

And that, I thought in annoyance, was the stupidest thought I'd ever had. He wasn't all and sundry because he was a *reaper*, and he didn't care if I was clothed or naked, upside down or inside out. The only thing that mattered to him was achieving his mission. Nothing more, and nothing less.

"That is not entirely true," he said softly.

I closed my eyes as I turned on the water. Damn it, why couldn't I just stop thinking such stupid thoughts? "Why isn't it?"

"I care for your safety. I care that you are not looking after yourself properly."

"Only because my carelessness could affect your mission." I stepped into the shower and simply stood there for a moment, letting the hot water sluice down my body, washing away the worst of the sewer grime as well as the remnants of my clothing. Then I took a deep breath and blew it out slowly. "You know, we've had this argument before. I really need to get over it, don't I?"

"Yes."

I grinned and glanced at him over my shoulder. He

was leaning against the far wall, his arms crossed and his expression dispassionate. Valdis sat in her sheath, yet little amber fireflies of energy flew around her hilt. Not indicating his anger, I thought, but something else—though what that something else might be, I had no idea.

I grabbed the shampoo and tried to concentrate on the mundane task of washing my hair rather than the very *un*mundane man behind me. "Did you find anything on the body?"

"Nothing at all."

"What do you mean, nothing?" I said, a little confused.

"No wallet, no identification, no phone, nothing."

I frowned. "What about a holster?"

"No."

"Why would he have a gun and not a holster?"

I was thinking out loud rather than asking an actual question, but Azriel answered anyway.

"Maybe he doesn't normally carry a gun and only grabbed it once he was running from you."

"He didn't have time to grab anything. He simply ran."

"Then logically, he was carrying it all along."

Logically, yes. But I still couldn't escape the itch that something about the whole situation was off.

"Then you need to listen to instinct," Azriel commented.

I sighed. "The trouble with that is that instinct isn't giving me a whole lot more than vague feelings of unease."

"You'll get more, if you give it time."

And time was something we didn't seem to have a lot of. "Was his soul collected by a reaper?"

"No. His death did not follow the ordained order, so his soul will roam the wilderness between this world and the gray fields."

"Could you find it? Question it?"

"No. He is in the lost lands. I can see the lost ones, but I am not able—nor am I allowed—to communicate with them in any way." He paused. "But you might be able to. Adeline Greenfield said you had more of your mother's talents than you were aware, and your mother communicated with both the dead and the lost ones."

"I might be able to see ghosts, but I've never known how to communicate with them. And right now we haven't got the time for me to learn." Although if things kept going against us, I might just have to find the time. "Did Ilianna get her books and equipment okay?"

"Yes."

"So why didn't you come riding to my rescue when I had the car accident?"

"Because the Raziq attacked us at the house."

I spun around. "What? Is Ilianna okay?"

"Of course. They attacked in force, which meant I had to flee rather than fight."

I studied him for a moment, hearing the annoyance in his voice even though it didn't show in his features, then turned around and squirted some soap into my hand. "And you would rather have fought?"

"Of course. The more Raziq I destroy, the fewer there are to find and use the keys."

"So why not gather together a group of Mijai and hunt them down?"

"Because," he said patiently, "that is against—"

"—the rules," I finished for him. "Whoever made these rules of yours really sucks, you know that?"

"There are times when I think a certain amount of absurdity has been added to the whole process," he agreed solemnly.

I glanced at him again and saw the brief twinkle in his bright eyes. "It's hard to believe that, when I first met you, I thought you were devoid of humor."

"I'm afraid it's merely a side effect of holding this form."

"How can holding human form affect whether or not you have a sense of humor?"

"It's not just a sense of humor we gain." He hesitated. "We are not without emotions, as I have said, but holding this shape for any length of time sharpens certain emotions, and that is often inconvenient."

"Meaning it makes you more like us?"

"No." Again he hesitated. "It simply makes us more . . . susceptible . . . to certain types of emotion."

"What types of emotion?"

He shrugged and his game face came back down. "That very much depends on the situation we find ourselves in."

"So if you find yourself guarding a totally annoying woman who won't listen to reason and who insists on seeing an Aedh you distrust intensely, you're liable to become more angry and more unreasonable the longer you hold this form?"

Amusement briefly touched his lips. "More than

likely. Luckily for us both, I am not stuck guarding a woman who totally ignores reason. She just ignores it when it suits her best."

A smile twitched my lips. "Ah, but she *is* seeing a fallen Aedh."

"I didn't say she was perfect."

I laughed and he smiled. It made his whole face seem warmer, more alive. More handsome. *And I shouldn't be noticing*. I turned around and finished washing myself.

"Did you discover anything else about Forman when you examined him?" I asked as I turned off the taps then reached for a towel.

"No. And there certainly wasn't enough of his brains left to enter his mind and read the lingering shadows of his thoughts and life."

"Yeah, Lucian did get a little trigger-happy." I walked across to my locker and began dressing. "I would have loved to have questioned him about his boss."

"So Forman did not set the magic?"

"No, and it wasn't an Aedh, either, because the magic had a different feel. It was darker."

"Suggesting a sorcerer or Charna, perhaps?"

"Perhaps." I finger-combed my hair. "But why would either of those want control of the gates?"

"Power," he said simply. "Especially if we're dealing with a dark sorcerer."

"And if the dark sorcerer is also behind the buy-up of the businesses around Stane?"

He shrugged. "West Street sits on a major ley line junction. That would be a huge draw to someone after power—especially if he cannot naturally walk the gray fields."

I raised my eyebrows as I grabbed my bag of clothes and closed the locker. "How could a junction of ley lines help a sorcerer walk the grey fields?"

"As I have said, these intersections are places of such power that they can be used to manipulate time, reality, or fate. But they can also be used to create rifts between this world and the next."

I frowned. "So a powerful enough sorcerer could enter the gray fields and presumably find the gates, even though he doesn't have that ability naturally?"

Azriel nodded. "Although it is not so easy to find the gates in the fields. We are attuned to them; the sorcerer would not be."

"But that might not matter if he finds the keys."

"Which is why we must find the keys first."

"Well, we won't be able to do that until Ilianna creates the void for the book." I hesitated. "But there's one thing I don't get. What was the point of buying up all the businesses around the ley lines? Why not just buy the building where they intersect?"

"Potions and spells do not require protection circles, but *real* magic—be it big or small—does. When it comes to an intersection this large, a prudent practitioner would want to build something rather more substantial than just a normal protection spell."

"Something more permanent?"

"If they intend to use it more than once, yes."

Then I guess the buyout made some sort of sense. "I think I'll head to my hotel room to grab some sleep."

"Get something to eat before you do," he said, his tone indicating it was an order more than a suggestion.

"Are you always this bossy?" I said, exasperation in my voice as I headed for the door.

His lips once more twitched. "Only when the person I am supposed to be guarding is less than cautious about her own well-being."

"And do you guard such people often?"

"This is the first and—more than likely—the last time I will undertake such an endeavor."

I stopped next to him and met his gaze. "If you don't like the mission, why not ask for a transfer?"

"It is my duty, and no one else's." His gaze didn't waver, and yet something in those blue depths—something fierce and raw—made my stomach quiver. "And I never said I didn't like it."

"You've a funny way of showing it then, my friend."

"That is because," he said softly, "I fear it more than I like it."

And with that, he winked out of existence, leaving me with dozens of questions I knew would probably never find an answer.

"Damn you to hell, Azriel," I muttered, and clomped down the stairs.

Tao raised an eyebrow as I entered the kitchen. His brown hair was covered by an old baseball cap worn backward, and his white chef's jacket was splattered with a colorful array of the evening's cooking.

"You don't look happy," he commented. "Do you need a shoulder, drink, or food?"

"Mostly the last option, but a little of the others wouldn't go astray right now, either."

He caught my elbow and led me over to a chair in the far corner. "Sit," he ordered, "while I rustle up a meal and a drink."

I did as ordered. Tao, like most wolves, tended to be on the lean side, but he worked out religiously and, as a result, had not only wonderful shoulders and arms but a nice V-shape to his body as well. And he moved with a grace that belied his height.

"So," he said, coming back ten minutes later with a thick steak sandwich and a huge glass of Coke, "what's been going on?"

I updated him on everything that had happened over the day as I ate, and when I'd finished talking, he frowned. "So the first priority now has to be tracking down this Harlen fellow."

"Stane's not going to make much headway until we can get a full name," I commented, grabbing a tea towel and wiping my hands on it. "I think we're better off trying to find the man in charge. I mean, how many dark sorcerers can there be in this city?"

"Probably more than you or I are aware of," he said grimly, crossing his arms as he leaned a shoulder against the wall. "And Ilianna is probably getting close to using up all her goodwill at the Brindle."

"Which is why I'm going over there myself tomorrow to talk to them." I wanted to see their reactions when I told them someone had raised a Maniae and had sent it after members of the high vampire council.

"You want company?" Tao asked.

I hesitated, then shook my head. I had Azriel and, at this point, it seemed wiser to keep contact with those I cared about to a minimum. At least until we sorted out the Aedh problem. They'd already gone after Ilianna—they might try Tao next.

Which only meant it was all the more urgent that Ilianna find the wards my father had set and try to reuse them around our place.

Of course, as Azriel had already pointed out, I was probably endangering both Ilianna and Tao just by being here at the café. I finished my Coke and stood up with a sigh. "I'll be staying at the Langham for the next few days. You'll need to find someplace else to stay, too."

He grinned. "Finding a place to bunk down will *not* be a problem, let me assure you."

I eyed him for a minute, then said, "How are you and Candy doing?"

"Sadly, it was just a fling, and now she's moved on to greener pastures."

I blinked. "You almost sound upset."

"I am. It's usually me doing the dumping, not the other way around."

I leaned forward and kissed his cheek. "Well, I can't say I'm sad she's out of your life, but I doubt she'll find a better lover than you."

He smiled and touched my chin lightly. "Damn right," he said, a smile teasing his lips. Then it faded a little. "Be careful, okay?"

"I will." I kissed him again then headed out of the café, catching a passing cab and heading to the Langham. Once in my suite, I crawled into bed and went straight to sleep.

The sharp trilling of my phone woke me. I groped for it blindly and croaked, "Hello?"

"Risa? It's Mike."

It said a lot about my state that it took me several moments to remember that Mike was our accountant. He'd also been Mom's accountant and, I suspected, a whole lot more—although *that* was something neither he nor she had confirmed.

"Mike," I said, rolling over onto my back and wiping the sleep from my eyes. "What's up?"

I glanced at the clock as I said it and discovered it was nearly midday. I'd slept a whole lot longer than I'd intended.

"I need you to come in and sign some documents so we can complete the transfer of several of your mom's assets," he said. "I'm free at three—does that suit?"

I somehow restrained a yawn and said, "I guess."

"Good. I'll see you then." He hung up, but the phone rang again almost immediately. This time, the vid-screen opened up, revealing Stane.

"Hey," he said, sounding far too cheerful for someone who spent his entire life sitting behind com-screens. "How's it going?"

"I've had better weeks," I replied honestly enough. "What's up?"

"I've done a sweep of your place and removed several bugs. You'll be pleased to know there were no monitors." He paused, then added a little dramatically, "And I've had a minor breakthrough."

My heart skipped several beats. "You've found the missing man behind the consortium?"

"Nope."

"You've discovered who our mystery man known only as Harlen really is?"

"Remember, I used the word *minor*," he said drily. "So no."

"Then what?"

"Remember that rat-faced guy you were looking for? The one who delivered the Dušan's book and the first letter from your father?"

"You've discovered who he is?"

"Better than that. I know where you can find him. And he's there right now if you want to talk to him."

Chapter Eight

THE CAB PULLED UP SEVERAL DOORS DOWN FROM the run-down building. I paid the driver and climbed out, the wind snatching my coat ends and flinging them backward. I shivered and zipped it up, shoving my hands into my pocket as I studied the building.

According to Stane, this area had recently been re-zoned from industrial to residential, but the demolition teams had yet to move in. As a result, the city's homeless had taken up residence.

The building the rat-faced courier had entered was a quaint two-story brown-brick building sandwiched between two bigger warehouses. Large windows looked out onto the street but there was little chance of anyone seeing me standing here, as somewhat grimy blinds had been drawn down in all of them.

"These are the premises we seek?" Azriel said softly.

I nodded. "Stane couldn't give us his name, but thanks to the traffic cams down the road, he spotted our rat-faced shifter enter here forty-five minutes ago. He hasn't come out."

"Then let us go in and find him." He drew his sword. Valdis gleamed brightly in the dull afternoon light.

"You do realize we can't kill him?" I commented as we crossed the road.

Azriel looked at me. "You seem to be of the opinion that I enjoy shedding blood."

"I am of the opinion that you'll do whatever is necessary to complete your mission. And if that means killing, then yeah."

"I cannot kill if it is not warranted—something you've been told several times."

Then he pushed the door open and stepped through, Valdis's fire imparting an eerie glow to the shadow-filled hallway.

His gaze swept the immediate vicinity, then he looked up. "There are three people upstairs, five people on this level, and one downstairs, in the basement."

"If he's a rat shifter, he's probably the one in the basement."

He nodded and advanced. I followed, sorting through the scents that filled this place as I did. It smelled of age, refuse, and unwashed humanity. I couldn't sense a shifter, but if he was down in the basement, then maybe the heavier aromas of oil and machinery were masking his scent.

No one came out to see who we were, although I did hear several movements. Maybe the homeless feared we were the police, sent to roust them out of their free lodging.

The stairs loomed out of the shadows. Valdis's light died, although if the man we were hunting *was* a shifter, then he'd smell and hear us coming long before the sword's brightness could announce us.

Azriel led the way down into the deeper darkness. I kept close to his back, the heat of him washing across my body and somehow making me feel more secure. When we hit the end of the stairs, the darkness became so complete I was virtually blind. I touched Azriel's shoulder, not wanting to lose him as we continued on.

Gossamer brushed across my face and I bit back my squeak of fright. A web—sans spider, hopefully, I thought with a shudder. Critters that possessed eight legs were definitely *not* on my favorites list.

Our quarry is on the move, Azriel said, his words warm as they whispered into my brain.

Stop laughing at my phobia. I might not be telepathic, but that apparently didn't stop him from hearing my thoughts loud and clear.

A point he'd proved time and again.

I wasn't laughing. I am merely bemused that anyone could fear a creature so small.

Australia has some of the deadliest creatures on the planet, I retorted, *and most of them are tiny!*

It was an empty web that touched your face, and you squeaked, he said, mirth still very evident. *Our quarry is now running.*

Should we?

He can't escape. I have a sense of his soul now.

And I had his scent. It was musty, sharp, and definitely rat-like.

We moved quickly through the blackness. Deeper shadows loomed, and the scent of oil and machinery sharpened. Azriel led me through the maze easily, obviously seeing a whole lot more clearly than I was.

There was a whisper of sound—dirt falling onto concrete—then the scent of the shifter faded sharply.

He's gone through a hole in the wall, Azriel commented. *I smell sewers.*

For fuck's sake, what was it with these people and sewers?

Rats do like them. Amusement rolled through his thoughts again. *You may stay here, if you like, and I shall retrieve him.*

You promise not to question him before bringing him back?

He studied me for a moment—something I felt rather than saw. *I would not, but if you wish me to promise, then I shall do so.*

It was a rebuke, even if it was a gentle one. I didn't answer and, a second later, the heat of him was gone. I crossed my arms, shifting from one foot to the other impatiently. But he was back quickly, the heat of his body announcing his presence long before the sharp scent of rat shifter hit the air and both men re-formed.

The shifter came into being screaming. "Fucking hell, what did you just do to me?"

Valdis's flickering light lifted the darkness. The shifter was built like a string bean, but there was a strength to his movements that belied his gauntness. His face was angular—sharp—and his small eyes dark. Azriel held him securely by the scruff of the neck, but the shifter didn't seem to notice, twisting from side to side as if to check that all the bits of himself had re-formed properly.

"You know what he did to you," I said flatly. "You work for an Aedh. You must have more than a passing knowledge of their abilities."

He jumped—a hard feat given how tightly Azriel was holding him—and his gaze settled on me. "Who the hell are you?"

"It doesn't matter who I am. Just answer the question."

"I would if I fucking knew what you were talking about!"

I studied him for a moment, sensing no evasion in his words and seeing no lie in his body language. Which was odd. "Several months ago, you were asked to deliver a package—and then a note—to a warehouse apartment in Richmond."

"Yeah, so?"

"So you're not a deliveryman, and the uniform you used was not yours. Who employed you to deliver those packages and how did they get in contact with you?"

He shrugged, his expression growing more uneasy. "The package was delivered here, with a page of instructions. I got paid once I did the job. I never saw the person and I never cared to, as long as I got my money."

"And did you get your money?"

"Of course I did! I'm not a sucker, lady."

I glanced over his shoulder and met Azriel's gaze. He no more believed the shifter than I did.

"So you never saw who left the package here?"

"No. Like I said, the guy just left it sitting there with the instructions."

"If you never saw him, how do you know it was a man?"

"Because girls don't like the dark and all the spiders down here, do they?"

No, they didn't, I thought with a shiver. Luckily, Valdis's light wasn't revealing any eight-legged critters in the immediate vicinity.

"Let me try," Azriel said, then touched his free hand to the shifter's forehead.

The shifter stilled instantly, and his face went slack. Azriel closed his eyes, and, for several minutes there was little noise other than the sound of both my breathing and the shifter's.

Then Azriel opened his eyes again. "He does not lie. However, he does not tell the truth, either."

"Meaning?"

"Meaning, Hieu has tampered with this man's memories."

No surprise there, I guess. Not when he didn't want to be found. "That still leaves the problem of how the book actually got here. I mean, my father no longer has a flesh form, and though this doesn't stop him from manhandling me, the fact remains that you can't carry anything in Aedh form unless it's in contact with your skin before you change shape."

Azriel nodded. His fingers were still resting against the rat shifter's forehead, keeping him still, keeping him compliant.

"Hieu did not entirely erase the event from his mind. There are remnants." He hesitated. "I can show them to you, if you like, but it will mean I need to go into your thoughts."

"You do that anyway."

"That is surface sifting. This would be deeper."

I studied him for a moment, wondering at the wariness I saw in him. "Is it dangerous?"

"For you? No. But you are not happy with my frequent incursions as it is, and this might just strengthen the link that already exists."

Well, wasn't *that* just great! But it wasn't like I had another choice, not if I wanted answers.

"You always have another choice," he said softly.

I snorted. "You're in my head one way or another, so let's just get on with it."

His gaze lingered on mine for a moment, then he nodded and tapped the rat shifter's head twice. The rat shifter dropped to the ground and didn't move. But he was breathing, so he wasn't dead.

"Handy trick," I muttered, crossing my arms in an effort to chase away the chill beginning to invade my bones. "Why didn't you do that with the half-shifter in the locker room? Why use the ropes?"

"Because Razan are harder to render unconscious by this means. The rope achieved the same result, but with less effort."

Azriel stepped over the shifter and stopped in front of me. The heat of him washed over my skin, filled with the vague scents of musk and man. When he'd first appeared in my life, he'd smelled of nothing. Holding flesh was obviously changing him in more ways than what he was saying.

"Are you ready?" he asked, his gaze steady on mine.

I licked suddenly dry lips, and yet I didn't know what it was I feared. I knew he wouldn't hurt me because he still needed me to complete his mission.

"I would never hurt you, mission or not." He raised his hands, lightly cupping my cheeks. Electricity flared instantly, burning past my skin into my body, right down to my soul—until it felt like there were thousands of fireflies buzzing around inside me.

Then they exploded and, in the midst of the energy surge, the two separate entities that were our minds became one. In that state, what remained of the shifter's memories and experiences were laid out before me like a picture book. The man who'd delivered the parcel was tall and powerfully built, but his face was blurry and he'd talked to the air. My father, undoubtedly, though the rat shifter had no sense of him. Then I felt the energy—an Aedh's energy, the same sort of energy that had attacked me when the Raziq had held me captive—flowing through the shifter's limbs, snatching away his memories, leaving huge swaths of nothingness rather than whatever conversation had followed the tall man's arrival. I saw the tattoo on the stranger's left shoulder as he departed—a dragon with two swords crossed across it. I saw a second tattoo—a ring of barbed wire—on his right shoulder.

Then, without warning, the contact deepened, flowing from an exchange of images to something both tempestuous and sensual—becoming a connection that went beyond mind, beyond body. It went beyond anything I'd ever felt before.

And it was a connection that was severed so abruptly I staggered backward, and would have fallen had not Azriel grabbed my arm.

I stared at him for several seconds, my breathing rapid and my heart feeling like it was about to explode out of my chest. His expression gave little away, but Valdis burned with orange fire, and it seemed to echo deep in the heart of his mismatched blue eyes.

"What the hell just happened?" I said, pulling away from his grip and taking a step back.

"Nothing," he said, voice clipped. "The connection simply became stronger than I'd intended."

"So you didn't cause—" I paused. "—whatever the hell that was?"

"No."

"Then how did it happen? And what *did* happen?"

He shrugged and glanced down at the rat shifter—not letting me see his eyes, I thought. Then, as Valdis's fire faded to blue, I realized he was simply getting himself under control. Which meant that whatever had happened had shaken him as badly as it had shaken me.

"We are Chi-linked. I did not expect it to affect the simple act of mind sharing, but it appears I was wrong."

"But that sensation was—" *Erotic.* A blush crept across my cheeks. Damn, I couldn't admit *that* out loud. Not to a reaper. Not to *him.* So I simply added, "Unusual."

"Yes. As I said, somehow the fact we are connected on a Chi level enabled the connection to deepen. What you felt—" He paused and rose, finally meeting my gaze. His expression was carefully neutral, and the fire in his eyes had disappeared. "What you felt was the energy of my true self."

It was more than that. He knew it, and I knew it. But he obviously wasn't going to admit it or explain it any more than he had.

I flexed my fingers, still feeling the energy of his touch on my arm—just as I could still feel the remnants of that connection burning deep inside. I suspected it wouldn't be something I'd easily forget.

Yet I had to. No good would ever come of it. Both instinct and head were suggesting that, and I believed them both.

"What do you wish done with the shifter?" he said calmly, as if he weren't aware of my thoughts or the tumult that still burned within me.

I took a deep breath that did little to calm anything, and said, "Can you get a name out of him?"

He nodded, then bent down and touched the shifter's forehead again. "James Larson. He's a small-time thief who generally survives by picking pockets at the St. Kilda market."

"I wonder why my father chose him to deliver the book."

Azriel shrugged as he rose. "That is something you will have to ask your father."

And my father was about as easy to get a straight answer from as Azriel. *And* he was a whole lot more difficult to find. "Can you erase any memory of us questioning him from Larson's mind? You never know; my father might decide to use him again."

"He will not remember us. I have already ensured that."

"Good." I glanced at my watch. I really needed to get going if I was going to meet Mike in time. Then I had to get over to the Brindle. And if I didn't start doing some work on Hunter's case, the shit was going to hit the fan—although Hunter herself had yet to come through with her list. Nor had Catherine Alston. It was rather hard to follow up on things when I wasn't getting full cooperation. But maybe that was the whole point. Maybe Madeline—or rather, the council—just wanted to see how I coped on my own.

"If these lists are important to solving this case, why not simply call her and ask for them?"

I snorted softly. "Because I'd really prefer to keep my contact with Hunter to a minimum."

"But would it not be better to solve this case quickly? That would at least prove to the council you are capable of such tasks."

Just what I needed—a practical reaper. "If I don't get them by the time I've seen Mike, I will call. In the meantime, you want to lead the way out of this maze?"

He nodded and brushed past me, his arm barely touching mine but electric all the same. This was crazy, I thought, following him out of the darkness. I mean, he was a reaper. He didn't *do* humans. There might not be any hope of a real and lasting relationship with Lucian, either, but at least with him I could settle for amazing sex.

Light began to filter through the darkness, and the stairs became visible. We climbed them quickly and headed out of the building.

"I shall keep my distance for the time being," Azriel said. "But call if you need assistance at the witch depository."

I nodded, although I didn't think the Brindle witches would take too kindly to an armed reaper walking among them. As he winked out of existence, I walked down the street and looked for a cab.

It was just after three by the time I got to Mike's. He lived within walking distance of our apartment, in a small single-fronted terrace that served as both his office and—on the floor above—his residence.

As the cab sped away, I climbed the steps and

pressed the intercom button. "It's Risa Jones, here to see Mike."

"Risa," a plummy, feminine voice said, "please, come in."

The door was buzzed open, revealing a small waiting room in which sat half a dozen plush, comfortable chairs. To the right there was a small desk and, behind it, a matronly woman with pale purple hair and sharp blue eyes.

I smiled at her. "How are you today, Beatrice?"

"Better than Mike," she said wryly. "It's tax time, and you know what that's like."

"I do." And I hated it. Which is why I tended to do mine ASAP, because I just wanted to get it all over with. But according to Mike, I was in the minority. Apparently, most of his clients tended to leave things to the last moment, then got into a panic.

"You can go straight in," she said. "He's been waiting for you."

I glanced at my watch in surprise. It was only ten past three. By Mike's usual standards, I was actually *early* for my three o'clock appointment.

Beatrice grinned and added, "Yeah, I know, it doesn't happen often. But several clients had to cancel this afternoon."

"At tax time? That's a little unusual, isn't it?"

She shrugged. "Strange are the ways of clients. Would you like a cup of coffee? Or maybe a Coke?"

"A Coke would be good."

She nodded. "I'll bring it in."

"Thanks." I walked down the short hallway to Mike's office, which dominated the back half of the small house. Unlike the rest of the downstairs area, which tended to be modern in its feel and furnishing, stepping into Mike's office was like stepping into another century. From the huge mahogany desk to the massive, Georgian-style, glass-fronted bookcases, the leather-and-mahogany chairs, and the wooden filing cabinets, the place looked—and smelled—old. And Mike only added to this impression, wearing close-fitting pants that looked suspiciously like breeches, a double-breasted waistcoat, a white linen shirt, and a plum-colored cravat. His hair was black but cut short, the dark curls clinging close to his head. I was never actually sure of Mike's age—he didn't look old, and yet he didn't seem young, either. And his eyes—a clear, striking gray—seemed to hold eons of knowledge behind them.

But then, Mom had once commented that he had a genius-level IQ, so that was to be expected.

He was standing near the bookcase as I entered, but turned around and gave me a wide smile of greeting.

"Risa," he said, his voice low and pleasant. "Lovely to see you again."

"And you." I kissed his cheek in greeting, then sat down on the chair he held out for me. "We haven't seen all that much of you recently."

"No." He walked around to the other side of the desk and sat down elegantly. "And I have very much missed my weekly dinners with your mother—" He paused for a moment, sadness flitting across his aristocratic features. "I suppose you've heard nothing more from the Directorate?"

"No. But the case is still open and they are working it."

"Ah." He sighed, then reached for several manila folders. While his secretary had the latest in technology and everything they handled went to the tax office electronically, Mike still preferred his old-fashioned ways, doubling up with actual paperwork and proper signatures rather than just electronic ones. "I just need your signature on these to complete the transfer to your name."

He opened the folders and indicated where I was to sign. I skimmed them all, noting the three businesses involved were the last three Mom had bought—the boutique hotel in St. Kilda, the ski lodge in Falls Creek, and the health spa in Hepburn Springs. All of them good, thriving businesses that didn't need a lot of input from me. Which is why I'd kept them rather than adding them to the pile I was selling off. Mom was hands-on—but I had enough on my hands just managing my café.

I signed in the spots indicated, then pushed the folders back. He collected them and said, "It'll take about a month for these to be fully finalized. Even in this instant age of ours, everything still seems to take forever."

I grinned and glanced around as Beatrice came in, carrying a tray holding a can of Coke and a mug of what smelled like seriously burned coffee. She placed the tray on the table, gave us a smile, and walked out.

I picked up my Coke, took a drink, then said, "But other than our tax liabilities, everything is pretty much finalized now?"

He nodded and took a sip of his foul-smelling coffee, then hesitated before saying, "I also wanted to tell you that if you ever need anything—outside financial matters, I mean—to please talk to me. Your mother and I—"

He stopped again and looked away, but not before I saw that flash of sorrow in his eyes again.

"Mom and you were close," I said softly. "I'm aware of that."

He nodded and seemed to get himself under control, because when he met my gaze again, there was little emotion in those steely depths. But then, there rarely was. I was never entirely sure what Mom had seen in him, but there had to be something pretty powerful between the two of them, because she'd had no other lovers. Or, none that I was aware of, anyway.

"We spent a lot of time together." Which is probably as close as he'd ever gotten to admitting they were lovers. "And I know she would want me to be of as much help as I could."

"Thanks, but—"

He raised a hand, stopping me. "I know you and I are not close, but your mother and I *were*. If you ever need help with any matter—even if it's simply an unbiased mind to talk to—then please, feel free to come here. Your mother would have wanted that, I'm sure."

"Thanks, Mike. I really appreciate the offer—"

"But you'd feel uncomfortable discussing personal matters with a man who is little more than a business adviser?" he said, humor in his eyes. "I can understand that, but the offer stands nonetheless. And remember, I do have quite a few interesting contacts through my business dealings. You never know when one of them might prove useful."

I smiled. "And if that was meant to tempt me into asking just what sort of interesting contacts, I think you might have succeeded."

He laughed softly. "I merely meant that I have business and personal relationships with people from all levels of society. They might prove useful one day."

I nodded and rose, drink in one hand as I offered him the other. "I was sincere when I said thanks for the offer, and I really will keep it in mind. I promise."

"Good." He shook my hand, his grip light, warm, and filled with a restrained strength.

It certainly wasn't the grip of a man in his twilight years, and again I wondered just how old he was. He'd been in charge of Mom's finances since I was born and, from what Mom had said, he hadn't exactly been a fresh-faced kid even then. Which meant he had to at least be in his fifties, if not older. Yet he didn't show it. Maybe he'd been blessed with good genes, I thought wryly, and wondered why I was even worried about it—especially given it had never seemed to concern Mom. And if anyone was going to sense anything off about him, it would have been her. She'd been one of Australia's most powerful and successful psychics, after all.

"Don't forget that the next Business Activity Statement is due soon," he added, getting back to business.

I grimaced, but suddenly wondered if the curious itch over his age had simply been a reaction caused by his stepping past our usual boundaries. Now that we were back on safe ground, the itch retreated. "Yeah, I know. And it's still a pain in the ass."

He laughed again. "Anything dealing with taxes generally is. But it keeps us accountants employed. I mean, if the system were simple, anyone could do it, and then where would we be?"

I grinned. "Sunning yourself on a beach somewhere?"

"Good Lord, I could think of nothing worse," he said, and added, with a mock shudder, "All that sand!"

I laughed, said my good-byes, and headed out. The weather outside had deteriorated in the brief time I'd been at Mike's and I shivered, wrapping my coat ends across my body in an effort to stop the wind from chilling me. But it didn't help much.

I looked around for my bike, then cursed when I remembered I was still doing the whole cab thing. "Damn it, Azriel, we really need to find a way to stop the Raziq attacking our home, because I do not want to be living out of a suitcase—or without my bike— for much longer."

The heat of his presence snatched away the chill wind. He materialized a second later, standing at the bottom of the steps staring up at me.

"The only way we could ensure that," he said, "is by not taking the book anywhere near your home. They need the book as much as you, and they will not make a grab for one unless they can attain the other. Their trap in the sewers was evidence of that."

His hands were resting on the railings on either side of the steps, effectively hemming me in. It was hard to say if it was deliberate or not because, as usual, his expression gave little away. And even though the fact he'd warned that the mind link would deepen our connection, I was getting zip from him—and maybe I never would. I wasn't actually telepathic, after all. Maybe all he'd meant was that the link would deepen on his end, not mine.

"Yet they attacked you and Ilianna yesterday when you both went there, and the book was nowhere near the house."

"Because they know I follow you and would presume I was with you rather than Ilianna. They would also have hoped that we possessed the book."

"My point exactly—they attacked without feeling the presence of the book."

"A move I doubt they'll repeat. They will wait and ensure all pieces are in place before they attack again."

I frowned. He seemed confident, but I wasn't so sure. The Raziq weren't exactly the sanest inmates in the asylum. "But the minute I touch the book and bring it out of the gray fields, they *will* attack—and you've already said you can't handle such an attack."

"No, I can't. But if your Aedh is right about the void, then we can keep the book safe in the brief moments it is here on earth while leading the Raziq in a completely different direction."

I studied him a moment, contemplating his words, sensing the slight edge of excitement rolling through the heat that surrounded him. "I'm guessing this means there *is* a locator spell on the book, and that you're planning to use it to lead them astray?"

He nodded. "We have managed to mirror the spell. Another Mijai has been assigned the task."

"But will the Raziq be stupid enough to fall for the charade for long?"

"The Raziq do not think much outside the box when it comes to human behavior. And the spell on the Dušan's book has been created in such a way that humans wouldn't be able to sense it."

"And yet they know a reaper is helping me, so you'd think they'd factor that into the equation."

He smiled. A real smile—the sort of smile that lit up his face and made my hormones do a weird little dance. "The Aedh, as a whole, have about as much respect for us as humanity does. In fact, at least humanity fears us. That is more than can be said for the Aedh."

"You like the fact that humanity is scared by the grim reaper image?"

"Of course not, and that is not what I meant."

"So what did you mean?"

"Simply that the Aedh rarely take our presence into account when contemplating whatever it is they spend their days contemplating. We are simply the messengers—the soul delivery people, if you will."

"Even the Mijai?"

"The Mijai only came into existence once the power of the Aedh began to wane. There was a need to be filled, so we filled it."

And it had been done out of their extraordinary sense of duty, I thought, rather than any real desire to fill the void created by the absence of the Aedh.

"It could be a dangerous task for the Mijai assigned the task of misleading the Raziq. They'll be far from happy if they realize what is going on."

He shrugged. "Danger comes in all forms and guises. You learn to live with it when you are a Mijai."

I studied him for a moment, wondering why I suddenly had the suspicion he wasn't talking about the Raziq or the things that broke through the dark path portal. "So if you're right, I can go home and retrieve my bike right now and be safe?"

"If I'm right, yes. If I'm wrong, we'll be running. Either way, I would not recommend staying there until our plan has fully materialized."

"I wasn't planning to stay, but I will need to grab some extra clothes and stuff."

He nodded. "Do so. Just don't be long."

A smile teased my lips. "There speaks a man who has no idea just how long it can take a woman to decide on what clothes to pack."

"No," he said, his expression as blank as ever but with a bright glint in his eyes. "But I am the man who will just grab the nearest items and whisk you both away if you linger unnecessarily."

"Now, there's a threat I'm truly scared of!"

"As you should be. Reapers have no fashion sense, after all." He released his grip of the right banister and stepped to one side. "You will head there now?"

"Yep. We're not far away, so I'm walking."

"Would it not be easier to become Aedh?"

"Not to my clothes, it wouldn't." I brushed past him and tried to ignore the tremor that ran through me as the warm, rich smell of him momentarily washed over me. He winked out of existence a moment later, and by the time I'd finished my Coke and walked home, my breathing had returned to a sensible rate.

Which obviously meant I needed to either see Lucian or go visit Franklin's. I mean, seriously, this hunger for the reaper was getting *ridiculous*.

I paused in front of our ugly building, my gaze searching it, trying to see—or feel—anything out of the ordinary. There was nothing. And even though I trusted Azriel's statement that the Raziq were unlikely to attack, every sense I had was on high alert the minute I entered our apartment. The air was still and smelled faintly of roses, honey, and rum—with undernotes of wolf. Tao had been here recently.

I headed into my bedroom and quickly collected clothes and various other personal items, then reset the alarms and went down to collect my bike. I couldn't help running my hand over her sleek metal, or the stupid grin that stretched my lips. I loved this bike—and not using her for this long had hurt.

I secured my packs, then started her up and headed for the Brindle. The traffic heading into the city was light, so it didn't take me too long to get there. I swung onto Lansdowne Street then right into Treasury Place. The Brindle was a white, four-story building that had once been a part of the Old Treasury complex. It look innocuous until you neared it—that's when its veil of power kicked in, in the form of a tingling caress of energy that burned lightly across your skin. Not hurting, just warning those who were sensitive to such things that this place didn't suffer fools or evil gladly.

I stopped in the parking lot along the edge of the area that had once held the premier's office but had long ago been reclaimed as a park, and left my bags where they were simply because the Brindle's magic secretly ensured no thief could ply his trade this close to her.

The last time I'd been here, they'd been waiting for us—three high-ranking witches, their tunic-clad bodies revealing little of their shapes and their faces serene as they'd forbidden us entry. This time the steps were empty, and the huge wood and wrought-iron doors were open, allowing a glimpse of the warm, shadowy interior. Several years ago I'd come here to deal with a ghost who was making life less than pleasant for some of the witches who lived in the rear parts of the old building, so I wasn't unfamiliar with the place. Even so, a sense of awe still struck me as I stepped through the doorway. This place—these halls—were almost as old as Melbourne itself, but they were so entrenched in power that mini comets of energy shot through the air at any movement.

The foyer wasn't exactly inviting, but the rich gold of the painted brickwork added a warmth that the somewhat austere entrance lacked. I walked on, my footsteps echoing in the stillness and little explosions of fire following in my wake. A woman appeared out of one of the rooms farther down the hall then stopped, her hands clasped together in front of her tunic-clad body.

"My name is Helena," she said, her voice like the water in a spring river—sweet but cool. "How may I help you, child?"

"I need to know if anyone has recently accessed the curse that summons a Maniae."

She paused. "That curse has gathered much interest of late."

Excitement had my heart skipping several beats. "Meaning someone has asked about it?"

"Several someones, I believe. This way." She turned and led the way to a room several doors down. The visitors waiting room, I knew from my past visit. You didn't get past this area without either a witch escort or special dispensation from Kiandra—the head witch herself.

Helena walked around a desk and opened one of several large books sitting on top of it. She flicked through the yellowed pages carefully, then said, "Ah, yes. Here it is."

She pointed to a spot about halfway down the register, then turned the book around so I could see it better. It was a spell register from the looks of it, with each page not only noting the name and location of the book that contained the spell, but holding a signed record of all those who had accessed it.

The Maniae curse only had three entries. The first, Charles James Highcourt, had accessed the book over two hundred years ago. The second, Deborah Elizabeth Selwin, had viewed it nearly three years ago. Which fit in rather neatly with Adeline's comment that Alston had hired her because of some nasty stuff going down on the vampire council nearly three years ago.

The third name . . .

My eyes widened and, for a moment, I couldn't believe what I was actually reading.

Because the third name—accessed only a few hours ago—was one Madeline Hunter.

Chapter Nine

I LOOKED UP QUICKLY. "MADELINE HUNTER? Is that Director Hunter, the woman in charge of the Directorate?"

She nodded and closed the book. "I believe so. Why?"

"Did she merely look at the register, or did she access the curse?"

"She asked about the specific details of the curse, but she did not ask for more than that." Helena studied me for a moment, then added, "We would not have allowed her to view the curse anyway. Too many of the older vampires have a working knowledge of magic, and this spell can be dangerous in the wrong hands. Besides, she is not a member of any coven."

"Would you have given her access if she had been?"

She smiled politely. "If she were a member of a coven, she would be a full practitioner, so yes, of course."

"Does that mean the more dangerous spells are not under strict control?"

"Of course not. All witches must make their own decision, and it is up to them to suffer the consequences should they take the wrong path."

I nodded thoughtfully. "The other woman—Deborah Selwin—I gather she *is* a coven member?"

"Yes."

"Can I ask which coven? I really need to talk to her if possible."

A small smile touched her lips. "Director Hunter asked much the same question."

"And did she get the same answer?"

"Of course. Selwin is a member of the Frankston coven. They meet weekly, as well as at the time of the full moon."

That odd smile still touched her lips, and instinct pricked up her metaphysical ears. "And the address?"

"They have special dispensation to meet at the Frankston Reservoir Park every Sunday evening."

"And will I actually find Deborah Selwin at these meetings?"

Her smile grew. "No, you will not."

Meaning *that* was a question Hunter *hadn't* asked—although I had to wonder why. She had far more experience hunting people down than I did—centuries of it, in fact. But maybe she'd simply slipped the information from Helena's mind—although that would be considered a breach of etiquette in this place, and might just put her on the outs with the Brindle. Even the vampire council wouldn't want that.

"Then where will *I* find her?"

"Ah," Helena said, "that is something of a problem. I can give you her home address, but we believe she has not been there for several weeks."

I guess if she *was* the one who'd raised the Maniae against the council, then she would have been smart enough to get the hell out of Dodge.

"Is there any one place she favors? A town or a building? Does she have a close friend or relative who might know where she is?"

"No relatives that we know of, but the Frankston coven might be able to give you more information."

Well, that was a lot of help. I forced a smile and said, "Thanks for letting me see the records. It was a help."

She inclined her head, then hesitated, cocking her head slightly, as if listening to someone else. "There is one other place you might try."

I paused in the act of turning around. "Where?"

Again she paused. "There is an old ritual site on Mount Macedon. Few people know of it these days, and even fewer would venture there, as the roadside is prone to slippage when it rains. But Selwin's mother was high priestess when it was a functioning coven site, so she would know of it. If she felt the need to find somewhere safe, then that place would be it. There is much ancient magic there."

"Did you also pass this information on to Hunter?"

Again with the small smile. "No, and we would ask that you don't, either. The council has no need to know of our more sacred places."

I nodded, even as I noted the use of *we* rather than *I*. She *was* in contact with someone else. "And the directions to find this site?"

"Will be here momentarily." She paused, obviously listening to that other voice again. "Be wary when you enter the site. If Selwin has raised a Maniae, she may well have stepped from the path of light. There is no telling just what else she is capable of."

"Thank you for the warning."

"Also, it is very likely your dark defender will not be able to enter. Those who are not true flesh and blood may be summoned into that place via magic, but they may not otherwise enter from outside its boundaries."

Unease slithered through me. I might have said many times that I was more than capable of looking after myself, but I'd learned very quickly that such was not the case when it came to the spirits and demons of hell.

And I had the sudden, gut-wrenching notion that, if Selwin had slipped from the path of light, I might just be facing those sort of creatures at the ritual site.

After all, she'd have to know that sooner or later the council would come after her, and she'd had plenty of time to prepare for that eventuality.

"Why would such a site be able to ban the entry of reapers and Aedh when a place as powerful as the Brindle cannot?"

"Because the Brindle is old, but it is not situated on an ancient site. There are places in this country that have been used for magic and ceremonies since long before European settlement arrived."

Which really didn't answer the question, but maybe she didn't actually know.

She glanced past me. I turned and watched a gray-clad young woman approach. She offered me an envelope, curtsied, then left.

"Please read the contents here," Helena commented. "We cannot risk the directions falling into the wrong hands."

Meaning Hunter and her council, I suspected. I tore open the envelope, scanned the directions carefully, then folded the paper into the envelope again and handed it back to her.

"Again, thank you for your help."

She nodded. "Just be careful, Risa. There are many things—and many people—in your life who are not what they seem."

And on that rather ominous note, I turned and walked out. But as I left the room, instinct had me glancing to the left. Down the far end of the hall, her willowy figure almost lost to the shadows, was Kiandra.

"The ancient site will protect you when nothing else will." Her voice, cool and distant, was whisper-quiet, but it floated down the hallway easily, as if there weren't any distance separating us. "But human blood must not be shed there. Not in anger, not in vengeance, and not in hate or fear."

I waited, but she said nothing else. She merely nodded my way once, then turned and disappeared through the closest doorway. Obviously, it had been Kiandra herself who'd given me all the extra information about the sacred ritual site.

For whatever reason, the Brindle witches were on my side.

Azriel appeared beside me as I walked across the park to the bike. "So you go to this sacred site next?"

I glanced at my watch. What I really wanted to do was go see Lucian and lose myself in a couple of hours of loving, but I guessed that really wasn't an option right now. Hunter was tracking down the same leads

I was, and faster, and maybe this test was my investigating skills against hers. And that was a test I would always lose.

As if to hammer home this particular point, my phone rang and Hunter herself appeared on the vidscreen.

"So," I said, by way of greeting, "when exactly were you planning to tell me you were working on this case yourself?"

She laughed softly, but there was very little humor in the sound or in her expression. "Did you honestly think the council wouldn't have other investigators on the case? How else would they judge your usefulness?"

"But it's not just any investigator—it's you. And you have a vested interest in keeping me alive, because you want the keys found."

"Which does not mean I will hesitate to erase you if I find the killer before you do," she said, with deadly calm. "And the council members are well aware of this."

Oh, fabulous, I thought sourly. The one person on my side really wasn't. "When were you planning to send me that list I asked for?"

"As soon as you forward Catherine's list to me." Cool amusement played about her lips—probably because she knew I'd be pissed off.

Which meant I couldn't give the bitch the satisfaction.

"She hasn't sent it yet. She's not dead already, is she?" I glanced across to Azriel for confirmation. He shook his head and held up five fingers. Meaning either five hours or five minutes, I guessed.

"No, and I am severely disappointed." She laughed again, the sound low and cruel. "The woman really does deserve it."

I bit back my instinctive retort—the one that went along the lines of Catherine not being the only one—and said, "I've talked to Adeline Greenfield, the witch who set up the magic protecting Alston's apartment. She mentioned that Alston requested it after something that happened at the council almost three years ago."

"Three years ago?" Hunter's perfect features creased into a frown. "I don't think—" She paused, and another cold smile touched her lips. "Ah, yes. The Whitfield affair. Ironically, his name does not appear on my list, and I doubt it will on Catherine's, either."

"What did Whitfield do, and why isn't he on your list?"

She paused, considering me. Weighing her options on just how much to tell me. "Robert Whitfield was a vampire with only a few hundred years to his name who went against council rules and created a nest for himself."

I frowned. "A nest?"

"A term we use for a large number of fledgling vampires created and controlled by one master. It is not considered a practical option in this day and age, as it is generally hard for a creator to either feed or control such a large number."

And we all knew what happened to vamps who couldn't control their fledglings—the Directorate stepped in and wiped them out.

"So what happened?"

"His nest was culled, of course, and he was severely punished."

"The culling of his blood kin wasn't enough?"

"Of course not. That was merely a practicality. Punishment needed to be rendered so that others would not be tempted to follow in his stead."

"So what happened to him?"

"He was drawn and quartered in front of the council, then a dozen of the younger members were allowed to feed from him."

Nice. *Not.* "I can't imagine he was too happy about that."

"It's hard to say, since he did not actually survive the experience."

Which was why he wasn't on the list. "You allowed the younger ones to kill him?"

"*I* didn't. The punishment was administered by the Melbourne council, not the high council." Mirth glinted in her cool green eyes. "His death was not intended, but things got out of control. It happens sometimes."

Meaning it *had* been allowed to happen. An arena filled with some of the strongest vampires in Melbourne could have easily controlled such a small number of younger counterparts.

"Then why did Alston fear retribution if Whitfield was dead? And who would be seeking it now?"

"If I knew the answer to that second question, you would already be dead," she said. "As to the first, Whitfield did have a number of friends on the council who swore vengeance. However, they saw the error of their ways, and I doubt they are behind the Maniae curse. They don't have the skills needed, for one thing."

Meaning they'd been threatened with a similar fate if Hunter's expression was anything to go by. "According to Greenfield, you don't need any sort of witch skill. You just need the spell and the desire."

"But it is a spell no one but a witch can get access to."

"We both know a witch did recently access it."

"Ah yes," she drawled. "I have already talked to the Frankston coven. They can tell us little of interest about Deborah Selwin."

"Meaning we've hit a dead end?"

"Meaning I have placed a watch on her home and her business, and I will interrogate her the minute she appears at either." She paused again. "Of course, it would be unfortunate for you if I *did* get hold of her first."

Which I doubted she would, if what I'd been told at the Brindle was any indication.

"You won't. I'll be in contact when I have her." It was said with more confidence than I felt. I signed off and shoved my phone into my pocket. "Did you hear all that?"

Azriel nodded. "It is troubling that I might not be able to get into this ritual ground."

"It just means I'll have to stay out of trouble." Or run like hell when it hit. "It would take some serious magic to stop you or an Aedh, though, wouldn't it?"

"From the sound of it, this place is steeped in magic."

I frowned. "Then it just might be the perfect spot to read the Dušan's book."

He eyed me for a moment. "Do you think the Brindle witches would approve of that?"

I remembered Kiandra's statement in the hallway and smiled. "I think they already have."

"Then it would be safer than attempting to read it elsewhere. But I recommend using the void regardless."

"You bet your sweet ass I'll be using it. Even if we are safe inside that place, that won't stop the Raziq from surrounding it and snatching us the minute we leave."

The ghost of a smile flitted over his face. "And why would you bet my ass on something like that?"

I snorted softly. "Now you're just teasing me."

"Perhaps," he agreed. "And I would hazard a guess that this is the first time you've called *any* reaper's ass sweet. Should I be honored?"

He was looking at me intently again, and again heat stole through my cheeks. Which was really, *really* weird. "Maybe."

"Then I shall have to work on said ass, because I'd really prefer a firm yes to an unconvincing maybe."

And with that, he winked out of existence again, leaving me wondering if—in his own weird way— he'd actually been flirting with me.

"No," I muttered. "You're imagining it."

No rebuttal came out of the air. If he was still following my thoughts, he was keeping his answers to himself. No surprise there.

I climbed onto my bike and started her up, firing out of the parking lot and into the traffic. But I didn't head immediately to Mount Macedon—not only because I needed to know what was happening with the void, but because I wasn't about to go up there without taking one or two precautions. And while that meant I should be talking to Uncle Quinn—who probably knew as much about demons and whatnot as Azriel—talking to him would no doubt result in me being chained to a chair unable to move for the next week or so. Neither he nor Aunt Riley had been overly impressed with the results of my last encounter with one of hell's minions.

I made my way to Mirri's and parked in a lot a few buildings down. After slinging my bag across my shoulder, I walked back, taking the stairs two at a time until I reached the third floor.

I pressed the doorbell and, in the distance, the tinny melody of "Witchy Woman" rang out. Sadness swirled; I'd used that same tune as Mom's ring tone. I blinked rapidly and forced a smile as the door was opened.

"Risa," Mirri said, her cheeks flushed and her clothing more than a little disordered. "We weren't expecting you."

"Clearly," I said, amused. "Do you want me to come back in half an hour or so?"

Her cheeks grew warmer. "No, no, of course not. Come in."

She stepped back and opened the door wider. I stepped through, my gaze sweeping the neat but small living area, admiring the comfortable old couches and the lovely old rugs that dotted the worn floorboards.

Mirri peered past me. "Reaper, if you're there, please materialize. We have a no-ghost policy in this apartment."

"I am hardly a ghost," Azriel commented as he gained flesh inside the room.

"When you're here but not here, you might as well be. And it's rude, you know. Sort of like eavesdropping."

He didn't comment as Ilianna came out of the bedroom, her expression exasperated as she tied the sash of her dressing gown.

"You really *do* have an impeccable sense of timing," she said. "What the hell do you want that couldn't wait?"

I grinned. "I did offer to come back in half an hour."

She snorted disparagingly. "You may like it rushed, but I don't. To repeat, what do you want?"

"What do you have on hand that I can use to ward off hellhounds and other possible nasties?"

She blinked. "And why would you be needing that?"

"Because I'm off to Mount Macedon to track down the witch who possibly raised the Maniae. The Brindle warned me that she might use dark magic to protect herself."

This time her surprise was more evident. "The Brindle helped you?"

"Yes. Kiandra herself gave me the information."

"That's one way of dealing with a problem without getting a threefold backlash."

I raised my eyebrows. "It was more than just a grab at a golden opportunity. They were actually helpful."

"Wow." Ilianna thrust a hand through her blond mane. "The Brindle actually helping an outsider? Things *have* changed. However, back to the problem at hand. Azriel's armed with a super-duper shiny sword. Why can't he take care of any potential threat?"

"Because I may not be able to get inside the sacred site in which the witch shelters. Have you made any progress on creating this void the Aedh spoke of?"

Ilianna's gaze ran past me, and her green eyes glinted with sudden amusement. "You just can't say his name, can you?"

"I could, if I wanted to, and if he was important enough." Even *I* was surprised at that. His voice might have been even, but there was definitely an undertone of antagonism. He added, "But that is neither here nor there. The void?"

"Is a work in progress. Unfortunately, there's no way to test its working without actually using it."

Azriel glanced at me. "Then the witch's solution could prove to be perfect."

"What solution?" Ilianna asked, before I could say anything.

"Kiandra basically gave us permission to use the old Mount Macedon site as a bolt-hole."

Mirri whistled. "Even I know that letting outsiders use a sacred site like that is a rather big deal."

"It totally is," Ilianna breathed, then shook her head, her expression concerned. "And it makes me wonder just what the hell the Brindle has seen coming. Although maybe we're better off not knowing."

I hadn't actually thought about Kiandra's sudden generosity, but now that Ilianna had mentioned it, it *did* seem strange. Trepidation stepped through me—and it spoke ill of what was to come.

I rubbed my arms and said, "Weapons for demons?"

"Oh. Yeah." She turned and walked back into the bedroom, reappearing a few moments later with her bag of tricks—one that I knew from long experience she never went anywhere without. "I don't have a whole lot on hand. Demons aren't something I generally have to worry about." She hesitated, frowning at Azriel. "Well, not until a certain sword-bearing reaper stepped into our lives."

"If I hadn't stepped into your lives, at least one of you would now be dead," he said softly.

I shot him a glance. He returned my gaze evenly, giving little away as per usual. But I knew who he meant—Tao. I shivered and watched Ilianna rummage through her case.

"Ah, here we go," she said, pulling out several items, then rising. She handed me three small smoky amber vials and a rather nasty-looking sharpened stake.

"I doubt vampires are going to be a problem at a witch ritual site," I said, studying the stake dubiously. It actually felt good in my hand—well-balanced and not too heavy.

"Stakes are good for more than just vampires," Ilianna said sarcastically, "and you of all people should know that."

I gave her a look and she made an annoyed noise. "It's white ash, which is not only a very strong wood, but also holds magical properties that make it dangerous to *all* creatures not of natural creation. And this one has been soaked in holy water, just to give it a little extra kick."

I frowned. "But vampires are of natural creation. Most of them were once human." Mainly because humans tended to hunger for eternal life, and vampirism offered that. Which didn't mean there weren't nonhumans who became vamps, just that there tended to be less of them.

"*Were* being the operative word. The process that makes them vampire is an unnatural creation. As are the creatures from hell—who may or may not have also once been human."

"What about Aedh and reapers? Is the wood dangerous to them?"

A grin teased her lips. "No creature, flesh or energy, would be too pleased about being staked. But I don't know if it will affect them magically or not. I certainly didn't read anything about it during my time at the Brindle."

I glanced at Azriel. He merely shrugged and said, "The only way to know is to try it, and you'll have to forgive my reluctance to volunteer. I do prefer my flesh as it currently is."

So did I, I thought, and felt heat touch my cheeks as he glanced my way. *Damn my recalcitrant thoughts to hell.* I cleared my throat and glanced at the three amber vials. "And these?"

"Holy water. Use it sparingly—you don't need a lot for it to be effective."

"Okay." I shoved the stake in my belt, then carefully placed the little vials in various pockets. "I'm not sure how long this is going to take, but if you don't hear from me by midnight, contact the Brindle for directions, then call Aunt Riley and let her know what's happening."

Ilianna nodded and gave me a quick hug. "Be careful, okay?"

I nodded, although it wasn't like I deliberately threw myself into danger. It just happened. Sort of like night following day, I suppose.

I gave Mirri a quick kiss on the cheek, then added, "Sorry for the interruption. Next time I'll call ahead."

She snorted. "I've been a part of this little family for long enough to know that you *never* phone ahead. There is an imp inside you, Risa Jones, that occasionally loves to upset the apple cart."

I grinned, but I couldn't deny the fact that I sometimes did take great delight in doing the unexpected.

"And that," Azriel said, his voice clear and bemused as we headed down the stairs, "might be more than a little frustrating, but it could also be your one saving grace."

I glanced at him. "Meaning?"

"Meaning that doing the unexpected has so far kept us one step ahead of the Raziq. Here's hoping it continues to work."

"Amen to that," I muttered. But even as I said it, I couldn't help thinking that, sooner or later, our luck would run out.

Mount Macedon was about forty miles outside Melbourne, so it took me a little under an hour to get up there. Dusk was settling in by the time I turned onto the rough-looking dirt road that apparently led to the sacred site—although to call it a *road* was something of a misnomer. *Goat track* was more apt.

I slowed considerably, avoiding the worst of the ruts and gunning through the ones I couldn't, splashing muddy water all over the bike and myself. The steep, tree-lined mountainside seemed to close in around me, filled with shadows and an odd sense of watchfulness, almost as if the trees were sentient.

I suppressed a shiver and rode on, the Ducati's lights coming on automatically as the dusk and shadows gave way to darkness. It wasn't the best time to be going hunting, especially in unfamiliar territory. I might have the keen nose of a wolf, but that wouldn't help me against the sort of traps a witch might conjure. And Selwin had had plenty of time to do just that.

A set of old wrought-iron gates came into view. I stopped, kicking out the bike stand but leaving the motor running and the lights on as I walked over to the gates—which, unsurprisingly, were padlocked. The lock was ancient and heavy, the chain as thick as my arm. It wasn't something I had any hope of breaking.

"Azriel, are you here?"

"Always," he said from behind me. He stepped forward, his arm brushing mine, sending little tremors of electricity scampering across my skin.

"Can you break the lock?" I said, oddly torn between wanting to press closer to him and needing to create space. In the end, I did neither.

"I can, but the lock is wrapped in magic. If I smash it, there is no telling how this place will react." He paused, his gaze on the heavy darkness beyond the gates. "There is much power here, and some of it is very old. And it is not quite as benign as you might presume."

"Great," I muttered, stepping back to first study the gates, then the old chain fence that disappeared into the darkness to either side of the main gate. I could jump over it no problem, but that would leave me without a fast getaway option should things go bad.

"You could always become Aedh."

"If the magic inside that place can stop both you and the Raziq from entering, what chance have I got?"

He shrugged. "You are part wolf—a flesh-and-blood being as well as an energy one. It could be a vital difference."

Could be. Could not be, too.

I returned to my bike and switched her off, then picked up my phone, checking to see whether I had service up here. I didn't, so I shoved it and my wallet into the under-seat storage before walking to the fence. I leapt up, grabbed the top of the fence, and hauled my ass—rather inelegantly—over.

Once I'd dropped down on the other side, I turned and glanced at Azriel. "Well?"

He shook his head. "I can go no farther."

"*Naturally*," I muttered. Then I mentally smacked myself for being annoyed. It wasn't his fault, after all.

But as I resolutely turned and followed the faint path through the trees and the darkness, I couldn't help my trepidation. There were some things that even I—trained as I was by two of the best guardians the Directorate had ever produced—couldn't fight alone. And I had a bad feeling that I was walking toward one of them now.

As my eyes became adjusted to the darkness, I became aware of shapes looming through the trees. Small buildings that smelled of incense, smoke, and ancient magic, as well as various silent, unmoving figures who hunched in the shadows—concrete monoliths hung with moss and lichens.

It wasn't really what I'd imagined a witch's ritual site would look like, but then this place was supposedly far older than even the coven that no longer used it.

The path meandered its way through the trees, sometimes widening into broader clearings but generally remaining little more than a goat track.

The wind was cool and fresh, smelling faintly of decomposing forest matter, eucalyptus, and the musky hint of animal. Probably kangaroo, given they were considered a pest in the Macedon region.

But the farther I walked into the mountain's heart, the stronger another scent became—humanity, accompanied by the faint hint of roses. The scent of a woman rather than a man.

I slowed my steps and proceeded more cautiously. Ahead, through the trees, the darkness was lifted by a fierce orange glow that sent sparks cascading into the air and filled the night with the raw aroma of burning greenwood.

My fingers twitched with the need to reach for the stake, but as yet nothing and no one had threatened me. To walk in there expecting trouble might just encourage it.

The light of the fire grew stronger, until the shadows and the night were banished and the air rode with warmth and electricity.

It wasn't a normal fire. Not completely. The flames moved and danced in a manner that seemed almost controlled—as if there was a being inside them that stirred them to life.

And yet I could feel no life other than myself and the woman who stood so close to the fire.

Fear tripped lightly down my spine, but I ignored it, pausing in the cover of the trees to study the clearing beyond.

The fire dominated the center of the rough circle, the wood piled high and burning fiercely. The witch stood so close to the flames that her skin had an orange glow and her hair seemed to flicker. There was no one else in the clearing. My gaze swept the grass. I couldn't even see a protection circle, which seemed unusual.

"I know you're there," she said, her voice clear and untroubled. "The magic of this place warned me the minute you breached its boundaries."

I walked into the lighted clearing but stopped halfway to the fire. The heat of the blaze scalded my skin, and I had no idea how she was managing to stand so close.

Her clear blue gaze swept me before rising again. "You're not what I expected."

"I daresay I'm not *who* you were expecting, either."

"I daresay," she agreed. "What is it you want?"

"Answers."

She smiled. It was a real smile, a warm smile—the sort of smile that would have normally tugged a response from my lips. But there was something off-kilter about her, about the look in her eyes. Not to mention the edge of wariness that swirled across the clearing, mingling with the wood sparks and stirring the leaves of the nearby trees.

"The vampire council sent you?"

I hesitated. "In a sense. But I am not an assassin."

"If I thought you were, you would already be dead." She cocked her head and studied me for a moment. "I must admit, you intrigue me. I cannot determine exactly what you are."

"I'm a half-breed, but that's neither here nor there. And its not what I'm here to discuss."

"Obviously," she said. "I suppose you want to know whether I am responsible for the rise of the Maniae?"

"I do."

She nodded and returned her gaze to the flames again. "I did not expect the Brindle to help the council, I must admit."

"They're not helping the council. They're helping me."

"A minor difference when you are here as a representative of the council."

She might have considered it minor, but I doubted the Brindle would. "So you did raise the Maniae?"

"Of course." She glanced at me. "Why else would I access the spell?"

She was, I thought uneasily, extremely chatty about her deeds. And that was never a good thing when it came to bad guys—or so Aunt Riley claimed—because it usually meant they had something devious planned. "Then my next question has to be, why?"

"Ah, that is far more complex."

"I have all night."

She smiled again—and this time there was nothing real or warm about it. "Perhaps. Perhaps not."

I resisted the urge to rub my arms and said, "Why did you raise the Maniae?"

"Because they killed my master."

It took a moment for her words to hit. *Shit, she was one of Whitfield's fledglings!* One they'd obviously missed during the cull.

"Which master are we talking about?"

She gave me a long look. "You know which master. You are not stupid, young woman."

"Then we *are* talking about Robert Whitfield?"

"Of course! How many others has the council allowed to be drained and killed recently?"

"To be honest, who the fuck knows? It's not like the council actually advertises their business."

"That's true." She crossed her arms and studied the fire for a moment.

As the silence stretched on, I said, "Why wait so long for your revenge, then?"

"Because while I have merely undergone the blood ceremony and not the conversion, Robert's death was almost my death. It took a toll on my strength and my will." She looked at me again, her face bitter and suddenly gaunt. "But I could have survived that. I could have survived his death and moved on with my life, had it not been for one discovery."

I raised an eyebrow, and she continued almost savagely. "By killing Robert and declaring that his entire nest be erased, they have sentenced me to madness when my death finally comes and the conversion takes place."

I frowned. "Why? I mean, it's not like another vampire couldn't help you."

"But they won't. Robert's line has been sentenced to death—each and every one of us. I am the last of his fledglings-in-waiting, and no vampire would dare take me into his care for fear that going against the council's edict would doom their own nest."

My frown deepened. "Fair enough, but I still don't see why you'd be sentenced to madness when you're converted. I mean, you seem sane enough now." Or as sane as anyone hell-bent on revenge could get. "Why would that change when you die and become a vampire?"

"Because the step from life to unlife is a traumatic one—not just because you die and are reborn, but because every new vampire is hit with a veritable sensory overload. It takes years for *any* newborn to learn to eat, walk, and talk, and it is no different for a newly turned vampire. That is why a fledgling's master is so important. They keep us safe, keep us in line, and—most important—teach us."

That being the case, I could understand her bitterness and need for revenge—and it didn't make my task here today any easier. I might sympathize, but I still had a job to do. One I had to finish if I didn't want to end up a victim of the high council.

"Look, the council's full of bastards, we both know that, but murdering them isn't going to solve your problem. You've killed two already. Why not call off the Maniae—or, at least, offer the council a trade?"

"And why would I do that?"

"Well, it's not so much Whitfield's death that has pissed you off, but the fact that you'll be left in isolation thanks to their ban on helping his fledglings, right?"

She nodded, amusement bright in her blue eyes. I had a sudden suspicion she was only humoring me, that she was waiting for something—or someone—else.

I resisted the urge to look around, although every sense I had seemed to be on high alert, and the hairs on my arms were standing on end. But other than the increasing sense of wariness and the strange way the fire was moving, nothing appeared out of the ordinary.

I continued, "So with two councilors already dead, why not contract the council and offer a trade? Their lives for yours? It seems a sensible option to me—especially if all you really want is the opportunity to survive."

She considered me for a moment, then turned her gaze to the flames again. After a moment, she nodded. "It is, indeed, a sensible option."

"Meaning, I gather, that you're not into sensible right now?"

"Not when it comes to the council, I'm afraid. They enjoyed Robert's passing far too much when they could have—and should have—stopped it."

And how, exactly, did she know that? She couldn't—not unless she was there, and there was no way she would have been. Whatever else this woman was, right now she was still human. As such, she would never have gotten anywhere near a council meeting.

"So who's your source on the inside?"

She smiled. It was a cool, calm, and altogether too-collected smile. "And why would you think I'd tell you that?"

"Because you have something planned that you don't think I'll survive," I replied evenly, "And therefore you have nothing to lose."

She laughed. It was a warm, rich sound, and the flames seemed to shiver away from it, as if afraid. I eyed the fire curiously. It really did seem alive, but that was ridiculous.

Wasn't it?

God, I wished I knew more about not only magic, but also the creatures that inhabited the realms beyond my own. I had a bad feeling I might be confronted by one of them soon.

"You could be right," she said, leaving me wondering if she was answering my thoughts or my comment. She studied me for a moment, then added, "but I've always hated those movies where the bad guy just blabs about all his plans, and then everything goes to hell and the good guy saves the day. So I don't think I'll be saying anything more."

Well crap, I thought, and flexed my fingers. I was going to have to do this the hard way.

"Look, as I said, I'm not here to harm you. But by the same token, I *will* have to take you back with me."

"And I," she said calmly, "have no intention of going anywhere."

"Please don't make me force you—"

She gave a cold, humorless laugh. "My dear child,

there is no way in heaven or hell you could force me to do *anything*. Now please, leave this place."

"I can't—"

She sighed dramatically. "I suppose it was too much to hope that you would."

With that, she flicked a hand, the gesture almost casual. But there was nothing casual about the result.

Because the fire came to life.

Chapter Ten

THE FLAMES ROARED SKYWARD, FORMING A thick, columnar mass more than six feet tall. Fingers of fire shot out from its center, forming trunk-like arms and legs. There was no head, just a seething mass of flame. In the center was a gaping maw, from which came a low growl that crawled ominously across the silence, stirring fear deep inside me.

It tore itself free from the main mass of the fire and stepped onto the damp ground, dripping molten globules. The ground sizzled but didn't burn, and the wariness in the air increased, the energy of it crawling across my skin.

It was as if this place did not welcome the fire demon. And if that were the case, would it do anything to protect the woman who had raised it?

I guessed I'd have my answer soon enough. I backed away from the fire and drew the ash stake. It seemed woefully inadequate as a weapon.

"Selwin, call off your creature." But even as I spoke, it moved. Its steps were ponderous, as if its flaming trunk-like legs were a weight it could barely lift. I watched it warily and continued to back away. It might not have eyes, but it seemed to have an uncanny sense of my location, shifting direction every time I did. "It's not too late to take the sensible course."

She snorted softly. "There is no sensible course when it comes to revenge."

"If this was just about revenge, you would not have been able to call the Maniae."

The creature raised a massive paw and swiped at me. I jumped away and the blow missed, but the heat of it rolled over me, furnace-like in its intensity. Sweat beaded across my brow and began to roll down my spine—although I couldn't honestly say it was all due to the heat. Some of it—most of it—was fear.

"This is about justice, not revenge. Closely related, but different enough. They stole my future, so it is only fair that I steal theirs." Her gaze rested on me—a contemplative weight. "You actually sympathize with my plight, so why go through this charade? Why not save yourself?"

"Because it's either bring you in, or die myself."

The creature swiped again. Fire sprayed across the darkness, splashing the ground around me, sizzling where it landed. I let the blow skim past my chest, the heat of it singeing my clothes and scorching the fine hairs on my arms, then raised the stake and slashed it across the creature's body. The sharp point hit the creature's fiery essence, slicing through it as easily as a hot knife through butter, cutting its trunk in half. For a moment, nothing happened. Then, like a great tree that had been sawed in two, it split asunder and fell, each half hissing and screaming in pain.

But instead of being extinguished, the two halves began to dance, to grow, until what stood before me was not one fiery being with limbs and no face, but two.

The stake didn't kill them. It just created more of them.

Fuck.

I shoved the stake back into my belt, ducked under a blow from the nearer creature, and reached for one of the bottles of holy water. Another fiery limb whistled toward me, its flames trailing behind it like a whip. I ducked, trying to undo the bottle's top as I did so. But this time, the blow didn't whistle past. With a sharp cracking sound, the trailing tendril snapped forward, roping itself around my body, wrapping me in a ring of fire that set my clothes alight. I screamed, but somehow managed to get the top off, splashing water over my skin as I poured it over the fiery leash that held me.

The water extinguished the flaming cord around my waist, and a good part of the creature's limb. It roared—a sound of anger and pain combined—and staggered backward, leaving my clothes smoldering and skin burning. I dropped and rolled on the damp ground, extinguishing the flames but not the pain. Then I noticed that where the droplets of holy water had splashed, my skin was already beginning to heal.

I grabbed another bottle and poured it over the bigger areas of raw, exposed flesh. My skin hissed and the pain sharpened abruptly, bringing tears to my eyes and sending a rush of agony through every nerve ending. Yet even as I clamped down on another scream, the fiery sensation turned to ice, and the twisted mass of burned flesh began to disappear.

But I had no time for relief, and no time to wonder at the healing properties of the holy water. I scrambled to my feet, barely avoiding one club-like foot as it thumped down where my head had been only moments before. The force of it shook the ground and almost knocked me back off my feet—and the sheer closeness of all that fire threatened to set me alight again. So I turned and ran. Not for safety, because I doubted there was any place in this forest safe from these creatures.

Instead, I ran for Selwin.

It was obvious I wasn't going to beat the fire demons with the tools I had. The ash stake only created more of them, and while the holy water *did* work, I needed buckets of it, not the remaining bottle I had. So Selwin herself was my only hope. Short of running for the gates and hoping that Azriel could defeat these things, anyway.

And that might *yet* be an option.

But before I could get anywhere near the witch, a third creature appeared, stepping out of the fire to stand between us, its massive body flaring outward and upward, creating a huge barrier of fire that appeared all but impenetrable. It also meant I was trapped among the three of them.

Fuck, fuck, *fuck*.

I had no choice. I had to keep going. Selwin was the key to getting out of here alive, and if I had to go through one of these creatures to achieve that, then that's exactly what I would do. So I grabbed the last bottle of holy water and uncapped it as I ran. The creature raised itself up even farther, towering above

me—a huge sheet of flame that looked ready to top-
ple down around me and burn me to cinders.

Oh God, this was going to hurt . . .

But I just kept running. The heat grew more intense
the closer I got, until my whole body felt ready to
burst into flame. Then I threw the water.

It arced through the air—a thin silver ribbon that
seemed to get lost in the fiery maelstrom that was all
but enveloping me. Then it hit the creature's stomach
and the flames there retreated, the creature screaming
as a hole gaped open in the middle of its body.

A hole that I dove through.

Fire and heat and energy assaulted my skin, and for
the briefest of moments it really did feel as if I were
aflame. Then I was through, hitting the ground on the
other side and rolling to my feet.

Selwin's eyes widened as she saw me. She raised her
hands, and energy began to crawl from them. She was
attempting to raise more creatures.

I called to the Aedh within me, hoping like hell that
Azriel was right, and that as a half-human I would be
able to become Aedh when the magic of this place
barred full-bloods.

I shouldn't have doubted him.

The magic within me erupted, flowing through my
body, snatching away pain and sensation as it began
to change me from flesh to energy. I dove forward and
wrapped my arms around Selwin's waist, dragging us
both to the ground. Her scream of anger became one
of fear as the Aedh change swept from me to her, but
it was abruptly cut off when her body and mine swept
from flesh to energy.

I could feel her in me—feel the seething mass of anger and fear and shock twisting and turning like a malignant canker deep inside. The weight of her forced me low to the ground but I swept as quickly as I was able through the trees. The light of the fire creatures soon faded and the darkness closed in again, but the air remained alive with that odd awareness. So far, the forest had not reacted to anything that had happened. I could only hope it would remain so once I neared the exit, because I had a feeling this place could bring to life a far deeper and darker magic than what Selwin had called forth.

The gates came into view. For an instant blue fire flared across the wrought iron—a shimmer that was reflected in the old wire fence to either side. The energy of it slapped across the air, hitting like a ton of bricks and halting my progress in an instant. I hung suspended, unable to move, as that unseen force swept through me.

Then it was gone, and I could move again. I fled through the gates, saw Azriel, and called to the Aedh. The energy swept through me again, picking apart particles, separating me from Selwin, re-forming our beings into two separate people.

We fell to the ground in a tangle of arms and legs. I rolled away with a groan, my head on fire and my heart pounding so hard it felt ready to tear out of my chest. In fact, *everything* hurt. For several seconds, it was a battle just to breathe.

Then a warm, strong hand clasped mine, and energy began to flow through me, batting away the pain and hurt and forcing strength back into my limbs.

Someone was moaning, and despite that influx of energy, it took me several minutes to realize it wasn't me but Selwin. Which meant I'd put her back together okay, and that was a huge relief. I wasn't exactly experienced at shifting into Aedh form with someone else in my arms. Nor did I really want to be—not when it took such a toll on my body.

I forced my eyes open. Azriel was kneeling beside me, his expression fierce. When his gaze met mine, the fierceness faded, as did the flow of strength from his fingers. But he kept hold of my hand and I was glad. There was something oddly comforting about the way his fingers clasped mine.

"Are you all right?" he asked.

I nodded. The movement, although slight, made my head pound, but it was nowhere near as fierce as it usually was after a shift.

"What about Selwin?" My voice sounded croaky, harsh. I swallowed heavily then added, "Did she re-form okay?"

His gaze flicked briefly past me. "Almost."

Almost? Oh, fuck! "What have I done to her?"

I tried to get up, but his grip on my fingers tightened, pushing me back down and keeping me still.

"There is no major damage. She is merely missing a few minor appendages. It could have been much worse, believe me."

I closed my eyes. Minor appendages? Like what? God, he was right, it could have been much worse, but that didn't make it any better. Didn't make *me* feel any better.

Especially when the groaning became hysterical screaming.

"We need to get her back to the Brindle," I said, my voice almost lost in the wash of noise.

He nodded. "I'll take her. You follow on your motorcycle when you are well enough."

I pulled my hand from his, pushing backward and upright. The sudden movement made my head swim, and my stomach rose abruptly. I swallowed bile and forced a smile. "I'll be right behind you in Aedh form."

"Risa, you are in no condition—"

"I need to see this sorted out," I cut in, a little surprised by the anger in my voice, and not entirely sure if its cause was guilt over my actions or his obvious concern about me. I took a deep breath and released it slowly. "The sooner we do this, the sooner we can get back to the business of finding the damn keys."

His expression lost its warmth. He studied me for a moment, then said, "And the sooner we do that, the sooner you will have me out of your life?"

I eyed him warily. "It's what we both want."

"Yes."

It was said in that same flat tone, and yet there was an odd hostility coming from him that made no sense. But then, nothing about this reaper really made any sense. Not him, not his actions, and not his reactions.

And certainly not mine.

He rose and offered me a hand up. I hesitated briefly, then accepted it, letting him pull me easily to my feet. Pain stabbed into my brain, and I had to close my eyes and breathe deeply for several seconds before the sensation eased.

"Yes," Azriel said, pulling his fingers from mine. "It is obvious that you are totally okay."

"Sarcasm does not become you, reaper."

"And stupidity does become you."

He moved past me. I took another deep breath, then opened my eyes and carefully turned around. Selwin was still on the ground. Her clothes—like mine—were shredded, hanging in fibrous bits from her body, but she obviously didn't know or care. She was staring at her fingerless hands, her wailing getting louder and louder.

I'd done that. I'd maimed her.

And the knowledge that she'd intended to do far worse to me didn't ease the guilt.

Azriel squatted down beside her. Valdis's blade flickered with blue fire, as if in expectation. Azriel raised an arm and lightly touched two fingers to Selwin's forehead. Valdis's fire swirled down his arm and jumped from his fingers to her skin. She stilled instantly, her screams dying on her lips and her expression curiously blank.

"Can you re-form her fingers?" I asked softly as the blue fire spread from Selwin's forehead, down her face, to her body.

He didn't even glance at me, but I could feel the annoyance rolling off him as clearly as I could feel the watchful energy still haunting the air. "I do not know. I will meet you at the Brindle."

And with that, he and Selwin disappeared.

For several moments I simply stood there, staring at the spot where they'd been, irritated not only by the fact he'd disappeared but by his refusal to even look at me. And I honestly had no idea why he was so annoyed. I mean, Azriel wasn't a friend and he wasn't even here by choice, so why would he care if I pushed myself to my limits or not? Unless, of course, he merely wanted me in a fit state to find the damn keys.

I shook my head and walked across to my bike. Even that short distance had exhaustion trembling through my limbs. There was no way on earth I was going to have the strength to become Aedh and journey all the way back to Melbourne. It would kill me. Which left me with little other choice than to do as he suggested. And *that* was even more annoying. I retrieved my phone and said, "Madeline Hunter."

The voice-recognition software swung into action, and the screen put on its psychedelic show as the number was located and dialed.

"Risa," she said, as her cool features appeared on the vid-screen. "It appears your reaper was right. Catherine Alston staked herself this afternoon. Good news from you will be the icing on this day's cake."

Although her voice was light, there was something in her expression that suggested I wouldn't have wanted to be the bearer of bad tidings. "I found Selwin."

"Where?"

"The where doesn't matter. I offered her a deal."

Darkness flared deep in her green eyes. Darkness and anger. "You had no right—"

"If the Melbourne council wants to be free of the Maniae curse," I cut in, "then they will agree to the deal. Selwin is the only one who can stop the creature, and she has to do it willingly."

Hunter's expression remained stony, and yet I still saw death in her eyes. "What did you offer her?"

"This all began because Whitfield was killed and

his fledglings sentenced to death. Selwin underwent the blood ceremony with him, but has not yet turned."

"Ah," Hunter said softly. "Now it all makes sense."

"She only wants to live. If you offer her another master, she might call off the curse."

"I cannot imagine the councilors will want to spend the rest of their lives looking over their shoulders, so I cannot see that they have any other option." She paused, and once again something dark and vicious flared deep in her eyes. Ice curled through my veins. Though I'd never had any doubt that Hunter wasn't someone you'd want to be on the wrong side of, that brief but stark glimpse of her true self was a more-than-ample reminder. Especially when she added—in a low, chillingly cold tone—"Though really, all they'd want to do is drain the bitch of blood and watch her die in brutal ecstasy."

There wasn't a whole lot I could say to *that*, so I simply said, "I'll let the Brindle know that the council will agree to the deal."

A cold smile touched her lips. "And the Brindle is the one place she is safe from us. Does that mean you do not trust the council, little Risa? Or just me?"

No one possessing a brain would trust the council *or* Hunter herself. "The Brindle can contain her magic. I couldn't."

"You really *do* need to master the art of lying, my dear." Her smile grew more ferocious. "But I'm sure the high council will be pleased that you've solved this case so quickly."

And with that, she hung up. I sighed in relief, though I'm not entirely sure why. I may have solved the case—and found Selwin before Hunter—but that didn't mean the high council would now view me as useful rather than a liability.

Trepidation crawled through me, but I ignored it and did a search for the Brindle's number, then called them.

"This is the Brindle depository," a pleasant voice said. "How may we help you?"

"I'd like to speak to Kiandra, please."

"I'm sorry, but that is not—"

"This is Risa Jones," I cut in, "and it's a matter of some urgency."

"I'll put you straight through," she said almost before I'd finished talking. Meaning Kiandra had been expecting this call.

There was a click, a brief, soft hum of music, then Kiandra's cool features came onto the screen. "If you're calling to tell me your reaper is about to deliver a somewhat traumatized Deborah Selwin, you are too late."

She didn't mention the fact that Selwin was missing some extremities, and I hoped like hell that meant Azriel had been able to undo my mistakes. "I thought you might want to know that Selwin raised several fire demons in the ritual site. You'll need to do something about them, because the fire that created them doesn't seem to be burning itself out and the magic in that place is not happy about their presence."

Her eyebrows rose. "You felt that?"

"Yes."

"Interesting."

I frowned. "Why?"

She shrugged. "It implies you are a sensitive, and that is unusual in one who is not a magic user."

I might not be a magic user, but I'd been around one a good part of my life. That would surely make me more sensitive than most. "This all started because Hunter and the council killed her vampire master and condemned all his fledglings to death. Hunter's going to revoke the death sentence if Selwin calls off the Maniae."

"Then we shall attempt to talk sense into her. But it must be her decision, made of free will, for the curse to be successfully revoked."

"I know. But I suspect she might agree."

"Yes," Kiandra said, her expression somewhat amused. "Karma can be a bitch when it hits, and I suspect that no matter how much dear Deborah might want revenge, she will not want to chance more retribution for her actions. I think she's finally realized life is precious, no matter what might await at the end of it."

Meaning, obviously, that Azriel hadn't pieced her back together. I closed my eyes for a moment and tried to ignore the image of fingerless hands that rose like a ghost to taunt me. "Hunter knows you have her at the Brindle."

"Then she knows she is safe here. I'll be in contact to let you know, one way or the other, what Deborah's decision is."

"Thank you."

She nodded, then hung up. I retrieved my wallet from the under-seat storage, then shoved it and the phone into my pocket and climbed onto my bike. My clothes were in tatters, but I hadn't thought to bring a change, so it was going to be a long cold ride home.

But at least it was dark and my near nakedness would be less noticeable.

I started up the Ducati and turned her around. The journey back across the mountainside was hell, every bump jarring my still-aching head and body. When I finally reached the freeway, I would have cheered, except I simply didn't have the energy. It was all I could do to keep upright and pointed in the right direction.

I parked under the hotel, then shifted form and flowed up the elevator shaft until I reached my floor. Even that short trip just about did me in.

Twenty minutes later, after a quick shower to wash away the worst of the fabric threads, I crawled into bed and fell into a long, exhausted sleep.

When I finally woke, it was to the realization that I was no longer alone. The scent of lemongrass, suede, and musky, powerful male filled each breath and I smiled, recognizing not only the scent, but the muscular body that was pressed so warmly against mine.

"That's odd," I murmured, snuggling back against the hard press of his erection. "I don't remember issuing an invite."

"Ah," he murmured, his lips nuzzling the back of my neck, "but I'm the man who intends to ravish you senseless."

And I couldn't imagine a better way to greet a new day—even if that new day was already half over. "And just how did my would-be ravisher get into the room? I don't believe the hotel staff would have let you in."

"Oh, they didn't, but after living on this world for as long as I have, you tend to learn a thing or two about picking locks. Even electronic ones."

His hand slid upward from my waist, and my breath caught in expectation. His palm lightly brushed my nipples and I shuddered, arching a little into his touch, wanting— needing—more. He chuckled softly and kissed my earlobe.

"You seem overly eager this afternoon, my dear."

"You have no idea," I said, and twisted around to face him.

In the shadow-wrapped confines of the hotel room, his beautiful jade-green eyes glowed with a ferocity that was both otherworldly and yet very human. It spoke of ruthlessness, power, and, in the deeper depths, an almost chilling lack of emotion. But it was also a gaze filled with lust, and it was the combination of all four that had desire surging. Female wolves tended to gravitate toward the strongest male, and there was enough wolf in me to be bowled over by not only the sexuality of this man, but the sheer unyielding force of him, too.

Only he wasn't actually a man, but a being of energy just like Azriel. Whom I totally *didn't* want to think of at a time like this.

I ran a hand up the muscular length of Lucian's thighs and hips, feeling the tremor that ran through him and rejoicing in the way his cock leapt, as if eager for my touch. I let my fingers slide teasingly around his belly, almost, but not quite, touching the sensitive tip. He groaned, thrusting against me even as his mouth claimed mine and he kissed me fiercely. As ever, his kiss quickly transcended heat and passion and desire, sweeping me beyond such human emotions and into a world that was all fierce and electric ecstasy.

But as good as that kiss felt, I wanted more. I wanted a connection that was flesh if not emotion, and I was never going to get that with his kiss. I broke away and pressed my hand against his shoulder, forcing him down onto his back. I quickly straddled him, then lowered myself onto his cock, watching his eyes, watching the anticipation burn ever brighter and feeling its echo deep within me. I was so slick and ready for him that he slid in easily—yet still I took it slow, descending inch by torturous inch. He groaned again and reached for my breasts, teasing and pinching my engorged nipples, sending pleasure rippling across my body. I thrust down hard, until the thick length of him was buried deep inside of me. For a moment neither of us moved, and I simply enjoyed the pleasure of being so intimately and intensely connected.

Then he caught one nipple in his mouth and began to suck on it fiercely. I groaned in sheer delight and began to move, rocking back and forth, my movements becoming faster as pleasure intensified, until I couldn't think, couldn't breathe, and it felt like everything was about to break.

Then everything *did* break, and I was shuddering, shaking, and moaning. He came a heartbeat later, groaning fiercely as his body stiffened against mine and his juices flooded deep inside.

I collapsed against him and rested my forehead against his. For several minutes, neither of us moved. Then he kissed my nose and gripped either shoulder, pushing me back a little.

"As foreplay goes," he said, his grin wicked, "that wasn't half bad."

I laughed softly and sat fully upright. He was still deep inside me and already half erect again. Werewolves had *nothing* on this man when it came to stamina. "You haven't exactly explained just what you're doing here at this hour of the morning."

He began to move his hips again. "I thought it was rather obvious."

"Besides that, I mean."

"Ah, well." His expression became slightly distracted as he ran a finger up the inside of my thigh. "You may not be too pleased about the answer to that particular question."

His finger met the junction of our bodies. I shifted slightly and his touch slipped between us, finding my clit then brushing it teasingly. A moan escaped me and I closed my eyes, enjoying the sensation even as I tried to concentrate on the conversation.

"Meaning?"

"Meaning," he murmured, rubbing his finger back and forth through my slickness, "that I sensed through our connection that you were about to attempt to find the keys, and I wished to be a part of it."

Alarm stirred. I stilled my movements and opened my eyes. His expression was still distracted, and he didn't seem to notice my sudden lack of participation. "Why?"

"Because the priests will not ignore such an attempt, and I wish to offer my help. I am, after all, Aedh, even if a maimed one, and I know more than a little about fighting them."

"But if we do as you suggested and create a void, they will not even know we've accessed the book, let alone retrieved the key."

His gaze rose to mine, studying me for several heartbeats. Then he gripped my arms and expertly reversed our positions, pinning me underneath him with the full length of his body.

"The Raziq will feel it the minute you touch the keys, because they are part of the process that created them—even if it was the blood of your father that provided the building blocks." Despite his words, there was little in the way of concern in his expression, only a fierce determination. He wanted this fight badly, but it wasn't for the reasons he was stating. "They will go to any length to retrieve those keys, and one lone reaper will not be enough to keep you safe."

"Azriel can call on others—"

Lucian snorted softly, and it was a disparaging sound. "If that were possible, don't you think he would have done it earlier? How many times have the Raziq attacked you now?"

"There was no need before now—" I started, but again he cut in.

"Was it a question of need, or is the real truth the fact that there were no resources?" He shifted his weight onto one elbow and lightly ran one finger down my cheek before circling my lips. Though the caress was light, it felt heavy, as if the weight of the conversation were bearing down on it. "The Mijai are few, and they are kept busy hunting the demons who slipped into this world during the brief time that the three keys were tested."

And how did he know all this? Just how deep a connection had he formed? I wriggled, trying to get out from underneath him, but he pressed me back down. "Damn it, Lucian, let me go!"

"Not until I get an answer. I want this, Risa. I *need* this."

My heart hammered at the edge in his voice, and again I saw that fierceness. And suddenly, I realized why. "This is about revenge for what they did to you, isn't it?"

His smile was a savage and wholly human thing. And it was yet more proof that Lucian was very different from other full-blooded Aedh.

"Totally. And if feeding my need helps your cause, why is that a bad thing?"

"So basically, your presence here isn't about sex, but about gaining access to information on the Aedh that you might not otherwise get." Even as I said the words, bitterness swirled through me. It seemed everyone new in my life wanted something from me. Lucian, Azriel, the Raziq, even my father. They were here for a purpose rather than any real caring.

Lucian studied me. "In truth, are we not using each other? I have a need for revenge, and you have a need for information about the Aedh. While we each pursue our goals, we take our ease in each other's bodies. I cannot see how that is not a worthwhile exchange."

Put that way, I guessed it was. Except that I thought he was a safe harbor, the one place I could go and *not* be on guard.

"You're using the connection created through sex to steal information. That's not right, Lucian."

"I did not know who you were or what you were involved in when I intervened in the fight between you and the Razan," he retorted. "It was only after we'd become intimate that I realized the truth and seized the opportunity to combine my desires. And do not doubt that I desire you, regardless of what else I might seek from you."

I couldn't doubt his desire when the fierceness of it was pressed between us. It was a fierceness I fought to ignore, even though half of me wanted nothing more than to lose myself in the ecstasy of sex rather than a lingering sense of loss.

Although really, what had I actually lost? The truth was, we didn't have anything in common other than an almost insatiable need for each other and great sexual chemistry. It was never going to be more than that, and I'd known that going in. He was Aedh, and they didn't do emotions as we knew them. So why the hell was I angry?

I didn't know. And there seemed to be a whole lot of *that* in my life of late, too. Between Lucian, Azriel, and my goddamn absent father, it was a wonder I wasn't more of a mess than I was.

"How can I be really sure that you're telling the truth?" I said, an edge in my voice.

"You can't. But how can you be sure any of us is telling you the truth? Everyone has their own agenda, Risa, even the reaper who supposedly guards you."

He pressed his knee between my legs and moved them apart, then thrust himself deep inside. Despite my apprehension and anger, it felt so good that I wanted to moan. But I didn't—though only because I was fiercely holding on to the need to question him. If I gave into pleasure, I'd be giving in to a whole lot more. Even if I wasn't entirely sure what that *more* was.

"But not everyone has direct access to my mind," I said, my words a little breathless as he began to move, only—damn him—this was no slow seduction of the senses, but rather a ravishment filled with forceful and furious intent. And it felt so good that I had to battle to ignore the sensations threatening to engulf me.

"The reaper has, and his link is far deeper than anything I have achieved. If you want to fear anything, fear that."

Before I could reply, before I could even digest the import of his words, he claimed my lips with a kiss that was as harsh as his lovemaking. From that moment on there was no more talking, only an intense and brutal sort of pleasure that swept me swiftly into rapture and then far beyond it.

For sometime afterward, I could only lie there, replete, exhausted, and still furious. But eventually, I pulled free from him, climbed out of bed, and strode to the shower.

"You're angry," he said, sounding oddly surprised. Like he hadn't just seduced the hell out of me in an effort to get what he desired—information, if not consent.

I flicked on the shower and waited for the water to heat up. After a second or two, he seemed to realize I had no intention of answering him, and sheets rustled as he climbed out of the bed.

"Don't touch me," I said, long before he could. Not because of the anger, but because I knew that, once he did, I'd be putty in his hands again. I couldn't resist him; or maybe I simply didn't *want* to resist him. Either way, I simply wasn't in the mood. I wanted to hang on to my anger just that little bit longer, even if it was stupid and unreasonable.

He stopped in the doorway and crossed his arms, leaning a powerful shoulder against the door frame. "I don't understand why you feel this way."

He didn't understand, and Azriel didn't understand. Two sides of the same coin, and both of them incapable of giving me what I truly wanted.

And you knew this from the beginning, so what the hell is your problem? And what the hell do you want from the reaper?

Honesty, I thought. *That's what I want. That's what I've always wanted.*

I stepped under the water and raised my face to the needle-sharp spray, enjoying its sting against my skin. But I was also aware of the weight of Lucian's gaze on me.

After a while, I reached for the small bottle of shampoo and finally met his gaze. "I'm sick of people not telling me truth, Lucian. Everyone is playing their own game, and everyone is using me to do it, and yet no one is bothering to fill me in on all the details. And it's pissing me off."

"I only have one endgame, that I can promise you."

I raised an eyebrow. "Revenge?"

"Yes." His expression hadn't changed, but suddenly there was something very dark about him— something deep and dangerous and alien. This was the man I knew, and yet it wasn't, because this version was consumed by a hatred so deep it was breathtaking. *He will do anything, absolutely anything, to get his revenge.* And that knowledge chilled me even more than the alien darkness. "And I cannot see why you would not put that need to good use. If they attack en masse, you *will* need my help. And if they don't, then you have lost nothing."

It made sense, yet still I hesitated to agree and I wasn't sure why. My gaze searched his, looking for lies and finding nothing but honesty. But that didn't mean a whole lot given he'd been bound to earth for many centuries. I was betting he could lie so well that even someone with the most sensitive of bullshit detectors wouldn't know it.

But what if he wasn't lying? What if he was actually telling the truth? We probably would need help retrieving the keys, and the only other person I could really call on who would be of any use against the Raziq was Uncle Quinn. And I wouldn't do that to Riley—even if she'd be madder than hell if she ever found out that I *hadn't* asked him.

I sighed, more than a little frustrated by the twisting of my thoughts, and said, "Even you and Azriel might not be enough if they attack en masse."

"The reaper has his sword. I have weapons of my own. Trust me when I say we will hold them off long enough to get you and the keys to a safe place."

I finished washing my hair, then met his gaze again and said, "And how are you going to do that when all you want to do is kill the bastards?"

He grinned, and it was a ugly thing to behold. "Because merely killing them outright is not good enough. I want them to suffer as I have suffered. Finding these keys and having all their plans turn to dust is but one means of ensuring that."

I believed him. It was impossible not to. "Okay," I said slowly. "When we go look for the keys, you're in. But not before."

He frowned. "Will you not need help when you go read the book?"

"No."

He studied me for a moment, then shrugged. "I don't think that's wise, but this is your game, not mine."

His words had a trepidation stirring, and I couldn't help wondering if I'd made my situation better, or much, much worse.

Chapter Eleven

THE CAFÉ WAS PACKED WHEN I ARRIVED, AND several staff members had called in sick, so both Ilianna and Tao were in as replacements and working the floor. Which, in Tao's case, was a rare event that pleased his many fans—some of whom were young, many of whom weren't, but all of whom were female. Given most of them were wolves who were not afraid of grabbing what they wanted, Tao ended the shift with a sore butt and more phone numbers than even *he* could handle in a year. But he wasn't the only one who'd scored—although in my case, it was offers of drinks rather than actual dates. Obviously, I'd looked as if I'd needed to drown my sorrows, even though I'd tried to be my usual cheerful self.

As the evening shift swept in and took control of the madness, the three of us retreated upstairs, beers in hand. I didn't drink often—except when Ronan was around—but sometimes, when things got really insane, there was nothing more refreshing than a crisp, cool beer.

And *insane* was certainly an apt description of my life at the moment.

"So," Tao said, as he rolled the chilled bottle across

his forehead. "Ilianna tells me you've found a way to read the book without alerting the Raziq. When you attempt it, I want to be there to help."

I opened my mouth to say no, then shut it again and took a drink instead. I'd known Tao long enough to realize he wouldn't be dissuaded. And the truth was, with both Azriel and Lucian barred from entering the sacred site, we might just need him. Ilianna wasn't a member of *any* coven, let alone the one that owned that ancient site, so there was no telling how the forest was going to react once she raised her magic in its midst.

And while she might be a powerful witch in her own right, she couldn't help me and protect herself at the same time.

"You'll need to wear every magical charm Ilianna can lay her hands on if you do," I said, meeting his gaze evenly. "The place we're going is almost sentient. There's no telling what will happen once Ilianna creates the void."

He nodded, looking pleased and somewhat bemused. "I was actually prepared for a rather long and drawn-out argument. I think I'm almost disappointed."

I chuckled softly. "I'm not stupid, no matter what some people think. And I rather like the thought of having someone at my back whom I can completely trust."

Tao opened his mouth, but before he could say anything, Azriel said from behind me, "I gather by the rather ill-disguised sarcasm in your voice that *that* particular sentence is aimed at me?"

"At you, at Lucian, and at everyone else looking for these keys," I retorted, not bothering to swing around and look at him. I didn't need to—not when I could taste his rising anger in the air around me. "I just want you all out of my life. I'm sick of the lies and the endless threat of danger. I want everything to go back to normal."

"Then we had best get moving and find these keys," Azriel said, his voice still cool and collected, even if the air still boiled with his emotions.

"Which all sounds well and good," Ilianna said as her gaze swept between me and Azriel, "but this spell must be done at the break of dawn. And that's quite a few hours away."

"By the time we gather everything you need and drive to the site, it won't be." I hesitated, then added, "You'll need your four-wheel drive rather than Tao's Ferrari. This spot is a bitch to get to."

She nodded, then swigged the last of her beer and rose. "I left everything at Mirri's, but it won't take me long to get there and back."

My gaze flicked to Tao, and he said instantly, "Feel like some company? I might be tempted to help out in the kitchen if I hang about here too long, and that would annoy Jacques."

Jacques was the sous-chef we'd recently employed, and while he was a damn fine chef, to say he was somewhat temperamental would be an understatement. He respected Tao as the boss and co-owner, but when it came to his shift, he was in charge and interference was not appreciated.

Ilianna smiled and patted his cheek. "You lie so prettily. No wonder the girls all love you."

"The Raziq have already had one go at snatching you," he said evenly. "I might not have a magic sword, but I can arrange a good old-fashioned barbecue if any of them turns up."

"Given how they've turned our lives upside down, I might enjoy seeing that." She gathered her jacket from a nearby chair, then looked at me. "Play nicely until we get back, children."

I snorted softly. I had no intention of playing with *anyone* right now, let alone a reaper who seemed to be gathering too many human traits.

As Tao and Ilianna trooped down the stairs, I rose and walked across to the fridge, getting myself another bottle of beer before walking across to the windows. Outside, Lygon Street was alive with laughter, life, and music. I closed my eyes for a moment, losing myself in the sound and briefly imagining that everything was normal, that this was all some crazy dream.

But it wasn't, and no amount of wishing was going to make it so. Part of me wondered if things would *ever* be normal again, even after this whole mess was resolved.

I opened the beer, took a drink, then said, "Lucian tells me that the Raziq will know our location the minute I touch the keys."

"That is more than possible," Azriel agreed.

"So why did he have to tell me that? Why couldn't you?"

"Would it have made the situation any easier?"

No, but that wasn't the point. "He also suggested that you're unlikely to get help from other Mijai. He said you guys are rather thin on the ground at the moment."

"That is also true."

I turned around and faced him. He was still standing on the far side of the room, his stance casual and his hands clasped behind his back. But there was nothing casual about the feel of the air that boiled around him, or the fierce light that burned in his different-colored blue eyes.

"So just how did you intend to protect me when I retrieved the keys?"

"With all that I have. With my life, if need be."

"And a fat lot of good that'll do," I retorted, "if you die and I'm stuck trying to undo this mess by myself."

He raised an eyebrow and said, rather cuttingly, "There is still the Aedh."

"He's not you. He could never be you." The words were out before I could even think about them, and sort of hung in the air between us.

And it hit me then that, as frustrating as this reaper could be—and as much as I wanted the whole situation to be finished and my life back to normal—I'd actually miss him when it happened.

I *liked* Azriel. More than I should. Certainly more than was sensible.

I swung away from him and took a long drink of beer. I was insane. This whole mess had driven me insane.

Azriel was undoubtedly following my thoughts, but for once he didn't comment. Maybe he thought silence was the better part of valor.

"Lucian's offered to help us when we go find the keys," I said eventually. "I've accepted."

"I do not think that is wise—"

"We don't have much choice," I cut in. "I don't want you to die, and there are few others we can call on for help. Lucian is an Aedh, even if he has been damaged. He knows how to fight them, and he's eager for revenge as well."

"Do you trust him? Do you honestly think he is telling the truth about what he's truly after?"

"He *is* after revenge. I'm certain of that, if nothing else."

"That doesn't entirely answer the question."

No. But it was the only answer I could honestly give.

"Then I guess I have no choice but to trust your judgment." He hesitated, then added softly, "And another warrior would make things easier."

I smiled, recognizing an olive branch when I saw it. How long that offer of peace lasted was another matter entirely. "I'm able to fight, but I don't think any of my weapons will actually work against the Aedh, especially if they don't take human form in the attack."

"Which is why I bought you Amaya."

"And what the hell is an Amaya?" I said.

"This," he said, drawing a sword from the sheath at his back, "is Amaya."

The sword was shorter than Valdis, and much finer. Its steel was an inky black, and in the shadowed confines of the room it seemed little more than a threatening shadow. Yet with every movement, energy dripped from her like lilac rain—a rain that matched the color of my eyes and the Dušan on my arm. I doubted it was a coincidence.

"It isn't," he agreed. "I am attuned deeply enough to you now that I was able to uncover a weapon that would accept you as her master."

"Accept me?" I said, studying the sword a little warily. Did I really want a weapon that had a life and a mind of its own?

"Amaya, like Valdis, was forged during the death of a demon." He stopped several feet away from me. The sword's energy rolled across my skin—a dark and dangerous caress that had goose bumps rising. My gaze met his. His expression was neutral and— for some reason—that scared me. "It breathes life into the steel, and gives it the power to destroy the dark ones. They do not submit to a master easily, but once accepted they will serve you well."

"What's the catch?" Because there had to be one. The seriousness of his expression told me that, if nothing else.

"You must offer them blood."

"Naturally," I muttered sarcastically, but with more than a trace of fear. "It couldn't be something easy, could it?"

No smile touched his lips, and his bright eyes remained as ungiving as his expression. Fear sharpened, sweeping through me, making me tremble like a leaf in a storm. "Just how much blood are we talking about?"

"You must bury the sword in your flesh. She must become a part of you to serve you fully."

Oh, *fuck*. I gulped down my beer, but it did little to

ease the dryness in my throat. I thumped it down on a nearby table and crossed my arms. "You know, I really don't think I'm that desperate for a weapon."

"If the Raziq attack, and if the Aedh and I fall, then all you will have is your wits and your strength. Against the Raziq, that will not be enough."

As had already been proven when they'd kidnapped and tortured me. I swallowed heavily, my gaze sinking to the sword held so lightly in his hand. It still dripped lilac rain, and I had an odd sense it was waiting.

I licked my lips. "I have the Dušan. If I fled to the gray fields—"

"If the Raziq attack en masse, even the Dušan will not be enough."

If the Raziq attacked en masse and both he and Lucian were killed, I seriously doubted if even a demon sword would make a difference.

"Do not doubt her capabilities," he said softly. "Swords forged in demon fire are stronger—and more dangerous—than you could ever imagine."

And it would only work if I plunged it into my flesh. I rubbed my arms and said, "How can you know for certain that Amaya will accept me?"

"As I said, I am attuned to you enough to sense her willingness. All you have to do is make the sacrifice."

"But won't burying a sword in my flesh kill me?"

"She will heal you as a gift for your sacrifice. From that point, she will be yours until your life's end."

Oh great, I was going to have a fire-dripping sword constantly strapped to my back. And wouldn't *that* please the customers?

A small smile broke the seriousness of his expression, and it felt like sunshine breaking through a storm—warm and welcome. "Amaya belongs to the shadows. You can see her, and I can see her because of our connection, but no one else will. Nor will anyone feel her—not unless you bury her in their flesh. And you do not have to wear her all the time. She can be put aside when you sleep." He hesitated, then added, "Or when you have sex."

"I'm sure my partners will appreciate that," I muttered. I ran a somewhat shaky hand through my hair. I could do this. I *had* to do this. "Okay, so what do I need to do?"

He raised the sword, offering it to me hilt first. "Take her."

I wrapped my hands around the night-dark hilt. Fire flared along the blade's edge, thick and dangerous. The hilt itself felt warm against my palm, and something within it pulsed, as if it had a life and a heart of its own.

And given it was forged during a demon's death, maybe it *did*.

I licked my lips, then raised my gaze to Azriel's. "Now what?"

"Place the tip against your stomach."

I closed my eyes against the rush of fear and did as he asked. The metal hummed—a sound that vibrated through every nerve ending.

"Now we perform the bonding ritual. Repeat after me; *we are one mind, me and thee*."

I repeated the words softly. Energy stirred, caressing my skin and making the small hairs at the back of my neck rise.

"We are one spirit, me and thee."

The power in the air increased as I repeated the words, crackling like lightning through the darkness, until it felt as if I were standing in the eye of a storm.

"We are one body, me and thee, spirit within flesh, bound together until life is over and the soul has moved on."

I repeated the sentence. The words seemed to hang in the air, electric and alive. The sword burned against my palms, throbbing with life and hunger.

"Now," Azriel said softly, "make the sacrifice."

I hesitated. I couldn't help it. Lucian's warning returned to haunt me and, for the briefest of moments, I wondered what the hell I was doing—and why I trusted Azriel so damn much.

Then I thought of the Raziq, and the danger they represented—not just to me, but to the people I loved. People like Ilianna and Tao, who were putting their lives on the line to help me. If bonding with the sword could help mitigate that danger, then I had no other choice.

I tightened my grip on the sword hilt and drove it into my flesh.

For several heartbeats, nothing happened. The blade carved through skin and muscle as easily as if they were air, until the sword broke out the other side and I was standing there skewered by a blade that was little more than shadows itself.

Then the power surged all around me, becoming a tornado that tore at my skin, my hair, my body, until it felt as if it were stripping me of all that I was, making me as shadowy as the sword.

Then it exploded, the pain hit, and all I could do was scream. Scream and scream and scream as the sword became a part of me.

And then there was nothing. No shadows, no power tearing me apart, just a deep pit of unconsciousness that I fell into gratefully.

Of course, my life being what it was of late, I didn't get to remain in that peaceful void for long.

As consciousness returned, it became apparent that I was no longer standing. I lay on my back, stretched out on the carpet, my head resting against thighs that were as hard as steel and as hot as a furnace. Gentle fingers brushed sweaty strands of hair from my face.

"Don't try to speak," Azriel said softly. "Your throat will be raw."

From the screaming, no doubt. God, what would the customers think? And why wasn't a squadron of cops beating down our door right now?

"The magic that binds also contains. The only person who heard your screams was me."

There was an odd edge to his voice, and I opened my eyes and looked up at him. There was concern and regret in his expression, and maybe even a hint of censure. But at himself rather than me, I suspected.

"You are correct," he confirmed. "I did not think the binding would affect you that way. It doesn't us."

I licked dry lips and somehow croaked, "I'm not Mijai. I'm a half-breed nonhuman."

A slight smile touched his lips—an echo of warmth that curled through my being, chasing away the chill. "But a very brave one."

I snorted softly. "Okay, who are you? The Azriel I know wouldn't be saying shit like that."

He paused. "Why is it that many humans—or in your case nonhumans—are reluctant to accept a compliment when it is given?"

"I don't know about anyone else, but for me, I don't deserve the compliment. I was scared shitless."

"My point exactly."

I grimaced and pushed upright, needing to get away not only from the heat of him, but from the gentle caress of his fingers. I glanced down at my body. There was no blood on my shirt, no dark stain on the carpet. I was whole. It was as if the shadowed sword had never been a part of me.

And yet she was.

I could feel her. She was a distant hiss of static that was almost a heartbeat and lingered at the edges of thought, coiled and ready to be unleashed at the slightest notice.

I shivered and rubbed my arms. There was darkness and danger in that static—for me, and for those who opposed me.

"Amaya has accepted you," Azriel said. I glanced around as he pushed to his feet, the movement economical yet somehow graceful. "You will feel her presence everywhere you go, in everything you do. Learn her song. She is more than just a blade."

He offered me his hand. I clasped it and he pulled me up lightly. "I'm not Mijai. I can barely understand you, let alone a bloody sword."

"You understand me more than you might wish to let on," he countered. "And Amaya's voice will become clearer as you grow used to each other."

Maybe. Maybe not. While the sword might have accepted me, it didn't necessarily follow that we would ever understand each other. After all, according to him, I shouldn't have felt the pain that I did during the binding. So heaven only knew what else would differ.

"So where is she now?" I said, looking at the floor but not seeing the shadow-wrapped weapon.

"She's where she always will be, unless you purposefully remove her. In her sheath at your back."

If I was wearing a sword, then I couldn't feel it. I reached back and felt the coldness of steel. *Damn.* I wrapped my fingers around the hilt and slowly drew the sword free. While she was little more than shadows, she was far from light, though her weight rested comfortably in my hand. At my touch, her whispering grew stronger, filled with an eagerness to rend and tear. Another shiver ran through me. I swung her back and forth, watching the lilac fire that caressed her sharp edges spray across the floor, and wondered if—like Valdis—she'd scream when she sliced into flesh. Somehow, I suspected not.

Then I placed her back into her sheath, only briefly feeling the weight of her across my back.

"Are you sure no one can see or feel her? I really don't need to get arrested for carrying a weapon right now."

Footsteps clattered up the stairs. Tao and Ilianna returning.

"No one will see her except those whose life you are about to extinguish," Azriel said.

"Whoa," Ilianna said, her gaze widening as she came into the room. "Where the hell did that sword come from?"

I raised an eyebrow at Azriel. A smiled touched his lips and lightly crinkled the corners of his eyes, and my pulse did its usual stupid dance. "Well, no one except someone like Ilianna."

Tao came up behind her, his gaze swinging from me to Azriel before frowning down at Ilianna. "What sword?"

I smiled and waved a hand. "Long story. You two ready to go?"

Ilianna hefted the large canvas bag she was carrying. "All manner of magical whatnot present and accounted for."

I grabbed my purse and swung it over my shoulder. It settled into place easily, as if there weren't a shadowy sword strapped to my back. I shivered again, then said, "Then let's get this show on the road."

Before the inner voice whispering dark warnings of trouble ahead became too loud to ignore.

We arrived at Mount Macedon an hour before dawn. In the glow of the four-wheel drive's lights, the old metal gates seemed even older and stronger than they had the other morning—a barrier that seemed to forbid passage.

Ilianna leaned her forearms on the steering wheel, her gaze sweeping the gate and the fence to either side of it. "The magic in this place feels ancient."

"According to Kiandra, it is." I opened the SUV's door and climbed out. "It seemed almost sentient to me."

"I don't think I'd go as far as that," Ilianna said, frowning as she walked to the front of the vehicle, "but there's certainly a great power residing here, and there *is* a level of awareness within it."

"There's also some sort of fire burning," Tao commented, his hands on his hips as he stopped beside us. "I can feel its heat."

I swore softly. "The fire elementals must be still present."

He raised an eyebrow. "Fire elementals? As in, World of Warcraft, Lord of the Rings fire elementals?"

I blinked. "What?"

"You know, that creature Gandalf battled when he was in the pits of Moria?"

"Wasn't that a Balrog? They're demons, not elementals."

"But it was associated with fire—"

"Enough," Azriel cut in, as he appeared in front of us. His expression was impatient. "The elementals remain near the fire that gave them life. If Ilianna creates the void just inside the gates, we should be able to retrieve and read the book before they become a problem."

"*Should* being the operative word." I'd learned the hard way not to rely on shoulds.

His gaze met mine. "We have little other choice."

That was certainly true enough. I sighed. "Go get the book. I'll meet you on the gray fields."

He nodded and winked out of existence. I glanced at Ilianna. "Time to go see if the ancient power will accept your magic."

I strode forward, Ilianna and Tao a step behind me. The gates were still locked, but as we approached, the lock fell away and the gates slid silently open.

"I think that's your answer," Ilianna said softly. She walked past me, her expression awed. "I can feel it. Around me. In me."

I shivered and rubbed my arms. I knew all about feeling magic inside of you—Amaya was a dark heat that stirred restlessly on the outer edges of my consciousness. Something about this place seemed to be making her uneasy—or was I transferring my own unease and trepidation onto her?

"The fire elementals are on the move," Tao murmured as we followed Ilianna off the path and into the trees. "They must have sensed our presence."

Or the magic of this place was hedging its bets—welcoming us, but at the same time opposing. I met Tao's gaze grimly. "Will you be able to cope with them?"

He shrugged. "Do we have any other choice?"

"No, but—"

"Ris," he said, gently squeezing my arm, "I'll keep Ilianna safe. I'll keep *me* safe. Just do what you have to as fast as you can."

I nodded. There was nothing else I could do. Nothing else I could say. I knew what the elementals were capable of, but Tao was a fire-starter. If anyone had a hope of containing those things, it was him.

We hit a clearing. Ilianna stopped in the middle of it and said, "We can do it here."

"What do you need us to do?"

She glanced at me, her gaze still glowing with an almost otherworldly luminescence. "You need to stand here. I will create the protection circle and containment void, then invite you in."

I frowned. "But you can't be in the circle. It's too dangerous, Ilianna." We didn't know if there were other spells woven into the fabric of the book, and had no idea what would happen once I opened it. The containment spell was aimed at protecting them as much as the void was meant to stop the Aedh from sensing what I was up to.

"I won't be," she said. "Once the circle and void are in place, I'll create a doorway. As long as we use only that doorway to enter and exit, then the circle will remain active."

"If there's a door, then other things might be able to get in." Or out.

"They won't. It's a modified spell that will be attuned to our resonance alone. Nothing else will be able to get in or out." The odd glow in her eyes died suddenly and she smiled. "It'll be fine. Stop worrying."

How? They were risking their lives for me, in a place filled with magic, not to mention walking bonfires. I took a deep breath that did nothing to alleviate the fear twisting my guts, then glanced at Tao, who gave me a brief thumbs-up as I walked across to Ilianna. But his gaze had already moved on, scanning the trees, his expression touched with concern. I bit my lip and wondered just how close the elementals actually were.

"When everything is ready," Ilianna said, making me jump a little. "I'll say, *How do you enter the circle, Risa Jones*? Your response should be, *In complete trust of the powers that reside and protect within.*"

When I nodded, she returned to her bag of tricks and withdrew her athame, four candles, and a box of matches. She placed these on the ground, then marked a large circle in the dirt around them. Next she picked up the candles and placed them at four points—the green one to the north, yellow to the east, red in the south, and blue in the west. I knew from past experiences that these points represented the four elements—earth, air, fire, and water.

With that done, she raised her arms and made a sweeping motion. "Let this space be cleared of all negativity and inappropriate energies, and may any lost souls inhabiting it be returned where they need to be."

Air stirred and became imbued with warmth. I clenched my fingers but otherwise remained still.

Ilianna bent to light the first candle. "Guardians of the east, I call upon you to watch over this circle and guard the two allowed to enter. Powers of knowledge and wisdom, guided by air, keep watch over us and let no others enter by body or deed."

Then she moved to the red candle and lit it. "Guardians of the south, I call upon you to watch over this circle and guard the two allowed to enter. Powers of energy and will, guided by fire, keep watch over us and let no force or ill intent enter."

She moved on. The blue candle was next, then finally, the green. "Guardians of the north, I call upon you to watch over this circle and guard the actions of the two allowed to enter. Powers of endurance and strength, guided by earth, we ask that you protect us against deeds of strength and might."

When the last of the ritual words had been spoken, she picked up her athame and said, "The circle has been cast. How do you enter the circle, Risa Jones?"

I took a deep breath and blew it out slowly. "In complete trust in the powers that reside and protect within."

She slashed her athame across a small section of the circle, first to the right, then to the left. "Enter."

I did. She caught my fingers in hers as I stopped beside her and squeezed lightly. "Good luck."

"Thanks."

Then she stepped out of the circle and made that slashing motion with her athame again, effectively closing the circle.

I blew out a breath, then sat down, legs crossed. I closed my eyes and took a deep breath. As I slowly released it, I released awareness of everything and everyone else around me, concentrating on nothing more than the slowing beat of my heart. The world around me began to fade as the gray fields gathered close. Warmth throbbed at my neck—Ilianna's magic at work, protecting me as my psyche, my soul, or whatever else people liked to call it, pulled away from the constraints of my flesh and stepped gently into the gray fields that were neither life nor death.

But on the gray fields, the invisible became visible. The real world might fade to be little more than shadows, but those things not sighted on the living plane gained substance when viewed from here.

The Dušan was one of those things. She exploded from my arm, her energy flowing through me, around me, as her lilac form gained flesh and shape, until she looked so solid and real that I wanted to reach out and touch her. She swirled around me, the wind of her body buffeting mine as her sharp ebony gaze scanned the fields around us, looking for trouble. I wondered if she was actually sensing it, or if she merely reacted to the knot of fear growing in the pit of my stomach.

I saw Azriel before I felt him—he was a blaze of sunlight in this ghostly otherworld, a force whose very presence seemed to throb through my body. As if he, like the Dušan and Amaya, were a part of me. And I guess in many respects he was, given he was attuned to my Chi.

He stopped in front of me, his energy so fierce and bright that I winced. He gave me the book and, like everything else in this place, it appeared ghostly. Yet it felt heavier here than it had on earth.

The second I touched it an odd twist of power seemed to shudder across the fields, then sparks exploded from the book. But these were no ordinary sparks flying high then dying. These sparks converged into several separate masses, each one dancing around the other, growing bigger with each movement, gaining flesh in much the same manner as the Dušan had.

Only *these* things weren't dragons—winged or otherwise—but rather snakes. Fat, ugly snakes with bodies as thick as my torso and fangs longer than my arm.

The Raziq had spelled the book all right—just not in the way we'd expected.

"Go," Azriel commanded, drawing his sword. Valdis burned with blue fire, her scream echoing across the silence of the fields. It was a scream that found an echo as his Dušan exploded from his back—a winged black dragon who spat blue fire. "Read the book and find the keys' location."

"But I can't leave you—"

"Go!" he shouted, then raised his sword as the first of the serpents coiled in.

I swore softly but clasped the book tightly to my chest and closed my eyes. Valdis's scream echoed through my body as my soul stepped briefly back into my flesh. I placed the book on the ground and opened it. I was vaguely aware of heat and noise and shouting, and wasn't sure if it was coming from this place or the gray fields. Then I thrust it all aside as the pages began to flip on their own accord. The movement stopped several pages past the one that had held my Dušan, but there was no writing on it. No pictures.

Because the words can only be read while I'm on the grey fields. Fuck.

I closed my eyes and pulled free of my body once more. The moment I stepped onto the gray fields, my Dušan appeared again, but this time she screamed, her fire burning all around me as something fat and sleek lunged in my direction. The fire hit it head-on, exploding in a rush of air that rocked me sideways but seemed to do little more than push the serpent aside.

I shivered, knowing I was in trouble, my fingers itching to reach for Amaya. Her song was a hiss of anger that burned through me. She wanted out. She wanted to taste serpentine flesh and blood.

I licked my lips, ignoring her, ignoring the shadowy, sinewy shapes that twisted and turned just beyond reach. I had a book to read. The sooner I did that, the better.

I stepped forward, closer to the edge of the fields, until there was only the thinnest of veils between this world and my own. Viewed from here, the book—

like everything else—was a shadow without substance or weight, but the words unseen on Earth glowed like fire when viewed from the gray fields.

The keys wear the veils of an ax, a dagger, and a shield, respectively. The first was sent to the west of Melbourne, to where the wild—

Something hit me hard, knocking me sideways, away from the book. I staggered, trying to regain my balance, vaguely aware of screaming—high, harsh screaming. I twisted around and saw the Dušan and a serpent coiling around each other, each creature's teeth tearing into the flesh of the other. Then another serpent appeared, coiling past my Dušan to lunge at me. I threw myself sideways and drew Amaya. She didn't scream, but she spluttered and hissed, the sound so ferocious it reverberated through the shadows of the gray fields.

White fangs slashed at me. I swung Amaya, her purple fire dripping like venom. The blade hit the serpent's oversized teeth, slicing through them as easily as a hot knife through butter. Liquid gushed, thick and yellow, stinking to high heaven and stinging like acid. I swore and jumped back as it lunged at me again, this time attempting to use its head as a battering ram. I ducked under the blow, twisted around, and brought Amaya down as hard as I could just behind the serpent's neck. It felt like I was hitting stone. The force of the blow reverberated up my arm and made my teeth ache. For a moment, nothing happened. Then the blade hissed and burned, her fire crawling across the serpent's back like a living thing. And as the creature coiled its body around to face me again, Amaya began to burrow down, into flesh and then bone. The serpent screamed—a high pitched, almost human scream—and began to flop and twist its body, trying to shake Amaya off. It pulled me off my feet, throwing me around like a rag doll, but Amaya kept her grip. She kept slicing into flesh—a demon sword with blood on her mind and murder in her heart.

Then she was through, and the serpent's head dropped clear of its body. As Amaya's hissing became victorious, I hit the ground and rolled clear of the dying serpent, coming to my feet, demon sword at the ready once more.

But the gray fields were suddenly still. Quiet.

My Dušan pulled free of the coiled form and swirled around me once more, her purple scales battered and bloody looking. I wondered suddenly if they could die, and hoped not. I had a feeling I was going to need her more often as the years wore on.

I took a deep breath that did nothing to ease the tension still coiling through me and looked around for Azriel. He was standing where I'd left him, in a sea of broken, twisting bodies.

He looked up and said, "Did you read the book?"

"No." I sheathed Amaya and stepped across the snake's still-twitching body. "A serpent hit me before I could get full directions."

"Then get them now."

A horn rang across the silence—a long, haunting note that oddly filled me with fear. I bit my lip, my gaze searching through the shadows of the gray fields, seeing little. No ghosts, no reapers other than Azriel, nothing that seemed out of place. And yet, something *was*.

"Hurry," Azriel said. "The Aedh hunt the gray fields. They are coming this way."

I swore and stepped closer to the edge of the fields. The book came into view, but whatever magic had allowed me to view the words had dissipated.

The page was completely empty.

Chapter Twelve

I SWORE AGAIN. VEHEMENTLY.

Azriel was beside me in an instant, his heat and tension washing across me, leaving me breathless. "There is a problem?"

I flung a hand toward the book. "The words are gone. I didn't get the full directions for the key."

"That *is* unfortunate, but there is nothing we can do about it now." His voice held an edge that was part anger and part frustration. "The Raziq grow near. You must leave this place."

"What about the book?"

"It is safer to keep it where it is than retain it in the fields at the moment. The Raziq are as restricted by the magic of the coven site as we are. That is not the case here." His gaze met mine. "Go."

I hesitated, and saw the annoyance flash through his expression. And he had every right to feel that way. Hesitation was *stupid*. There was nothing I could do against the force of the Raziq, not in this place and not in my own world. Staying here was only putting him in greater danger.

I pulled free of the fields and stepped back into my flesh. For several minutes I did nothing more than sit there, regaining my equilibrium.

After a few minutes, the awareness of my surroundings returned. The air was hot enough to burn my skin and it was filled with shouting—Tao and Ilianna, in trouble.

Fear surged again and I opened my eyes. The clearing was in flames. Everything burned—the trees, the ground, even the air itself seemed to be on fire.

I blinked, positive that I was imagining it, that my vision was faulty, but it didn't help. The world *was* on fire.

The elementals.

I scrambled to my feet and twisted around, looking for Ilianna and Tao. I saw Ilianna first—she was running backward, intermittently yelling abuse and flipping the contents of two small bottles at the elemental that trundled after her. Given the way the creature's fiery form reacted to the spray, I knew it had to be holy water. It kept the creature at a respectful distance, but she didn't have an endless supply and would need help soon.

I swept my gaze past her. Tao was on the opposite side of the circle, his body ablaze as he stood his ground, going toe-to-toe with a second elemental, battling fire with fire. *His* fire didn't seem to be having much effect on the creature, but at least the elemental's fire didn't seem to be hurting him. Which was something to be thankful for.

The third elemental was nowhere to be seen, but instinct said it wouldn't be far.

I drew Amaya free from her scabbard and ran through the circle. This would destroy any protection it offered and leave the book open to attack, but I didn't have any other choice. Ilianna had just thrown the first of her bottles at the creature, which meant she was out of water.

I screamed and raised the sword high above my head. Amaya's hissing was an electric, vehement sound that filled the clearing and made the creature shudder. It turned around, its movements heavy yet rapid.

I swung Amaya. Lilac fire splattered through the air in a wide arc, whipping around the creature like a leash, burning where it touched. Then the blade hit it. Unlike the white ash stakes I'd used the last time I'd confronted these things, Amaya didn't slice through the elemental, allowing it to divide and regenerate. She simply consumed it.

The creature's flame seemed to wrap around the black of her blade, and then it melted away, as if its energy were being drawn into the sword itself. The blade shuddered and glowed, the ethereal steel glinting and flaring as the purple leash of her fire drew tighter and tighter, until the elemental was little more than a flicker of flame, and all I could hear was Amaya's fierce hissing and the elemental's dying screams.

Then the last of the fire creature was gone, and Amaya felt heavier in my hand—almost as if her belly were full. I shuddered, then thrust the thought aside and looked at Ilianna.

"You okay?"

She nodded and wiped a hand across her sweaty forehead. "Just fucking hot."

No doubt thanks to both the elementals *and* fires they'd lit in the forest. Fires the sentient forces residing in this place weren't happy about, if the seething mass of energy filling the air was anything to go by.

"Keep alert, because there's a third elemental around somewhere."

She nodded and bent, withdrawing a knife from her left boot. It looked and felt like silver, and I wondered if it would do any better against the elementals than the white ash.

Then I turned and ran for Tao.

He and the second elemental were still trading fiery blows, but Tao's flames were no longer as bright or as fierce as they had been. I raised Amaya and screamed again, drawing the attention of the creature.

It swung around and aimed a ponderous fist at me. Fire spat from Tao's fingertips, forming a rope of flame that spun around the creature's wrist and snapped it back. Tao stepped away—his flame dying everywhere except for that one band around the creature's wrist—and pulled with all his might.

The creature stumbled sideways, arms flailing as it struggled to regain balance. I leapt close, letting the heat of the thing wash over me, feeling the burn flush across my skin as I swung Amaya at the elemental's head.

This time, the sword didn't consume. She simply killed.

Black steel met with flame and the creature exploded. The force of it knocked me backward, and I landed on my butt several feet away. I grunted as the shock of the landing reverberated up my spine, but nevertheless tightened my grip on my sword and scanned the clearing.

Where the elemental had been standing, there was now a large patch of burned, sooty-looking ground. Several feet to the other side of that was Tao. He looked beat, his face drawn and ashen, as if the force of his flames had drained every ounce of life out of him.

But he gave me a tired smile when his gaze met mine. "I think you timed your reentry into our world almost perfectly. Another few minutes and I would have flamed out."

I pushed to my feet, sheathed Amaya, then walked over to Tao. Every step felt heavy, as if the sword's weight had somehow become mine. Or maybe it was simply exhaustion. Walking the gray fields always drained me, and I'd done that *and* battled creatures on both that plain and this.

I pulled Tao to his feet, then gave him a quick hug and said, "Thank you."

He snorted softly. "We are family, and a family stands together."

"I know, but—"

He placed a gentle finger against my lips. He smelled of flame and fierceness and also, oddly, elation. He'd actually *enjoyed* fighting the elementals. "As I've said before, you are not doing any of this alone—"

He paused and frowned suddenly, his gaze going past me. "What the—" He swore, pushed me aside, and ran. "Ilianna, watch out!"

I swung around and instinctively bolted after him, fear slamming through me as I saw what he'd seen. The last elemental was forming out of the flames that engulfed a eucalyptus, and it was oozing down toward Ilianna.

I drew Amaya and flung her as hard as I could at the elemental. The sword whooshed high above Tao's head and hit the creature in the midsection. But it did little more than make it falter and scream, because the force of my throw sent the blade right *through* the creature's body and thudding into a tree at the edge of the clearing.

At least it gave Ilianna time to get out of the elemental's reach. While she scrambled backward, Tao launched himself at it, his body arcing through the air like a bullet, flames licking across his skin as he hit the creature hard and ripped it from the tree.

"Tao!" I screamed, as the two of them went tumbling, a seething mass of flames and arms and screams. Tao's screams. Horrible, pain-filled screams.

Oh God, oh God . . . No!

I ran past their tumbling, twisting forms, wrenched Amaya free from the tree, and swung her high. But as I did, there was a weird sucking sound—it was almost as if the fire creature was consuming every ounce of air around it. A second later I realized it *wasn't* the creature. It was Tao. And his flames were growing brighter, fiercer.

He was drawing the creature's energy into himself!

"Tao, don't!" I screamed again, but the words were lost to another explosion—one powerful enough to throw me the full length of the clearing. I hit a tree trunk hard, heard a crack, and knew something inside me had broken. Pain washed through me as I dropped like a stone to the ground and for a moment there were so many stars dancing in front of my eyes that I couldn't see anything else.

Damn it, it *hurt*. It would hurt more to move. And yet move I did, wanting—needing—to know if Tao was still alive.

I pushed to my feet and staggered back across the clearing, holding a hand to my side and feeling pain every time I took a step or drew a breath. The heat of the fires that still burned all around us was nothing compared with the burn inside me. Sweat broke out across my brow and my stomach twisted, threatening to rebel. But I staggered on, my gaze on the unmoving Tao.

He couldn't be dead. He just *couldn't*.

I dropped on my knees beside him. The action jarred my whole body, but I swallowed heavily and studied my friend, searching for some sign of life, but fearful of actually touching him lest I find none.

I couldn't see him breathing, but his skin was red and the heat within him burned so fiercely it washed over me like flame.

He *couldn't* be dead. Not when the fire was still burning so ferociously inside of him.

"Risa?" Ilianna said tentatively, from somewhere behind me. "Is he . . . ?"

"I don't know." My voice broke as I said it. I swallowed heavily, then gathered the remnants of my courage and touched his neck. It was as if I'd inserted my fingers into the heart of a cauldron. It *hurt*. Burned.

I jerked my fingers away before they blistered, but not before I'd caught a pulse. It was thready and erratic, but it was there.

I closed my eyes and released the breath I hadn't realized I'd been holding.

"He's okay," I said, even though I knew that wasn't necessarily the case. He'd sucked in the energy of a fire elemental—consumed it, in much the same manner as my demon sword had. But Tao was a half-breed were, not a sword forged in the death of another demon, and who the hell knew what the merging of his flesh and an elemental's would do to him?

Ilianna dropped down beside me. "God, he's burning up," she said, her voice still distressed. "Inside and out."

"Have you got any holy water left?" I said, suddenly remembering how it had healed my wounds. It might not work on whatever was happening within him, but it sure as hell would help with his outside.

She nodded and scrambled up again, returning a few seconds later with a small bottle. "It's all I have, though."

"Then drizzle it over the worst of his wounds. His wolf healing capabilities should take care of the rest."

I pushed wearily to my feet. Pain rolled through me, catching in my throat and, for a second, sending those stars dancing again.

Ilianna frowned up at me. "You're hurt."

"Yeah." And if I *had* cracked a rib, as I suspected, then there was nothing I could do but grin and bear it. At least until I got my hands on some painkillers.

"You should let me see—"

"Ilianna," I said softly, "the only cure for a cracked rib is rest and time. I can't afford either right now. Just take care of Tao until I get back."

Her frown increased, and her green eyes searched mine worriedly. "Why? Where are you going?"

"I'm going to find the first damn key and attempt to finish this whole stupid thing."

"But that could be dangerous—"

"Yeah. Which is why you and Tao will stay here for now."

"But Tao needs more medical care than I can give him. We can't just leave him here!"

"Ilianna," I said, as gently as I could, "he took an elemental into his own body to destroy it. I have no idea what that's done to him, and I very much doubt anyone else will, either. I certainly don't think there's anything modern medicine can do for him that you and his own natural healing abilities can't."

"But if he's in a coma—"

I hesitated, studying him, torn by the need to do whatever I could to help him and the growing desire to protect them both. "Look, if you think he needs it, call in some healers. But don't leave this place. The Raziq are on the prowl, and this is the only place we know for sure they can't penetrate."

"But we can't stay here forever!"

"I know, and we won't. It's just for the next twenty-four hours." I squeezed her shoulder gently. "It'll be okay. I promise."

"God, I hope so." She took in a long shuddery breath, then added, "Be careful, won't you?"

"I will." And bit back the instinctive urge to tell her the same, to warn her that Tao might not be the person he was if and when he woke. But on some instinctive level, she'd be aware of that—and as a powerful witch, she'd certainly be aware of the energy storm deep with Tao.

I gave her a tense smile, then walked back across the clearing to grab Amaya—and stopped when I saw the Dušan's book. Or rather, the remains of it. It must have been caught in the last explosion, and it had been all but destroyed.

Damn it, could nothing go our way for a change?

I knelt and gently picked the book up. The leather binding crumbled under my touch and was blown away in cindery pieces by the gentle breeze. There was little left of the pages inside—just browned remnants as fragile as the cover. So much for Azriel thinking it would be safer here than on the gray fields.

I dropped it back on the ground, brushed my hands free of its grit, and stood up. There was nothing I could do about the book, and certainly no chance that I'd learn the location of the rest of the keys. I just had to rely on what I had.

And what I had wasn't a lot.

I picked up Amaya and cased her back into her sheath. Her song was a strand of anger that buzzed at the far reaches of consciousness. It was slightly stronger than before, but certainly no clearer. And right now, I was happy about that. I wasn't sure I was ready to understand the language of a sword who relished death and destruction so much.

I strode out of the clearing. Many of the trees were still on fire but, oddly, the fire wasn't spreading. Maybe whatever forces lived and breathed awareness—if not life—into this old ritual site were somehow containing the spread. Right now I was willing to believe just about anything, including a forest that was more than it seemed.

The gates were closed, but opened as I approached. A chill went through me. *Far too aware,* I thought, as I stepped through them.

Azriel was waiting on the other side. His gaze swept

me, and a slight frown marred his otherwise impassive features. "You are injured."

Which was stating the obvious given I was still clutching my side and breathing as shallowly as I could. And hell, I could be *just* as obvious. "And you escaped the fields before the Raziq could grab you."

He either didn't get the sarcasm in my voice or was ignoring it. I rather suspected the latter.

He said, "They were diverted."

I blinked. "Diverted how?"

"The how does not matter, just the result. How is your side?"

I shrugged, annoyed that he wasn't telling me how he escaped yet not entirely surprised. "I'll survive. We need to find those keys."

He studied me for a moment, then nodded. "What clues did the book give?"

I told him what I'd read, and he shook his head. "That's not much to go on."

"No. We need to sit down and try to work out the possibilities." I hesitated. "We'll need Lucian's help."

"There is no need—"

"Azriel," I said wearily, "right now I have a friend who may or may not die, another who is scared out of her wits, and I'm injured and tired. I just need it all to be finished. I don't really care what you do or don't think about Lucian. *I* think we need his help when we go get the keys, and I'm going to use him, whether you like it or not."

"Tao won't die," he said. "And you must live with whatever consequences arise out of using the Aedh."

Knowing Tao would live didn't relieve any of the tension still riding me, because living and remaining the man we'd grown up with and loved were two entirely seperate things.

"Azriel, I've been living with the goddamn consequences ever since you, the Raziq, and my father all decided to screw up my life!" I thrust a hand through my sweaty hair and sighed. Arguing with him wasn't going to get me anywhere. "I'll meet you back at the hotel. I'm gathering it'll still be safe there?"

He shrugged. "It's probably safer than your apartment."

"Then I'll see you there."

He nodded and winked out of existence. I reached for my phone and called Lucian.

"Hey," he said, his vid-screen dark and voice brisk, almost edgy. I'd obviously caught him in the middle of something. Or someone.

"Hey, yourself," I said. "You interested in meeting me at the hotel for a little key-finding strategy?"

Excitement swelled in his voice but didn't really lift the edginess. "You've read the book?"

"Some of it. Unfortunately, we were attacked before I could read all of it."

"Unfortunate, as you said." He paused. "But afterward?"

"Afterward we were attacked by elementals and the book was incinerated."

He snorted. "You're not having a good run of luck, are you?"

"No, but we've got enough to at least find the first key. That's a place to start."

"I agree. Where would you like me to meet you?"

"I'm heading back to the hotel now."

"Then I'll see you there in twenty minutes." He

hung up, leaving me staring at the black screen, wondering why our short, sharp conversation had my senses tingling.

I frowned, but shoved the concern aside as I put my phone into my pocket. Holding it tight, I reached inside and unleashed the Aedh. Her energy didn't rush through me—indeed, it was little more than a trickle, as if there was an inner awareness that I'd pushed my limits and was walking the edge of exhaustion.

The change swept over me gently, shifting me from one to the other. Even in Aedh form, I felt heavy, as if I was weighed down by more than my own flesh. And I guess I was, I thought, suddenly remembering Amaya. God, I had to hope that she didn't become a part of me for *real* when I re-formed.

I headed back for Melbourne and the Langham. Neither Azriel nor Lucian was in the room when I arrived, and of that I was glad. I re-formed flesh, not only imagining the sword as a separate entity but, for the first time, imagining my wounds as fully healed. I hit the floor with a heavy splat that left me shuddering in pain and gasping for breath, my head spinning so badly I wavered between wanting to throw up and falling into unconsciousness.

"You are such a fool, Risa Jones." The words seemed to come out of nowhere. I'd been so distressed that I hadn't even felt the heat of Azriel's presence.

Yeah, I wanted to reply, *you're not telling me anything I don't know.*

Hands touched me and energy flowed from them, bright and sharp and reviving. I wanted to jerk away from it—tell him I didn't need his help—but the truth was, I did. If I wanted to see this craziness through to the end, then I had to at least be able to open my eyes and walk. Right now neither of those seemed a possibility.

The energy continued to flow, and my body grew warm again. I opened my eyes and met his. "Thank you, Azriel, but that's enough."

He raised an eyebrow, but did as I bid and took his hands from my side. "You are not yet at full strength."

"No, but giving me strength more than likely drains you, and it's more important that you're whole than me. You're a better fighter."

"Having seen you fight, I'm not entirely certain that's true."

I snorted softly, and regretted the action almost immediately. "God," I groaned, "whatever you do, don't make me laugh. I think I'll die."

"I'm a reaper. I don't do jokes." I merely eyed him in disbelief, and he smiled. "Do you wish help to rise, or would you prefer to lie here until the Aedh arrives?"

"What I prefer is a shower. And that means getting up."

"Would you like some help?"

"No, I can manage."

He looked skeptical but didn't actually say anything. I blew out a breath and slowly—carefully— pushed to my feet.

Azriel rose with me, one hand out, as if ready to grab me should I fall. I pushed the sweaty strands of hair out of my face and gave him a weak smile. "See? I told you I could manage."

"I think the word for it is *stubborn*," he commented. "Have your shower. I will order food for you."

"Oh, will you now?" I said, not sure whether to be surprised or annoyed. "And who made you my mother?"

"No one, obviously, as that is not physically possible," he said, face as inscrutable as ever. Yet I sensed he was both amused and frustrated, and suddenly wondered if the Chi link between us was becoming strong enough that it was giving me a clearer glimpse of him.

I removed Amaya, placing the sword on the bed, then turned and carefully headed for the bathroom. A long hot shower revived me a little more, although I had scant success in scrubbing all the fibrous remnants of clothing from my skin. I was going to be pulling bits out for days.

After turning off the water, I grabbed a towel and carefully dried myself. A sudden knock at the door made me jump, but a second later the delicious scent of roast lamb invaded the room and I couldn't help grinning. Azriel had ordered my favorite—and no surprise, given he seemed to have an all-access pass to my memories and thoughts.

I left the towel on the bath's edge and walked out. He turned, his gaze scanning me briefly. Something flickered in his eyes—an emotion or reaction that disappeared too fast to name—then he waved a hand at the food.

"This is sufficient?"

"More than sufficient." God, there was even *Coke*. I drank half the bottle then grabbed a piece of lamb, munching on it as I walked across to my bag. After

pulling out underwear, jeans, T-shirt, and a sweater—
I skipped the bra because I really didn't want any
pressure on my newly healed ribs—I got dressed. Azriel's gaze was a weight that heated my insides and
stirred things that had no right to be stirring. Not
when it came to him.

"So," he said abruptly. "This first clue—"

"Any discussion will wait until Lucian gets here." I
glanced at the clock as I sat down to eat my meal.
Forty minutes had passed. It was unusual for Lucian
to be late for *any* date, let alone one that might give
him a shot at the vengeance he was so hungry for.
Concern stirred, but I thrust it aside. If anyone was
capable of defending himself against attack, it was
Lucian. Although why anyone would want to attack
him, I had no idea. It wasn't as if he'd been involved
in our quest before now.

I finished my meal and was on my second cup of
coffee—feeling more alive if not more energetic—by
the time he arrived.

Azriel opened the door. For a moment, the two men
stared, reminding me of combatants in a boxing ring,
each one measuring up the other. Then Azriel stepped
aside and Lucian's gaze met mine.

It was the gaze of the Aedh, not the lover. He was
here for business, nothing more. Even the kiss he
dropped on my lips was perfunctory, containing little
in the way of warmth or desire.

He pulled out a chair and sat beside me. "What are
we searching for?"

"The first key is veiled as an ax, but all I managed
to get from the book before we were attacked was: *It
was sent to the west of Melbourne where the wild*—"

I shrugged. "Wild what I have no idea. Nor do I know if it's literal or cryptic."

"The Aedh don't do cryptic," Azriel commented. He'd stationed himself on the other side of the table, his arms crossed and face impassive. Yet dark blue flames flickered across Valdis's sides, and I wondered if that was a sign of his annoyance or merely a reaction to Lucian's presence.

His gaze flicked to me. *Both.*

Seriously, you need to stop reading my thoughts.

I cannot. Live with it. His mental voice was short and sharp, and I wanted to laugh.

You know, if I didn't know better I'd think that was an edge of emotion creeping into your tone.

As I said, there are drawbacks to holding this shape for long periods of time.

The ability to become emotional being one of them? Interesting. And of course, the perverse part of me suddenly wondered if, with emotion, came desire.

And naturally, that was one internal question he *didn't* answer.

"So," Lucian said, "the mention of wild could mean anything from half the name of a sports team to a museum filled with stuffed animals."

"Or a zoo." I paused and frowned. "Although I can't imagine that the Raziq would be daft enough to hide an ax in a sporting club."

"And I couldn't imagine a zoo having much need for an ax," he retorted.

I leaned back in the chair at his tone, and he grimaced. "Sorry. Vengeance is so close I can taste it, and it's making me a little edgy."

Understandable, I guess, but that didn't excuse it. "It's not certain that finding or touching the keys will bring the Raziq to us. None of us has any idea just what magic went into the making of these keys *or* their disguising, and neither my father nor the Raziq was actually expecting to lose them."

"Your father may have disguised and stolen the keys, but the rest of Raziq would not have allowed him to be the sole provider of blood when it came to the actual making of them. That would be handing one man too much power, and even the Raziq would be wary of that."

"You seem to know an awful lot about the motivations of the Raziq," Azriel commented.

Lucian's gaze flicked to him, and it showed the contempt that Azriel was managing to hide. "I am a very old Aedh, and I have firsthand experience at just what the Raziq are capable of."

I frowned. "Just how firsthand are we talking? I thought it was the priests who stripped you of your wings and power, not the Raziq."

"It was," he said, so evenly and flatly that I didn't doubt it was the truth. And yet something within me stirred uneasily. "But the Raziq were a growing power within the priests when I was full Aedh, and it was thanks to their influence that I was punished the way I was."

Hence his need to get back at them. I rose and walked across to the coffeemaker to make myself another cup. "So, the clue. If not a sports club or the zoo, then where?"

"A museum, perhaps?" Azriel said. "There would be lots of axes in such a place."

I took a sip of the steaming liquid, then wrinkled my nose. Not enough sugar. I tore open a couple of packets and added them. "Yeah, but a museum would hardly be described as wild, and there are only a couple outside of the metro area. Sovereign Hill is more northwest, and Rippon Lea more southwest."

"I do not think the instructions should be taken as gospel," Azriel said. "Your father may have sent them in that direction, but there is no telling where his Razan ended up."

"True, but I think we'd be better searching for the obvious first. You never know, we might get lucky."

"It is never wise to rely solely on luck," Azriel commented. "You tend to get disappointed."

Wasn't that the truth?

"So, the obvious," Lucian said, a little impatiently. "What's out west that holds wild whatevers?"

I grimaced, thinking. "There's the Werribee Open Range Zoo, but as I said, I can't imagine an ax going unnoticed there."

Plus, zoos were always undergoing renovation. It wouldn't exactly be the most secure place to keep a prize such as the key safe.

He leaned back in the chair. "So there is nothing else out there?"

"Well, there's the Werribee mansion."

He raised an eyebrow. "How old a mansion? And how would it tie in with *wild*?"

"The zoo is part of the mansion complex, and the building itself is very old. I think it was built only a hundred years or so after Australia was settled."

He gave me an old-fashioned sort of look. "An ax would *not* stand out in a place that old."

Given I wasn't really into visiting old houses, I really couldn't say with any certainty what was usual and what was not. "The mansion is open to the public seven days a week, which means we'll have to go in at night."

Lucian frowned. "If it is open to the public, then that gives us the perfect cover."

"Yeah, but if I touch the key and the Raziq *do* attack, then people—innocent people—are going to get hurt."

"Many more innocents will get hurt if the wrong people get their hands on these keys."

"Yeah, they will," I said, annoyance edging my tone. "But that doesn't mean we have to endanger anyone unnecessarily."

He grunted. It was a somewhat impatient sound. But then, he was Aedh, and though his many centuries here on earth had humanized his ways to some extent, they hadn't changed his core being. And that being didn't really care who or what was damaged in the course of getting what he wanted.

"Tonight then. They will have security, I gather?"

"Undoubtedly."

"Then I shall take care of the electronic stuff." His gaze flicked rather disdainfully to Azriel. "The reaper can handle whatever human security they have."

Azriel didn't comment, which surprised me, given his previous statements that he couldn't physically intervene without just cause. Although I guess knocking out the guards *did* aid his quest to find the keys, and that might be cause enough. He'd certainly had no qualms about knocking out the half-shifter who'd attacked me at the rail station.

"It gets dark around six tonight," Lucian continued, glancing at his watch. "Shall we meet outside the mansion around eight?"

"Outside the main gate, yes." I frowned at him. "You seem to be in a bit of a hurry today."

He grimaced. "Yeah, sorry, but I have a ton of work on my plate—tax time and all."

An honest enough—and believable—answer, so why did unease wash through me again? Or was the strengthening connection with Azriel giving rise to my flashes of doubt?

"Are you sure you can dismantle the electronic surveillance and any other measures they might have in place?" I asked as he rose.

"Yes." He leaned forward and dropped another kiss on my lips. This time, however, it held a little more warmth. "Maybe once this is all over and we both have more time, we can spend a week or two together in bed."

I snorted softly. "I have a café to run, remember?"

"And I have a well-paid but demanding job. But once the tax-time madness is over, I'll willingly cast it aside to lose myself in the delights of your flesh for a lengthy period." His sudden grin was decidedly cheeky. "And do not try to tell me you would not do the same. I feel the anticipation in your thoughts."

"You know," I said drily, "it'd be nice if *both* of you would just let me keep my thoughts to myself."

"Sorry, that's not going to happen," Lucian commented, echoing Azriel's earlier remark. "I shall see you tonight, my sweet."

And with that, he walked out. I watched until the door slammed shut behind him, then shook wistful, somewhat hungry thoughts from my mind and glanced at Azriel.

"What are you going to do?"

"That very much depends on what you plan to do."

An odd tightness still swam through him, and I frowned. "Azriel, Lucian is on our side."

"For the moment, it would appear so."

"Then why not give the distrust and anger up, because it's fucking annoying."

Something flickered through his eyes. Surprise perhaps. "I was not aware that it was affecting you so. I shall try to be more circumspect."

Which meant even more contained. I wasn't entirely sure I was happy about that, because as much as his doubts about Lucian irritated me, I couldn't deny the fact that I rather enjoyed getting these odd snatches of thought and emotion from him.

"You can't have it both ways," he commented softly. "The link between us will continue to strengthen the longer I am near. If I manage to contain the seepage of what I might be feeling in regard to the Aedh, then I will contain it all."

"So just how strong will this link get?"

He shrugged. "I don't know."

Liar, I thought, and again saw that flicker in his eyes. But all he said was, "You have six hours until we meet the Aedh. What do you intend to do?"

I let out a huge yawn that basically answered his question, and said, "What do you think?"

A small smile touched his lips. "Then I shall guard."

"What, you've got nothing better to do than watch me sleep?"

"Apparently not." The mirth died. "Rest, Risa. You need it."

My name sounded like chocolate on his lips—sweet and rich. I gave myself a mental slap and spun around, heading for the bed. I stripped and climbed in, not looking at him but at the same time very aware of his presence. I closed my eyes and felt exhaustion sweep over me. Even so, that awareness had curiosity—along with a whole lot of other things I didn't want to dwell on—stirring.

"Don't you ever sleep, Azriel?"

"I have no need to. We are not governed by the restrictions of flesh as you are."

"But you're wearing flesh, and you did say that the longer you remain in this form, the more dangerous it becomes."

"The danger does not come from the restrictions."

I opened my eyes. Even though awareness of him was a weight I could feel, he wasn't even looking at me but rather leaning, arms crossed, against the window, staring out. His expression was thoughtful. Distant. And perhaps just a touch wistful.

"Then what does the danger come from if not the restrictions?"

He didn't answer immediately. Then his gaze met mine, and in those bright, mismatched depths I saw bleakness.

"Sleep, Risa. I will wake you when it is time to go."

He had to be the most frustrating, pigheaded man I'd ever known—except he wasn't a man and I really *had* to stop thinking of him in those terms. But it was damn hard when he was wearing that form and—by his own admission—gaining more human characteristics the longer he remained in it.

I blew out a breath that contained more than a little irritation, then determinedly closed my eyes. Given everything that had happened over the last twenty-four hours, it wasn't entirely surprising that I quickly slipped into a deep sleep.

The smell of coffee woke me many hours later. I muttered something unintelligible even to me, then rubbed an eye and glanced blearily at the clock on the nightstand. It was close to six thirty.

I twisted around in the bed. Azriel was still standing near the window, but on the table between him and the bed was a small tray containing several plates and a steaming coffeepot.

"I ordered freshly brewed," he said. "As well as bacon, eggs, and toast. You will eat before we leave."

"And if I don't, you'll force it down my throat?" I said, somewhat amused.

"If it comes to that, yes." There was little happiness in his expression, and certainly no sense of it in the energy of him. "It is advantageous to my quest to keep you not only safe but in a fit condition to face whatever might be waiting."

"And the quest is all," I muttered, tossing off the bedcovers and reaching for my clothes.

"You wish me well away from you. Succeeding with this mission is the only way to achieve that."

I glanced up at him as I pulled on my jeans. He still wasn't looking at me, yet I knew he was as aware of me as I was of him. I could feel the electricity of it in the air. See it in the taut set of his shoulders.

"So if we don't succeed, I'm stuck with you following me around for the rest of my days?"

"Until either I am dead or the mission is in ashes." He finally met my gaze, but no matter what I might feel in the air, there was as little emotion in his expression as ever. "Eat, Risa. We will need to drive to this mansion of yours. I cannot risk a journey through the gray fields."

"But I can take Aedh form." I frowned as I sat down and poured myself a fresh cup of coffee. Coke would have been better, but beggars couldn't be choosers. "And why can't we risk the gray fields?"

"Taking Aedh form will weaken you too much. Besides, if the Raziq can track your father's energy, they may well be able to track yours." He shrugged, the movement eloquent. "And we dare not risk the fields because the Raziq still roam there. They were sidetracked, not vanquished."

"So you think they'll be able to find us if we enter?"

"I do not know, and I prefer to be safe."

I sipped the steaming coffee, then picked up my knife and fork and tucked into the bacon and eggs. Despite there being enough on the plate to feed an army, I finished it off in no time. After also finishing the coffee, I rose and strapped Amaya back on. The black blade spat and buzzed, as if angry about being left alone so long.

"You are her lifeblood," Azriel commented. "She *is* angry."

Oh great. I'd managed to piss off a sword. Was there no end to my talents?

"Apparently not." Azriel pushed away from the

window and picked up the jacket lying on the other bed, handing it to me. "Are you ready?"

"Not really, but it's not like I have a choice." Not with the threat hanging over both Ilianna and Tao.

Tao. I closed my eyes for a moment and prayed like hell that he'd come out of whatever the elemental had done to him okay.

Azriel didn't comment. Maybe even he didn't know what fate awaited Tao.

We grabbed a taxi outside the hotel. Despite the fact that rush hour had passed, there was still a fair amount of traffic on the freeway and the going was slow. I directed the driver to a house just up the road from the mansion's main gate so that he didn't think it odd or—worse—do something civil-minded like phone the police.

The night was clear and the air crisp. I shivered and zipped up my jacket, glad Azriel had grabbed it.

"The Aedh waits at the gate," he commented. I peered through the darkness but couldn't actually see Lucian. Then again he'd been around long enough to know how to remain hidden from prying eyes. "I will go inside and neutralize the guards."

I frowned. "I thought you said it would be too dangerous to walk the gray fields at the moment?"

His gaze met mine. "Only if I'm accompanied by you. Alone, I'm just another reaper on the fields. Your presence, however, is like a beacon to those attuned to you."

"And the Raziq are?"

"I cannot say for sure, but I am not willing to run that risk. Wait with the Aedh until I return."

And with that, he winked out of existence. I headed for the gates and, in the shadows of the signs, saw Lucian.

"Hey gorgeous," he said, stepping away from the back of the sign he'd been leaning against. "Why the hell did you arrive by taxi?"

"Azriel was worried that the Raziq might have been able to sense my presence in the gray fields." I let him sweep me into his arms, feeling the tension in him, the urgency—an urgency that spoke of the need to move, to fight. "For the same reason, I couldn't become Aedh."

"He's being overly cautious."

I shrugged. Maybe he was, but it was for my safety and I couldn't exactly argue with that. "Did you bring any weapons?"

He smiled. "A small armory, starting with two long knives strapped to my back."

"Knives aren't going to be much use against Raziq. They may not even take human form."

"Ah, but these knives are specifically designed to cut through energy beings."

"So Raziq." And reapers.

"Yes," he said, leaving me wondering if he was confirming one thought or both.

I pushed down the slither of unease again and asked, "Was there electronic surveillance?"

He nodded and slid his hands down to my butt, pressing me a little closer. Despite my certainty that passion wasn't part of his emotional makeup right now, he was fully aroused and as hard as a rock.

"The anticipation of an oncoming fight does that to me," he commented. "But I shall restrain the urge to ravish you senseless until after we complete our mission."

"Just as well," I said drily. "Because if you'd tried, I would have knocked you out."

"That wouldn't have been any use." He grinned as he tapped his head. "It's way too hard."

I snorted softly and pulled away from him. "Did you neutralize the surveillance?"

"No, but I do have contacts who have few scruples and who respect only the power of money. This entire area will be blacked out in—" He paused and glanced at his watch. "—three, two, one . . ."

Right on cue, the lights in the nearby houses went out. I raised my eyebrows. "And just how did they manage this, given said contacts don't sound as if they actually work for any power company?"

"It's easy to knock out a grid if you know exactly where to strike." He shrugged. "This way, it'll also look less suspicious."

True. Azriel reappeared and said, "The guards have been neutralized for two hours."

"And if we need more time than that?" Lucian said.

Azriel barely even glanced at him. "The mansion is not endless, and not all the rooms are furnished. Shall we go?"

That last was directed at me. I nodded, walked across to the white wooden fence, and leapt over it. And tried my best to ignore the ache in my side as I headed down the long, asphalt road. Crickets chirped loudly in the paddocks to either side, their song stopping briefly as we jogged by, then resuming once we were gone. The asphalt eventually gave way to stone, then the road split, one fork heading to the zoo, the other toward the mansion. We went over a second set of locked gates and continued down the road, the paddocks on either side giving way to trees, parking lots, and picnic areas.

"There is a gatehouse just ahead," Azriel said, his voice soft and oddly at one with the darkness. "The mansion lies to the right of the gardens."

I nodded, went over the fence to the right of the guardhouse, and pressed a hand to my side as we continued on. The mansion soon loomed before us, dark and regal in the moonlit darkness.

"How do we get in?" I asked as we walked to the main door.

Lucian produced an electronic lock pick. "How else?"

I smiled. "You do think of everything."

"Someone has to."

I wasn't entirely sure whether the barb was aimed at me, Azriel, or both, but annoyance slithered through me. I thrust it down. In truth, I *hadn't* really thought much about our task here, relying on the two men to get me in and out. And really, what option did I have? I might have been trained to fight by the best guardians the Directorate had ever produced, but that didn't mean I was proficient at anything else a guardian might do. Like breaking and entering.

Azriel caught my arm as we climbed the steps, stopping me abruptly.

"There is magic here."

Lucian stopped and looked over his shoulder, his expression disbelieving. "Why would there be magic here?"

Azriel hesitated. "I do not know. And it is . . . vague."

"Define *vague*," I said, wondering if the Raziq had somehow beaten us here.

"It does not have the feel of the Raziq," Azriel commented. "And it does not seem to be active. Rather, it waits."

"Waits? How can magic wait?" Lucian asked impatiently. "Magic is not sentient, reaper."

"Not as such, no," Azriel bit back, hostility briefly flaring in his voice. "But spells can lie inactive until set in motion by an event or action."

"Whether or not that is true in this particular case, we have no choice," Lucian said. "Not if you want to find this key of yours."

Azriel glanced at me. I shrugged. Lucian was right—we didn't have a choice. I motioned him on, and he pressed the lock pick against the door. After a moment, there was a soft click and the door opened.

I glanced at Azriel. "Any change in the magic?"

"No."

Maybe that meant Lucian was right. The two men flanked me as I stepped through the doorway. The hallway beyond was wide, and filled with shadows that did little to hide the opulence. At the far end of the hall, a grand old staircase swept upward, splitting to left and right on the landing before rising again. There were several doors leading off the hallway itself, but I couldn't feel any particular vibe coming from any of them. The dragon on my arm lay still and quiet—although to be honest, I had no idea if she'd react to the keys as she had the book. She'd come from the magic contained within the book, but the keys were entirely separate.

I stepped to the left, into what looked like a library. Though it was darker here than in the hallway, both demon swords flicked fire across the walls, giving me more than enough light to see by, but also stirring fear. The swords were reacting to something—and I had to hope it was merely the slither of magic in the air that Azriel had sensed, not something far worse.

My gaze swept the walls and bookcases, but I couldn't see anything resembling an ax. There was nothing coming through on the sensory lines, either.

We moved on into the other rooms, searching the opulent dining and drawing rooms, a billiard room that contained fierce-looking stuffed animal heads, and the half-furnished kitchen areas. Again, there was nothing resembling an ax—or anything else that kicked the psychic radar into gear—in any of them.

We mounted the stairs. And for the first time since entering the beautiful old building, energy slithered across my skin—a caress so light it barely brushed the hairs on my arm. But the Dušan stirred in my flesh, and my gaze swept the hallway above. It was here. It was somewhere up here.

"You've found something?" Lucian said, studying me with a frown.

"I think so." I paused at the landing, trying to catch hold of the elusive sensation. It came and went, as if there was still some distance between us.

I frowned at the long hallway visible through the richly painted arch. It didn't seem to be coming from down there, although the sensations caressing my skin were so fleeting it was hard to be certain.

"Risa," Azriel said softly, "we do not have all night. Pick a direction. If it is wrong, we can go the other way."

I bit my lip, studying the doorways to the left and the right, then abruptly turned left. I strode past a bedroom, not even bothering to look inside, drawn on by the faint pull of power. After a short series of steps, we entered another hallway—one less opulent than the others we'd seen. The rooms to either side appeared empty, aside from one that contained office equipment, but I didn't bother stopping. The pull was getting stronger, and it was coming from the room at the far end of the hall—the exhibition area, the sign near the door announced.

I stepped inside. It wasn't just a single-story room, but rather three, with an atrium in the middle and a soaring, white-painted, window-lined, wooden ceiling. Moonlight poured through the glass, giving the room a cool, eerie feel. I took several more steps forward, trying to pin down the location of the energy that was burning across my senses. The Dušan stirred and writhed, moving from the left to the right as she did so. I frowned, wondering if she was actually giving me a hint. I walked right. While bookcases lined the upper level and there was a café below, this level was filled with information boards and the artifacts that had been collected over the many years of restoration. I walked past several boards then stopped suddenly as the energy all but exploded, blasting heat across my skin and making Amaya hiss her fury.

It was here. Somewhere.

I scanned the half-height boxes, seeing the remnants of a rusted garden seat, the strap off an iron fence post, and a pickax.

It had to be that. *Had* to be.

"Have you found it?" Lucian asked softly.

"I think so," I said, reaching for it.

But my fingers had barely brushed the wooden handle when hell broke loose around us.

"What the fuck—?" Lucian said, spinning around.

"That dormant magic," Azriel said grimly, "is no longer so dormant. And we are no longer alone. We need to leave—now!"

I gripped the pickax's rough handle firmly as he wrapped his arms around me. Power surged—*his* power—running through every muscle, every fiber, until my whole body sang to its tune. But this time it failed to make us into energy beings, failed to transport us into the gray fields and away from the mansion.

Valdis spat and screamed—an echo of her master's frustration, I suspected.

"What's wrong?" I said, fear gripping me as he stepped back and drew the sword.

"The magic is preventing travel through the gray fields." His gaze went past me, and his expression became grim. I didn't even want to look. "Can you take Aedh form?"

I reached for her immediately. Her response was swift and harsh, no doubt due to the tension twisting my insides, but nothing happened.

"It is as I expected," Azriel said. "We have stepped neatly into another trap."

"Then we fight our way out of it," Lucian said,

drawing the long knives out of their sheathes and running to the right.

It was then I saw them.

Twisted, half-human, half-animal beings.

Fuck.

I drew Amaya. Her anger filled me, shoring up my courage. And I needed every ounce of it as I turned around and saw that there weren't just one or two of these creatures, but at least a dozen. Their inhuman faces were twisted by madness, and bloodlust shone in their eyes. Whatever—whoever—had done this to them, they'd killed any remnants of humanity left within them.

"Stay behind me," Azriel said. "We'll try to get to the door."

But even as he said it, the creatures surged forward. He swung Valdis, the blade screaming as her fire sent blue lightning flashing across the moon-cooled shadows. Body parts went flying but they didn't seem to care, just kept on coming—a relentless tide from which there seemed no escape.

They swarmed over him and lunged at me. I moved backward, Amaya gripped in one hand, the pickax in the other, swinging both as hard as I could. My arms shuddered every time a weapon hit flesh, but it didn't seem to make a difference to the tide of bodies in front of me.

And their stench . . . they smelled like humans who were now rotting inside. My stomach twisted and rolled, but I wasn't entirely sure the smell was solely responsible for that.

From the back of the pack, blue fire begun to erupt, and I knew Azriel was attempting to return to me. I had no idea where Lucian was, but I could hear the howls and screams of creatures to the right and guessed he was still doing damage.

A shadow leapt above the writhing mass of twisted flesh, coming at me with speed—a dark form with feline features and half-furred skin. It resembled a man-sized cat—a cat with twisted, yellowed canines and hands that ended in long sharp claws. I ducked, letting the thing arc high above me, and swung Amaya. Her hissing was lost to the inhuman sounds these things were making, but her black blade sliced through the creature's underbelly with ease. Blood and gore rained down on me as the creature's momentum sent it tumbling over the railings and down onto the floor below.

I didn't look to see if it was dead. I didn't have the time.

Another creature leapt at me. I backed away, hit the railing that ringed the void, and swung both weapons. The creature snarled and twisted, its clawed hands lashing out—not for me, but for the pickax. They were after the key, *not* us.

I tightened my grip on the ax's wooden handle as the creature tried to wrest it from my hands. It yanked me forward, into its body, clogging my senses with its reek as it snapped at my face with its teeth. I jerked backward, felt its canines slide down my cheek—marking but not cutting flesh—and lashed Amaya sideways, almost slicing it in half. Blood spurted and it howled, but it didn't let go, tossing me left and right as it tried to win control of the ax.

Then two more creatures hit us, their momentum so fierce they sent us all tumbling over the railing and onto the floor below. We landed in a screaming tumble of arms and legs, the jolt so fierce that my breath whooshed out of my lungs and knives of pain speared my newly healed ribs. The pickax went flying from my grip, but Amaya stuck like glue, her blade flaming and her murderous hissing strong and clear in my mind.

She wanted blood. I gave it to her, swinging wildly at the nearest creatures as they scrambled to get up . . . after the pickax or simply wanting to get clear of the murderous blade?

I pushed backward, out from underneath the last of the creatures, then staggered to my feet. I was barely upright when the creatures flung themselves at me. But even as I backed away, slashing left and right with the sword, the strangeness of their behavior had me frowning. If they were intending to attack, why wait until I was on my feet to do so? And why, when there were three of them, did they not simply attack en masse rather than one at a time?

It made no sense.

Not the way these creatures were behaving, and certainly not the fact they were even here. If the Raziq *were* behind this, why didn't they come themselves? Why risk sending these creatures when the three of us could never best a full complement of Aedh, no matter what Lucian and Azriel might think?

Claws lashed at me. I jumped back, hissing in pain as the movement jarred my ribs, but this time I wasn't quick enough to get out of the creature's way and its claws caught my jacket, tearing it to ribbons. But again, it didn't slice into flesh.

They definitely *weren't* trying to kill me. Despite the murderous light in their eyes and the desperate hunger that filled the air, something—or someone—had leashed them.

And there could be only one reason. Someone *other* than the Raziq, the reapers, and the vampire council was after the keys.

Even as the thought crossed my mind, energy caressed the room. An energy that was dark, ungodly, and bitter. My skin crawled in response, and Amaya's hissing became so fierce it just about shattered my eardrums.

It wasn't the energy of the Raziq. It was something else. Something that could make a demon sword burn with anticipation.

And she *was* burning. The black blade had given way to fierce purple flames that licked out across the shadows, burning everything she touched—be it flesh or furniture.

In the light of her fire, I saw the figure. It was man-shaped and indistinct, and it moved with speed, half searching under tables and in the deeper shadows.

It wasn't one of the creatures, and it was looking for the ax.

"No!" I yelled, and swung Amaya as hard as I could, battering away the nearest creature, forcing it backward with the force of the blow even as the black blade sliced it apart. Blood spewed, spraying across my face and body, covering me in its putrid, sticky stench, but I didn't care, diving toward the shadow in a desperate attempt to stop it.

Then the last of the three creatures who'd tumbled down with me hit my legs, dragging me down. My chin hit the edge of a chair and for a moment I saw stars. I cursed, kicking at the thing holding me. Bone cracked and more blood spurted, its scent stinging the air. The creature held on, screaming in fury and pain, but not attacking.

Ahead, the indistinct form bent and reached for something. The ax. I twisted and wildly swung Amaya at the thing holding me in place. The blade bit through the creature's neck and my legs, severing the creature's head but not even scratching me as it passed through my flesh.

Even headless, the fucking thing wouldn't let go.

And then it was too late, because the dark, bitter energy fell abruptly away, and the shadowy figure was gone.

As was the ax.

Chapter Thirteen

A DOZEN DIFFERENT SWEAR WORDS RACED through my mind, but I didn't bother saying them. I swung Amaya again, this time slicing away the arms that still held me so tightly. As the limbs fell away from the creature's body, I kicked it off me and staggered to my feet. Someone hit the ground behind me and I swung around, Amaya raised. It was Azriel. He was covered not only in the stinking blood of the creatures, but in his own. Wounds crisscrossed his stomach and right arm, and blood seeped down the fingers that gripped Valdis.

His gaze swept me, then he said, "The ax?"

"Gone. And it wasn't the Raziq."

He swore—at least I think he swore because it wasn't any language I understood—and thrust a hand through his damp hair. "I was not aware that there was anyone else after the keys."

"That makes two of us," I muttered, and glanced up as something moved on the floor above us.

Lucian appeared, leaning over the side, his face bruised, clothes torn, but a fierce light in his eyes. "Everyone okay?"

"Yeah, but the ax is gone."

He leapt over the railing, landing with grace and little noise. "The Raziq, I gather?"

I shook my head. "Not unless the Raziq use blood magic."

"Blood magic?" He stopped to one side of Azriel, smelling of sweat and blood and anger barely leashed. "Why would you think that?"

"Because I felt it, and because I saw the man involved."

"You saw him?" Azriel said quickly, then his gaze narrowed. "No. You only saw an indistinct shape."

"Enough to know it was a man. A tall man." I hesitated, squashing down the instinctive flash of irritation. As he'd said, there was nothing I could do about him accessing my thoughts, so I'd better get used to it. Which was easier thought than done. "It's a start, at least."

Azriel's expression suggested that as starts went, it pretty much sucked. "The magic that prevented us from leaving has dissipated. We should go."

"I can't. I'll need to report this." Because if I didn't and Rhoan got wind of it—which he undoubtedly would—then I'd be in deep shit.

Not that I wouldn't be in deep shit as it was.

I glanced at Lucian. "You'd better leave. There's no sense in you being here when the Directorate arrives. That'll only result in hours of questioning."

"And with my workload, that is not something I desire." He sheathed his bloodied long knives and bent to kiss my cheek. "Call me when you're free and we can plan our next assault."

I nodded. He touched my shoulder lightly, then

gave Azriel a somewhat dark look and walked across to the café's door, opening it with the pick then leaving.

I glanced at Azriel. "Are all the creatures dead?"

He nodded and replaced Valdis. Her blue fire had quieted, even though Amaya still hissed and spat. But flames no longer drenched her blade, and the café was no longer ablaze. So maybe her cry was a reflection of the anger and hurt that still burned inside of me.

"The magic that prevented us from taking our energy forms also smacked of the dark arts," he said. "I suspect the source is the same."

I nodded and wearily pulled out my phone. I eyed it for a few moments, knowing I had to call Uncle Rhoan as soon as possible but, at the same time, wanting to delay the inevitable for as long as I could.

"Who else could be after the damn keys?" I glanced at Azriel. "And why?"

"I cannot answer that."

"But would you, if you could?"

"Yes."

I grunted, feeling the truth of his words swirl somewhere deep inside. "I can't understand why anyone else would even want the keys! I mean, if they can't traverse the gray fields, they can't get near the gates, so what's the point of stealing them?"

"It can only be another Aedh—one we know nothing about—or someone like you. Someone who wears human flesh but is gifted psychically, and who has the ability to walk the fields."

"You left reapers out of that group."

"Yes, because no reaper can use black magic."

"Really? Why? Is it in your makeup or something?"

"In a sense, yes." He shrugged.

Meaning, that was all the information I was about to get. Although, to be fair, maybe he simply didn't know himself. "I may be able to walk the fields, but I've never seen the gates. In fact, as far as I know, I've never been anywhere near them."

"Which does not preclude the possibility of someone else possessing the same set of skills as you not seeing or knowing of them."

True. I rubbed a hand across my face, smearing blood, sweat, and God knew what else, then glanced down at my phone again and sighed. Better do it now, while I still had some energy to face him.

I pressed a button on the phone and said, "Uncle Rhoan." Colors swirled across the screen as the voice-recognition software jumped into action.

A few seconds later his cheerful features replaced the multicolored swirl. "Hey Ris," he said, but his smile quickly faded. "What the fuck has happened to you this time?"

"Long story. But you might want to get the Directorate over to the Werribee mansion. There's a whole heap of dead, half-human-shifter things here."

"Damn it, Risa, I told you to let me investigate the half-shifters!"

"I did. I *am*. This isn't related to that, but something else."

"The fucking keys, at a guess. Why didn't you call in help?"

"I *had* help." And probably better help than anything either he or the Directorate could provide—and safer, too, given Director Hunter's interest in the whole affair. I had no doubt I'd catch flak over my failure to keep her informed as to what we were up to, but that was something I was willing to face. The whole idea of the vampire council getting control of the gates made my skin crawl. "Look, please, just come down here, so I can tell you what happened and then go home to scrub myself clean."

He opened his mouth to say something, but the phone was ripped from his grasp as Aunt Riley appeared. "Are you okay? Are you hurt?"

"No, I'm fine."

"Do you want me there?"

It was on my tongue to say no, then I hesitated. One of the reasons Riley was still hooked to the Directorate was her ability to talk to the dead. Or rather, the *souls* of the dead. "Hang on." I glanced around, but couldn't see any reapers other than Azriel.

"There aren't," he said softly. "These deaths were not ordained."

I glanced back at the phone. "It might be worth trying to talk to the souls of these things. We might be able to learn something about their maker."

"Good idea. I'll bring some fresh clothes for you, too. You might want to clean yourself up first. Trust me, you'll feel better without all that gore over you."

I couldn't argue with that, so I signed off and looked at Azriel. "How long before whatever you did to the guards wears off?"

"Just under an hour."

"Time enough to find the bathroom, then." I hesitated, my gaze sweeping his bloodied, grimy torso. "Are you okay?"

He nodded. "This is merely flesh. I am unharmed where it matters."

"But you can be hurt—even killed—in flesh form, can't you?"

"Killed, yes, but the wounds affecting this vessel are not painful and will heal once I claim my natural form."

My gaze skimmed his body again. Some of those wounds looked pretty deep.

"I'm fine, Risa," he said softly. "Go find your water. I'm sure your friends will appreciate the effort."

In other words, I stank. I snorted softly and headed for the café door. It only took me a couple of minutes to find the bathroom and I quickly stripped off, rolling up my T-shirt and using it to wash off the worst of the gore.

Thankfully, the coat had protected my sweater, even if the left sleeve had been shredded by the shifter's claws. But my jeans were unsalvageable. I dumped them in the waste bin along with my undies, then washed my hands and headed out, suddenly glad that my sweater was long enough to cover my butt. Although the cold night air teased me in unmentionable ways that had my pulse rate humming happily.

Or maybe that was a result of the brief look Azriel gave me as I walked back into the room. *Intense* didn't even begin to describe it. And though it was a weight I felt deep inside, I wasn't entirely sure just exactly what it meant. Frowning, I walked around the other side of the café counter to raid the cookie jar, picking out a huge chocolate chip one as well as a macadamia and white chocolate.

"So," I said, meeting his gaze again, a little relieved that the intensity had been replaced by his more normal inscrutability. "How will we know if whoever has stolen the key has used it?"

"We will feel it."

"We? As in, you and I, or everyone who lives in this world and the next?"

"Those who are connected to the fields or who can walk them will feel it. That's how we became aware of the keys first being tested on the portals."

I frowned. "I didn't feel anything when they did that."

He shrugged. "It might have been nothing more than a sense of unease that you weren't able to place."

Maybe. And maybe he was overestimating my abilities. "These people might not have stolen the key to force the portals closed."

"No." Grimness briefly flickered through his expression before he caught himself. "And I do not know what will happen should the gates be eternally forced open. None of us do."

"How could it be worse than that whole human-race-becoming-zombies scenario?"

"That," he said, and this time the grimness did more than flicker, "would be a walk in the park compared to the hordes of hell being unleashed."

God, I thought, it would be hell on earth. Literally.

My phone rang, making me jump. I glanced down, saw it was Hunter, and mentally let loose a string of curses. I might be willing to face her fury, but I'd been hoping to get a few Cokes—or even something stronger—under my belt first.

I was tempted to ignore the call, but I was willing to bet that would just make her angrier. I answered.

"So," she said, her voice like the Arctic, "just when were you planning to inform me about this key-finding mission? One I gather has now gone spectacularly wrong?"

"When I had the key in my hand." Which wasn't exactly a lie. I would have told her; I just wouldn't have given it to her.

"Which you do not."

"No. A trap was set and, unfortunately, we sprang it."

"Why did you not call for help? The Cazadors—"

"If reapers and an Aedh could not stop this attack, what hope do you think the Cazadors would have?"

Her green eyes flashed dangerously. "Do not doubt the capabilities of the Cazadors. They are more powerful than you know."

I doubted that, given I knew a whole lot about them from Uncle Quinn. "Look, Aunt Riley's coming down—"

"I am well aware what Riley Jenson is up to. She is of no concern at this moment."

And I bet she'd *love* to know that. But all I said was, "Has Selwin lifted the Maniae curse?"

"Yes. And in return, she will receive the protection of a new master when she turns." Heat suddenly burned through the cool depths of her eyes. Heat and anticipation. "You have earned yourself quite an enemy, young Risa. I would watch your step if I were you."

"To be honest, she can take a number and stand in line, because she's the *least* of my worries."

"That is possibly true." She paused, and a small, cool smile touched her lips. Oh, *fuck*. The crap was about to hit the fan. "From now on, you will have a Cazador by your side. Day in, and day out."

"Oh come on," I retorted. "That's—"

"The way it will be. Or else." She stared at me, and though her gaze was as blank as her expression, a chill nevertheless went through me. Because that was the face of a vampire intent on a kill. And though I had Azriel and Amaya, I had a suspicion they wouldn't be enough if Hunter decided the council was right and I needed to die.

I licked my lips, my heart going a million miles an hour as I said, "No vampire is coming into my apartment. Not you, and not this fucking Cazador you're assigning me."

She inclined her head. "Do not try to lose the Cazador, or I shall lose you."

"Fine," I muttered, then hit the END button and glanced at Azriel. "This day just keeps getting better and better."

"Yes." He paused, his gaze turning to the café's door. "And I'm afraid it's not over yet. Your friends have just arrived."

"Bring them on. After all, what's one more bucketload given I'm swimming in a sea of it?" I stalked across to the refrigerator and pulled out several cans of Coke. What I really needed was to get stinkingly, mind-buzzingly drunk, but given that wasn't an option for several hours at least, Coke would have to do.

* * *

As it turned out, it wasn't as bad as I thought it would be. It wasn't *great*, but I think Riley's presence tempered the worst of Rhoan's anger. He merely yelled at me for five minutes rather than attempting to violently shake some sense into me like I think he wanted to.

I pulled another chocolate chip cookie from the jar—a jar that had started off full but was now half empty—and watched Riley. She was squatting next to one of the half-beasts, her face almost covered by the long sweep of her red-gold hair. What I could see of her expression was distant, but her lips moved. She was talking to the soul of the creature she knelt next to, which to me was little more than a wisp of fog. I didn't know what it was saying. And while I might yet be forced to learn how to communicate with them, I honestly preferred to stick to talking to the souls of the living. There was enough grief and pain in doing that. I didn't need to lump the anger and confusion of a ghost on top of it.

Behind Riley stood Uncle Quinn, her lover and the vampire who had taught me how to use my Aedh skills. He was, in every way, angelic, from his beautiful face that was framed by night-dark hair to his well-toned body. Of course, the angelic looks weren't exactly a surprise because he was Aedh. Not a full blood, but a half-breed just like me. Only he was older. Centuries and centuries older.

He wasn't just watching Riley, though. He was connected to her by the press of his flesh against hers and via the psychic link they shared, giving her an anchor to this world. As Riley's clairvoyant abilities had grown, so had the danger of her being permanently drawn into the between world. Using Quinn as her rock in this world greatly lessened the risk.

I continued to watch them, munching on my cookie and absurdly aware of Azriel's presence at my shoulder. His arms were crossed and he was watching Riley with something close to surprise.

Because there are few in this world who could even attempt what she now does, he said, not bothering to glance at me. *It is extremely dangerous to step into the lost lands as fully as she does.*

Hence the use of Uncle Quinn as an anchor.

Yes. His gaze flicked briefly to the man in question. *He was once a priest, was he not?*

He trained as one, but never completed it.

Then why do you not go to him for information about the priests? He would be of more use than your Aedh.

I flicked a hand toward them. *Riley needs him more. And to be honest, I've endangered enough people by including them in this fucking quest.*

There are casualties in any war, Risa.

Yeah, I snapped back, *but if I can avoid those casualties being my friends, I will.*

He didn't say anything to that. But then, he was well aware that anything he said would more than likely just make me angrier.

After several more minutes, Riley sighed and pushed to her feet. Quinn rose behind her, one hand under her elbow, steadying her. Her face was pale and her eyes haunted.

She brushed damp tendrils of hair away from her face, then said grimly, "These things were not willing recipients of the magic that changed their beings and their souls."

"It was forced onto them?" I said, not entirely surprised. It would explain the madness in their eyes, for a start.

She nodded and leaned into Quinn. He wrapped an arm around her shoulders and lightly kissed the top of her head. I smiled a little wistfully, and half wondered if I'd ever find a man to hold me like that.

"They were homeless before the change, and they don't remember much beyond being held captive underground for a long period of time."

Meaning they weren't Razan, which matched the fact that they weren't tattooed like the other Razan we'd caught or killed. "And they have no idea where that was?"

She shook her head.

"What of the practitioner?" Azriel asked.

Riley's gaze flicked to him, her expression neutral. She was waiting to learn more about the being before she passed judgment on him, and I knew her hesitation was no doubt caused by some of the comments I'd made previously. "That part of their memories has been burned away. I doubt whether we'd be able to retrieve it even if they were alive."

"We certainly tried with the other fellow we interrogated," Rhoan said as he jumped over the railing and landed lightly on our floor. "We didn't get very far—although the Directorate's witches said there was a decidedly dark flavor to the magic."

Riley nodded. "It's definitely blood magic from the feel of it, but it's more powerful than anything I ever felt before. And older."

Rhoan's gray eyes glimmered silver with the force of his anger as his gaze slammed into mine. "Which means you *really* need to keep your fucking nose clear—"

"Rhoan," Riley said softly. "Enough."

He gave her a sharp look, then thrust a hand through his hair and blew out a breath. "I'm only trying to keep you safe, Ris."

"I know, and I love you all for that, but my father has threatened to kill Ilianna and Tao if I don't continue to hunt down the keys. I really have no other choice."

"You may have no choice when it comes to the keys," Quinn said, his voice filled with the most gorgeous Irish lilt, "but you can choose *not* to undertake this search with only a reaper by your side. However handy with a blade that reaper may be."

My gaze flicked to Riley. She knew why I hadn't asked them. I could see it in the slight twist in her smile. "I learned the hard way that I needed to rely on others, Ris. Don't go through what I had to before you learn it, too."

It was a lesson I didn't need to learn. I was more than happy to lean on others for help—as long as it didn't place them in the path of danger. And Riley, Quinn, Rhoan, and his lover Liander had been through enough already in their lives. They'd earned their right to peace. This was my fight, and my turn.

"Might as well talk to a brick wall," Rhoan muttered. "She's listening, but she won't do it."

I didn't say anything. I couldn't—not when he was right.

"Send her home," Riley said softly. "If you need anything else for your report, you can talk to her in the morning."

"Okay," he agreed. "But for God's sake, be careful, Ris."

"Uncle Rhoan, those creatures weren't here to kill me. They were here to distract me. Whoever did this wants me alive."

"For the moment." He waved a hand. "Go. Just make sure you're contactable in case I need anything else."

I nodded and glanced at Azriel. *I need to go see Ilianna and Tao.*

He nodded imperceptibly. *Shall I meet you at the ritual site's gates?*

I hesitated, knowing that I wasn't up to much and yet very aware of the odd tension that still rode him.

Yes, I said eventually, and he immediately winked out of existence.

My own departure was a little less hurried, the change sweeping over me even more sluggishly. I was pushing my limits, and sooner or later the well would run dry and there'd be nothing left. Not even me. I'd scatter on the wind, broken and lost to both this world and the next.

But thankfully, that didn't happen this time.

Azriel was waiting at the gates when I got there. The heat of him washed over me as I landed—more accurately, splattered—onto the roadside, signaling just how close he was.

"Don't," I croaked, warding off the possibility of help even though I couldn't see him, let alone know for sure he was even going to offer.

He didn't. I stayed on my hands and knees battling to breathe as every inch of me shook and my head felt like it was about to split open.

After what seemed like ages, a pair of sapphire running shoes appeared in front of my somewhat blurry line of sight. I blinked, then recognized them. They belonged to Ilianna.

"Fuck, Risa, you've got to learn to take better care of yourself." Her jean-clad knees appeared as she squatted in front of me. "Here, drink this."

She shoved a thermos at me. I sat back somewhat cautiously but nowhere near slow enough, and madmen with red-hot daggers went insane in my head. I blinked back tears and reached for the container, my hand shaking so hard the contents splashed over the rim.

I sniffed it warily. It smelled vaguely of cinnamon and eucalyptus, but there were other scents in there I couldn't place.

"Oh, for God's sake," she said crossly, "it's not going to poison you. Just drink."

I did. The potion was thick and somewhat bitter, but I got it down and did actually start feeling better almost immediately. "How did you know I was here, let alone that I needed help?"

She raised an eyebrow. "How do you think?" She nodded toward Azriel, who remained near the gates, his arms crossed and his expression retaining its usual neutrality. But I still sensed the tension in him—though, to be honest, I'd never actually seen him look truly relaxed. Maybe tension was part of his makeup, or what made him such a good Mijai. Or maybe it was simply the end result of being forced to remain near me. Ilianna added, "He might not be able to enter the ritual grounds, but he sure as hell can yell."

Azriel? Yell? He vary rarely raised his voice, so it was hard to imagine him actually yelling. Besides, surely I would have heard it. He wasn't standing that far away. I handed her back the thermos. "How's Tao?"

She grimaced. "No better, no worse. The holy water and his own healing capabilities have fixed most of the burns, but I'm worried about what might be happening on the inside."

"We can't do anything about that."

She met my gaze. "*We* can't. But maybe the Brindle can."

I frowned and irritably brushed at the sweaty strands of hair that fell over my eyes. "The Brindle isn't a healing center. What could they do that you can't?"

"The Brindle is the home of all witch knowledge," she said grimly. "And some of the most powerful witches alive today are there. I don't know how to heal Tao, Risa, but they just *might*."

Her expression was determined, but deep in the recesses of her green eyes fear lurked.

"At what cost to you?" I asked softly.

"I don't know, and I don't care. I can't leave Tao like this. He saved my *life*, Risa. I can't not do the same for him."

"I know, but—"

She placed a finger against my lips. Her skin was even colder than mine. "I know the risks. I can guess what they will demand. But even if I'm wrong, even if they demand something more of me, it's a price I'm willing to pay to make Tao well again."

I gently caught her fingers in mine. "He may never be well again. We both need to face that."

"I will—but only when we've searched every damn book in the Brindle and done everything possible to help him."

There was no arguing with her. As much as we both knew Kiandra would use this to draw Ilianna back into the fold, if that was a price Ilianna was willing to pay, then there was nothing I could do to gainsay her. I wanted Tao whole as much as she did, but she was the one who'd be affected. If this was her decision—if this is what she was willing to do—then I could only support her—both now, and later, when the Brindle extracted its payment.

I squeezed her hand and said, "If you're sure, then let's call them."

"I already have." She grimaced and glanced past me. "That's them coming up the road now."

I turned around. My ribs—which I'd forgotten about in the agony of changing from Aedh to human form—sent me another sharp reminder that they weren't yet healed. I winced, blinking back tears as I studied the road below us. Two lights speared the darkness, and the sound of a car engine suddenly rode the night.

I met Ilianna's gaze again. "Who's coming?"

She shrugged. "I asked for people versed in healing, just in case his condition worsened on the trip down."

"So not your mother or Kiandra?"

She smiled slightly. "No. Mom's in season, so dad's

keeping her busy, and Kiandra rarely ventures out of the Brindle's confines."

I said, "Isn't your mom a little old to still be coming into season?"

She laughed and pulled her hands from mine. "A mare is never too old to come into season, and a stallion never too old to impregnate her. Thankfully, my father has accepted Mom's desire not to have more children."

"No doubt because he still has a whole stableful of mares to cater to his breeding instincts."

"Ten of them," she said cheerfully. "Some stallions never lose their virility, it seems."

I snorted softly. At last count, she'd had around thirty-five half siblings. It sounded like that figure was still increasing.

A long, ambulance-like van drove into the clearing and stopped beside Ilianna's four-wheel drive. She rose and strode over to talk to them. I blew out a breath, then pushed somewhat shakily to my feet and walked over to Azriel.

His presence swirled around me—a blanket of heat and something else, something that was oddly comforting.

And yet it made me ache far worse than any injury, because I wanted more than just a comforting swirl of energy. I wanted what Riley had. Someone to hold me, support me, to kiss me gently when I needed it, or to tell me off when I was being an ass. I wanted someone who loved me for *me*, warts and all, rather than loving my money or for who my mom might have been.

But I might never find any of that. Mom had never mentioned love and children in my future, and certainly it wasn't something my visions had ever hinted at. Besides, the depth of love and understanding Riley and Quinn had found seemed to be rare in this world—or at least, that was the way it seemed to me given Mom's experiences and mine. But that knowledge didn't dampen the desire.

Still, right now I had to settle for what I had. A fallen Aedh who was an excellent lover, and a reaper who was a protector if not a friend, and in whose presence I at least felt safe.

Even if that odd tension still rode him.

I stopped beside him, rubbing my arms lightly as I turned and watched Ilianna lead the two witches—who were carrying a stretcher between them through the ritual site's gates.

"If you are cold," he said, almost immediately, "you should go sit inside Ilianna's car."

"I will."

He glanced down at me. "And yet here you remain."

"Because I want to know why you're so tense. Are you expecting another attack?"

He hesitated. "There will be more attacks. We would be foolish to believe otherwise."

"Yeah, but that's not the cause of your tension right now, is it?"

"This person you saw stealing the key—was it your father?"

I frowned at the change of subject, although I wasn't entirely surprised. He tended to do that when hit with a question he didn't want to answer. "No. It didn't feel like him. Why?"

"Because I cannot escape the notion that he is the most logical person behind this attack."

"Why would he bother to attack us like that when we're doing what he wanted and finding the keys? That doesn't seem very logical."

"Aedh logic is not human logic."

"That still doesn't explain the fact that it makes no sense for him to be behind the attack."

"It would if it was some kind of subterfuge."

I shivered, and wondered if the night were getting colder or if the chill was simply the result of growing trepidation. "What kind of subterfuge?"

He shrugged. "Maybe it is simply a way of throwing the Raziq off his trail."

"Every time he interacts with this world—or with me—he reveals his presence to the Raziq. Why would he risk all that only to sabotage our efforts?"

"He would know that the reapers follow you. Creating a diversion and stealing the key ensures he gets it rather than us reapers."

"But he had no way of knowing we'd found the key," I said, frustration and perhaps a touch of fear sharpening my tone, "because he and I aren't connected and he can't read my mind unless he's in my presence. And I *would* have felt him if he were present. Besides, you sensed the black magic before we'd gotten anywhere near the key. Whoever was behind the attack, they were well prepared for our presence."

"Which, again, points to your father." He hesitated, his expression cooling a little—which I hadn't thought possible. "There's a spy in our midst."

I sighed wearily. I didn't have the energy for anything else, not even to raise the spark of anger. "Don't start on Lucian again. He was with us in that house and fought *against* those creatures, not with them. He isn't a part of some nefarious plot to steal the keys from underneath our noses."

"And you are one hundred percent sure of this?"

"Yes!" Exhaustion, it seemed, hadn't quite snuffed out the anger after all. "Lucian might be many things, but a traitor isn't one of them. Of that I'm positive."

Azriel looked away. "Then I must trust your judgment."

"And I've heard that fucking statement more than once. Maybe it'd be more believable if you actually did it rather than merely pay it lip service."

He acknowledged the words with a slight incline of his head. "If it isn't your father, then I am at a loss."

I bit my lip and resisted the urge to simply sit down and cry. I might be feeling weak, but tears wouldn't get me anywhere. So I crossed my arms, leaned against the trunk of the nearest tree, and thought about what I'd seen and felt in that room. And somewhere deep in the recesses, an idea stirred. "Maybe," I said slowly, "the dark magic itself will give us a clue."

I could feel his gaze on me but I didn't meet it, teasing out the idea, letting it grow. "This is not the first time we've encountered dark magic."

"The witch who raised the soul stealer can't be behind the theft."

"Of course not. She's dead." I raised my gaze to his. "But what about the third person in the consortium?"

"We do not know who that person really is, let alone if he's even a practitioner."

"Yeah," I said impatiently, "but the two we *did* find weren't witches or sorcerers, so how did they even know about the ley intersection and the potential power they'd gain by controlling it?"

"Maybe the witch told them."

"But they were buying up properties long *before* they employed her to raise the soul stealer. And that implies they already knew about the ley lines."

"Ley lines are not something a nonmagical person would be aware of, let alone see."

"Meaning the third person, whoever he is, is either magic-aware or a practitioner of some kind."

His gaze narrowed. "Why then would he employ another practitioner to do his dirty work?"

"Subterfuge. Remember, we caught the witch in the end, but we never caught the third member of the consortium." I shrugged. "It's only a theory . . ."

"But a plausible one."

Pleasure slithered through me—which was absurd and probably spoke more of my exhaustion than anything else. "Of course, unless Stane can uncover some paperwork that will give us a lead as to who that last person is, we really can't do anything more."

"Why not talk to the Brindle? They would at least know whether there are any dark practitioners active in the city."

I wrinkled my nose. "Ilianna is going to owe the Brindle big time as it is. I don't want her under a greater obligation."

"I didn't mean that she should talk to them. I meant that you should."

"Me?" I couldn't help the surprise in my voice. "I

doubt they'd discuss that sort of stuff with an outsider like me. I'm not even a witch."

"But did Kiandra not tell you where to find Selwin and then give you permission to come to this place? Did she not warn you that the Brindle is not safe from the Aedh? I think that one knows more about this situation than you currently believe."

"Ilianna might have said something to her mom. And we did ask her to translate the text in the Dušan's book."

He acknowledged the possibility with a slight nod. "I still think it's worth talking to her."

"Then I will talk to her. But not tonight." I glanced past him as Ilianna and her two stretcher bearers reappeared and pushed away from the tree trunk to join the procession.

"He's still burning up," I murmured, lightly touching Tao's gaunt face. It was as if the fires were consuming him from the inside out. I shivered and glanced up at Ilianna. "You'll let me know if anything changes in the next couple of hours?"

Relief washed across her face. "Don't tell me you're actually going home to rest?"

"If I don't, I'm not going to be of any use to anyone—even myself." I kissed my fingertips then brushed them across Tao's fire-touched lips. "Come back to us, my friend. We need you."

Ilianna gripped my hand and squeezed it lightly. "If there's a way to heal him, we'll find it."

As the two women loaded Tao into the back of the van, I gave Ilianna a hug. "Don't promise them too much," I whispered. "Your life is worth just as much as his. Don't exchange one for the other."

She pulled away and smiled, although we both knew it was forced. "A life for a life is not something the Brindle would ask."

I didn't mean literally and she knew it. "Kiandra wants you back at the Brindle. She may use this as a lever."

"If I was to go back to the Brindle, it would have to be done willingly, with no form of inducement. The building and the magic would not accept my presence otherwise."

I raised my eyebrows, but she waved away my questions before I even asked them. "Trust me to do what is best for both myself and for Tao," she said softly.

"I do." I gave her another hug then stepped away. She climbed into the back of the van with one of the gray-clad witches, then the driver closed the door and climbed into the front. Five minutes later they were gone and the normal night sounds of the forest returned.

I sighed and slowly walked across to Ilianna's car. Thankfully, she'd left the keys in the ignition, because I hadn't even thought to ask for them.

I opened the door, then stopped and looked across to Azriel. "You might have to come with me, just to make sure I don't fall asleep at the wheel."

"Why not let me transport you home? We can retrieve the car later."

Because I don't want to be that close to you. It was disturbing on far too many levels. Then I sighed, reached in, and grabbed the car keys. I was being an idiot again.

I turned and caught a brief glimpse of annoyance before his expression cleared again. I really, *really* needed to keep my thoughts in check.

I locked the car and forced a smile. "Okay, brave sir, whisk me away to safety on your wild white steed."

He walked toward me, his strides long and graceful. "I am not brave, but merely do what I am assigned to do, and I do not possess a white horse. That sentence does not make sense."

I didn't rise to the bait—and bait it was, given the amusement teasing the corners of his lips. He wrapped his arms around me, and I did my best to ignore his closeness and the way his body seemed to fit perfectly against mine, not to mention the musky, enticing scent of him.

Power surged—a song that ran through every part of me, taking what I was, making it more, making it less, until there was no me, no him, just the sum of the two of us—energy beings with no flesh to hold us in place.

Then the forest was gone and we were on the gray fields, and somehow everything seemed brighter, more beautiful, and so damn tranquil that I wanted to cry. It almost seemed like I was seeing it clearer than I ever had before.

And then something happened.

The gray fields shuddered. Shifted. *Leaned.* As if it were a structure from which one of its main supports had been removed. The brightness flickered briefly then returned, but the tranquility was gone, replaced by a sudden uneasiness.

Then the fields were gone and I was back in my room at the Langham. I pulled away from Azriel, my heart going a million miles an hour as I said, "What the hell just happened?"

"That," he said grimly, "was the answer to your previous question."

No, I thought. *No.* I licked dry lips and said, "And just which question are we talking about?"

And all the while, the litany inside my head was going, *No, no, no. Please God no.*

"Remember wondering what the thief planned to do with the key?" He thrust a hand through his matted hair, and the sheer depth of the anger and frustration rolling off him just about stole my breath. "Well, that movement we felt in the gray fields was our answer. They've forced the first portal open."

I all but collapsed onto the bed. "Oh, fuck," I whispered.

"Indeed," he agreed. "The shit has well and truly hit the fan."

And it was all our fault, because we'd had the key in our hands and still had managed to lose it.

"We need to stop this, Risa, before it goes any further."

I raised my gaze to his. "How? We're doing all that we can right now."

"But it's not enough. These people obviously seek the destruction of both our worlds, and they are still out there."

"That doesn't answer the question, Azriel."

"No." He spun away, walked to the window, every movement screaming of anger. "We do what we have to do—we track down these people by whatever means necessary."

By whatever means necessary.

I had a bad feeling the days ahead were going to get very long and very dark.

And very fucking bloody.

And if you missed it, be sure to pick up

Darkness Unbound

by

KERI ARTHUR,

the first exciting installment of Risa's story.

Available now.

Here's a special preview:

I'VE ALWAYS SEEN THE REAPERS.

Even as a toddler—with little understanding of spirits, death, or the horrors that lie in the shadows—I'd been aware of them. As I'd gotten older and my knowledge of the mystical had strengthened, I'd begun to call them Death, because the people I'd seen them following had always died within a day or so.

In my teenage years, I learned who and what they really were. They called themselves reapers, and they were collectors of souls. They took the essence—the spirit—of the dying and escorted them onto the next part of their journey, be that heaven or hell.

The reapers weren't flesh-and-blood beings, although they could attain that form if they wished. They were creatures of light and shadows—and an energy so fierce, their mere presence burned across my skin like flame.

Which is how I'd sensed the one now following me. He was keeping his distance, but the heat of him sang through the night, warming my skin and stirring the embers of fear. I swallowed heavily and tried to stay calm. After all, being the daughter of one of Melbourne's most powerful psychics had its benefits—and one of those was a knowledge of my own death.

It would come many years from now, in a stupid car accident.

Of course, it was totally possible that I'd gotten the timing of my death wrong. My visions weren't always as accurate as my mother's, so maybe the death I'd seen in my future was a whole lot closer than I'd presumed.

And it was also a fact that not all deaths actually happened when they were *supposed* to. That's why there were ghosts—they were the souls uncollected by reapers, either because their deaths had come *before* their allotted time, or because they'd refused the reapers' guidance. Either way, the end result was the same. The souls were left stranded between this world and the next.

I shoved my hands into the pockets of my leather jacket and walked a little faster. There was no outrunning the reapers—I knew that—but I still couldn't help the instinctive urge to try.

Around me, the day was only just dawning. Lygon Street gleamed wetly after the night's rain, and the air was fresh and smelled ever so faintly of spring. The heavy bass beat coming from the nearby wolf clubs overran what little traffic noise there was, and laughter rode the breeze—a happy sound that did little to chase the chill from my flesh.

It was a chill caused not by an icy morning, but rather by the ever-growing tide of fear.

Why was the reaper following *me*?

As I crossed over to Pelham Street, my gaze flicked to the nearby shop windows, searching again for the shadow of death.

Reapers came in all shapes and sizes, often taking

the form most likely to be accepted by those they'd come to collect. I'm not sure what it said about me that *my* reaper was shirtless, tattooed, and appeared to be wearing some sort of sword strapped across his back.

A reaper with a weapon? Now, *that* was something I'd never come across before. But maybe he knew I wasn't about to go lightly.

I turned into Ormond Place and hurried toward the private parking lot my restaurant shared with several other nearby businesses. There was no sound of steps behind me, no scent of another, yet the reaper's presence burned all around me—a heat I could feel on my skin and within my mind.

Sometimes being psychic like my mom *really* sucked.

I wrapped my fingers around my keys and hit the automatic opener. As the old metal gate began to grind and screech its way to one side, I couldn't help looking over my shoulder.

My gaze met the reaper's. His face was chiseled, almost classical in its beauty, and yet possessing a hard edge that spoke of a man who'd won more than his fair share of battles. His eyes were blue—one a blue as vivid and as bright as a sapphire, the other almost a navy, and as dark and stormy as the sea.

Awareness flashed through those vivid, turbulent depths—an awareness that seemed to echo right through me. It was also an awareness that seemed to be accompanied, at least on his part, by surprise.

For several heartbeats neither of us moved, and then he simply disappeared. One second he was there, and the next he wasn't.

I blinked, wondering if it was some sort of trick.

Reapers, like the Aedh, could become energy and smoke at will, but—for me, at least—it usually took longer than the blink of an eye to achieve. Of course, I was only half Aedh, so maybe that was the problem.

The reaper didn't reappear, and the heat of his presence no longer burned through the air or shivered through my mind. He'd gone. Which was totally out of character for a reaper, as far as I knew.

I mean, they were collectors of *souls*. It was their duty to hang about until said soul was collected. I'd never known of one to up and disappear the moment he'd been spotted—although given that the ability to actually spot them was a rare one, this probably wasn't an everyday occurrence.

Mom, despite her amazing abilities—abilities that had been sharpened during her creation in a madman's cloning lab—certainly couldn't see them. But then, she couldn't actually see *anything*. The sight she did have came via a psychic link she shared with a creature known as a Fravardin—a guardian spirit that had been gifted to her by a long-dead clone brother.

She was also a full Helki werewolf, not a half-Aedh like me. The Aedh were kin to the reapers, and it was their blood that gave me the ability to see the reapers.

But why did *this* reaper disappear like that? Had he realized he'd been following the wrong soul, or was something weirder going on?

Frowning, I walked across to my bike and climbed on. The leather seat wrapped around my butt like a glove, and I couldn't help smiling. The Ducati wasn't new, but she was sharp and clean and comfortable to ride, and even though the hydrogen engine was getting a little old by today's standards, she still put out a whole lot of power. Maybe not as much as the newer engines, but enough to give a mother gray hair. Or so *my* mom reckoned, anyway.

As the thought of her ran through my mind again, so did the sudden urge to call her. My frown deepening, I dug my phone out of my pocket and said, "Mom."

The voice-recognition software clicked into action and the call went through almost instantly.

"Risa," she said, her luminous blue eyes shining with warmth and amusement. "I was just thinking about you."

"I figured as much. What's up?"

She sighed, and I instantly knew what that meant. My stomach twisted and I closed my eyes, wishing away the words I knew were coming.

But it didn't work. It never worked.

"I have another client who wants your help." She said it softly, without inflection. She knew how much I hated hospitals.

"Mom—"

"It's a little girl, Ris. Otherwise I wouldn't ask you. Not so soon after the last time."

I took a deep breath and blew it out slowly. The last time had been a teenager whose bones had pretty much been pulverized in a car accident. He'd been on life support for weeks, with no sign of brain activity, and the doctors had finally advised his parents to turn off the machine and let him pass over. Naturally enough, his parents had been reluctant, clinging to the belief that he was still there, that there was still hope.

Mom couldn't tell them that. But I could.

Yet it had meant going into the hospital, immersing myself in the dying and the dead and the heat of the reapers. I hated it. It always seemed like I was losing a piece of myself.

But more than that, I hated facing the grief of the parents when—*if*—I had to tell them that their loved ones were long gone.

"What happened to her?"

If it was an accident, if it was a repeat of the teenager and the parents were looking for a miracle, then I could beg off. It wouldn't be easy, but neither was walking into that hospital.

"She went in with a fever, fell into a coma, and hasn't woken up. They have her on life support at the moment."

"Do they know why?" I asked the question almost desperately, torn between wanting to help a little girl caught in the twilight realms between life and death and the serious need *not* to go into that place.

"No. She had the flu and was dehydrated, which is why she was originally admitted. The doctors have run every test imaginable and have come up with nothing." Mom hesitated. "Please, Ris. Her mother is a longtime client."

My mom knew *precisely* which buttons to push. I loved her to death, but god, there were some days I wished I could simply ignore her.

"Which hospital is she in?"

"The Children's."

I blew out a breath. "I'll head there now."

"You can't. Not until eight," Mom said heavily. "They're not allowing anyone but family outside of visiting hours."

Great. Two hours to wait. Two hours to dread what I was being asked to do.

"Okay. But no more for a while after this. Please?"

"Deal." There was no pleasure in her voice. No victory. She might push my buttons to get what she wanted, but she also knew how much these trips took out of me. "Come back home afterward and I'll make you breakfast."

"I can't." I scrubbed my eyes and resisted the sudden impulse to yawn. "I've been working at the restaurant all night and I really need some sleep. Send me the details about her parents and the ward number, and I'll give you a buzz once I've been to see her."

"Good. Are you still up for our lunch on Thursday?"

I smiled. Thursday lunch had been something of a ritual for my entire life. My mom and Aunt Riley—who wasn't really an aunt, but a good friend of Mom's who'd taken me under her wing and basically spoiled me rotten since birth—had been meeting at the same restaurant for over twenty-five years. They had, in fact, recently purchased it to prevent it from being torn down to make way for apartments. Almost nothing got in the way of their ritual—and certainly *not* a multimillion-dollar investment company.

"I wouldn't miss it for the world."

"Good. See you then. Love you."

I smiled and said, "But not as much as I love you."

The words had become something of a ritual at the end of our phone calls, but I never took them for granted. I'd seen far too many people over the years trying to get in contact with the departed just so they could say the words they'd never said in life.

I hit the end button then shoved the phone back into my pocket. As I did so, it began to chime the song "Witchy Woman"—an indicator that Mom had already sent the requested information via text. Obviously, she'd had it ready to go. I shook my head and didn't bother looking at it. I needed to wash the grime of work away and get some sustenance in my belly before I faced dealing with that little girl in the hospital.

Two hours later, I arrived at the hospital. I parked in the nearby underground lot, then checked Mom's text, grabbing the ward number and the parents' names before heading inside.

It hit me in the foyer.

The dead, the dying, and the diseased created a veil of misery and pain that permeated not only the air but the very foundations of the building. It felt like a ton of bricks as it settled across my shoulders, and it was a weight that made my back hunch, my knees buckle, and my breath stutter to a momentary halt.

Not that I really *wanted* to breathe. I didn't want to take that scent—that wash of despair and loss—into myself. And most especially, I didn't want to see the reapers and the tiny souls they were carrying away.

I was gripped by the sudden urge to run, and it was so fierce and strong that my whole body shook. I had to clench my fists against it and force my feet onward. I'd promised Mom I'd do this, and I couldn't go back on my promise. No matter how much I might want to.

I walked into the elevator and punched the floor for intensive care, then watched as the doors closed and the floor numbers slowly rolled by. As they opened onto my floor, a reaper walked by. She had brown eyes and a face you couldn't help but trust, and her wings shone white, tipped with gold.

An angel—the sort depicted throughout religion, not those that inhabited the real world. Walking beside her, her tiny hand held within the angel's, was a child. I briefly closed my eyes against the sting of tears. When I opened them again, the reaper and her soul were gone.

I took the right-hand corridor. A nurse looked up as I approached the desk. "May I help you?"

"I'm here to see Hanna Kingston."

She hesitated, looking me up and down. "Are you family?"

"No, but her parents asked me to come. I'm Risa Jones."

"Oh," she said, then her eyes widened slightly as the name registered. "The daughter of Dia Jones?"

I nodded. People might not know me, but thanks to the fact that many of her clients were celebrities, they sure knew Mom. "Mrs. Kingston is a client. She asked for me specifically."

"I'm sorry, but I'll have to check."

I nodded again, watching as she rose and walked through the door that separated the reception area from the intensive care wards. Down that bright hall, a shrouded gray figure waited. Another reaper. Another soul about to pass.

I closed my eyes again and took a long, slow breath. I could do this.

I could.

The nurse came back with another woman. She was small and dark-haired, her sharp features and brown eyes drawn and tired looking.

"Risa," she said, offering me her hand. "Fay Kingston. I'm so glad you were able to come."

I shook her hand briefly. Her grief seemed to crawl from her flesh, and it made my heart ache. I pulled my hand gently from hers and flexed my fingers. The grief still clung to them, stinging lightly. "There's no guarantee I can help you. She might have already made her decision."

The woman licked her lips and nodded, but the brightness in her eyes suggested she wasn't ready to believe it. Then again, what mother would?

"We just need to know—" She stopped, tears gathering in her eyes. She took a deep breath, then gave me a bright, false smile. "This way."

I washed my hands, then followed her through the secure door and down the bright hall, the echo of our footsteps like a strong, steady heartbeat. The shrouded reaper didn't look our way—his concentration was on his soul. I glanced into the room as we passed him. It was a boy about eight years old. There were machines and doctors clustered all around him, working frantically. *There's no hope,* I wanted to say. *Let him go in peace.*

But I'd been wrong before. Maybe I'd be wrong again.

Three doorways down from the reaper, Mrs. Kingston swung left into a room and walked across to a dark-haired man sitting near the bed. I stopped in the doorway, barely even registering his presence as my gaze was drawn to the small form on the bed.

She was a dark-haired bundle of bones that seemed lost in the stark whiteness of the hospital room. Machines surrounded her, doing the work of her body, keeping her alive. Her face was drawn, gaunt, and there were dark circles under her closed eyes.

I couldn't feel her. But I couldn't feel the presence of a reaper, either, and that surely had to be a good sign.

"Do you think you can help her?" a deep voice asked.

I jumped, and my gaze flew to the father. Before I could answer, Fay said, "This is my husband, Steven."

I nodded. I didn't need to know his name to understand he was Hanna's father. The utter despair in his eyes was enough. I swallowed heavily and somehow said, "I honestly don't know if I can help her, Mr. Kingston. But I can try."

He nodded, his gaze drifting back to his baby girl. "Then try. Either way, we need to know what to do next."

I took a deep, somewhat shuddering breath, and blinked away the tears stinging my eyes once more.

I could do this. For her sake—for *their* sake— I could do this. If she was in there, if she was trapped between this world and the next, then she needed someone to talk to. Someone who could help her make a decision. That someone had to be me. There *was* no one else.

I forced my feet forward. The closer I got, the more I could feel . . . well, the oddness.

Pain and fear and hunger swirled around her tiny body like a storm, but there was no spark, no glimmer of consciousness—nothing to indicate that life had ever existed within her flesh.

It shouldn't have felt like that. And if death was her destiny, then there would have been a reaper here waiting. But there wasn't, so either the time for her decision had not arrived or she was slated to live.

So why couldn't I *feel* her?

Frowning, I sat down on the edge of the bed and picked up her hand. Her flesh was warm, though why that surprised me I wasn't entirely sure.

I took a deep breath and slowly released it. As I did, I released the awareness of everything and everyone else, concentrating on little Hanna, reaching for her not physically, but psychically. The world around me faded until the only thing existing on this plane was me and her. Warmth throbbed at my neck—Ilianna's magic at work, protecting me as my psyche, my soul, or whatever else people liked to call it pulled away from the constraints of my flesh and stepped gently into the gray fields that were neither life nor death.

Only it felt like I'd stepped into the middle of a battleground.

And it was a battle that had gone very, *very* badly.

Fear and pain became physical things that battered at me with terrible force, tearing at my heart and ripping through my soul. My chest burned, breathing became painful, and all I could feel was fear. My fear, her fear, all twisted into one stinking mess that made my stomach roil and my flesh crawl.

And then there was the screaming. Unvoiced, unheard by anyone but me, it reverberated through the emptiness of her flesh—echoes of agony in the bloody, battered shell that had once held a little girl.

Her soul wasn't here, but it hadn't moved on.

Someone—*something*—had come into the hospital and ripped it from her flesh.

Do you love fiction with a supernatural twist?

Want the chance to hear news about your favourite
authors (and the chance to win free books)?

Keri Arthur
S. G. Browne
P.C. Cast
Christine Feehan
Jacquelyn Frank
Larissa Ione
Sherrilyn Kenyon
Jackie Kessler
Jayne Ann Krentz and Jayne Castle
Martin Millar
Kat Richardson
J.R. Ward
David Wellington

Then visit the Piatkus website and blog
www.piatkus.co.uk | www.piatkusbooks.net

And follow us on Facebook and Twitter
www.facebook.com/piatkusfiction | www.twitter.com/piatkusbooks

piatkus